STRAY

by

LUX NOCTIS

www.luxnoctistales.com

Cover Art by Maja Cronvall
BleedingHeartworks

ACKNOWLEDGEMENTS

To my good friend **Ben "Kat" Cunningham**, who has read every version of this book throughout its various stages, more times than I dare to count. It's finally over. You never have to look upon these pages again. You must be over the moon.

To the beautiful **Catherine M. Regan**, who was for some time, my solitary motivation to continue working. I thank you dearly for keeping me on track, for believing in my (clearly limited) abilities, and for being my light in the darkness on countless occasions. You have a radiant soul, and no matter how hard things get, no one can take that from you.

TABLE OF CONTENTS

THE BEGINNING

Have you ever stared down at your own bloodied hands and wondered just what kind of monster you've become? Ladies and gentlemen, welcome to my fucked-up world. If you're looking for tales of love and companionship, of heroism and chivalrous deeds, then you, my friend, are about to be sorely disappointed. This is no fairy tale; it's not some bullshit fantasy of knights and dragons. This is far from being a case of good and evil, heroes and villains, rights and wrongs. There is no black and white here. No, here there are only shades of grey – thankfully, without the bondage.

Think of this as my confession of sorts. A documentation of my version of events because God knows no one would give me the chance to speak if I tried. They'd put a bullet in my head before I could take my next breath if they had the chance. When so many people are itching to kill you, no one's really willing to listen when you say you'd rather call it quits. So, this is my attempt at bringing a close to this whole screwed-up chapter. I realise the futility of that idea though; this ends when I'm dead, and nothing less than my untimely demise will do anymore.

If you think your adolescence is tough, you'll probably feel a little better about it once this is over.

■■■

"I can't believe I let you guys talk me in to this." I groaned as I answered the door.

The three of them stood in a line; at least two of them were thrilled by the fact that they'd pulled me in to be a part of their stupid and pointless endeavour.

"Come on man, you never do *anything*. You'll spend your whole life in that room at this rate. I'll drag you kicking and screaming if I have to."

Allow me to introduce you to Damian, who stood smirking and looking incredibly pleased with himself. He was the son of a single parent, same as me. His mom and dad weren't exactly on speaking terms to say the least; he had a home life far more troubled than my own.

Damian was on the tall side, easily surpassing the 6ft mark and laughing defiantly in the face of ticket-takers at adult-rated movies, and those little signs you get at theme parks that say 'You must be THIS tall to ride'. He was only sixteen years old, like the rest of us, but he looked like an adult, already sporting a healthy amount of facial hair. As for the hair on his head, it was short, black and gelled to within an inch of its life. With his morbid interests and taste for all things strange and/or Japanese he sat perfectly well with me.

"Come on, be a man! What're you, afraid of the dark or something?" Jackson spoke up, then created a poor facsimile of a ghost with his hands and let out a self-satisfied woo.

He was a scrawny little mote, pale as bone. He claimed he had a skin condition, which meant he couldn't be in direct sunlight for too long, lest he burst into flames I suppose. Then again he said lots of things that we were all sure were bullshit.

Jackson had a way of twisting the truth, but not in a treacherous sense; perhaps hypochondriac would be a more accurate way to describe him, although his dishonesty did extend to other subjects at times. It was sort of like he thought having all this weird stuff wrong with him made him special in some way. I personally wouldn't class illness, medical conditions or an intolerance to dairy products as anything to scream about but hey, each to their own I guess. Still young but not young at heart, already he wanted to be a politician. What better profession for a compulsive liar though, right?

Last, and probably least, there was Venn. He let out a small grunt in place of a greeting. Now, I know what you're thinking, and the answer is no, I don't know if his parents were drunk when they named him. He was another lofty one, slightly taller than Damian, although you wouldn't really be able to tell by looking. He was always hunched over, walking with his face to the ground.

His curly blonde hair sat awkwardly atop his head. I'm sure when he was younger he wouldn't have looked out of place in a sailor suit with one those giant swirly lollipops, but now he just looked like the before example in a commercial for acne cream. He had that kind of acne that makes your skin look all red and raw. It wasn't pleasant, but Jackson had comfortingly told him that 'Hey at this age, some are just doomed to hit puberty harder than a pikey hits his wife.' Yeah I know, the aspiring politician needed to do a little work on his diplomatic speech, but you've got to love the irony.

"Yeah, spending a night in the woods with three other guys… sure sounds manly to me." I replied snarkily.

"Well, there's no going back now. We already got the tent." Damian proclaimed and pulled a flimsy looking bundle of fabric out of an almost-as-flimsy carrier bag. Jackson looked at it with disgust.

"That's it?! That thing's gonna collapse faster than a pensioner in a harsh winter. No way are we making it through the night." Offensive as always. He shifted his thick black specs to get a better look.

"Well, you're welcome to sleep outside. Or you can piss off home now if it bothers you that much." Damian responded with a shrug.

"But what if it gets colder… or it rains? I don't wanna get sick!" His infinite sense of paranoia was kicking in yet again.

"Jackson, you're always sick…" I told him. "I'm surprised you haven't brought a pharmacy with you to be honest. I'm guessing the paramedics are on standby?" Damian let out a snort. Venn's breathy chortle sounded almost like he was choking.

"Fuck you Zack, you're such a douche!" The bespectacled boy helpfully informed me. I agreed with him and we finally set off towards our destination. We left my house and headed for the school, a mere hundred yards away.

"I don't get how you can live this close to school and *still* manage to be late every day." Damian spoke, sounding almost impressed. I shrugged. What could I say? It's a gift.

We began to round the building, planning to head across the school track and off into the forest beyond. As we turned the corner, our eyes fell on a group of hooded figures. One clung to a leash. A pitbull, white with brown markings tugged ferociously at the other end.

"Oh, shit." Venn mumbled, but no one paid any attention. "These guys are bad news." Damian groaned. We stood, hesitant for a moment. "Maybe we should go around."

"Man, fuck that, I'm not taking the long way 'round because of these pricks. Let's just walk past." Jackson ordered, and then set off on a confident march. The rest of us glanced at each other uneasily, wondering if one day his short-man syndrome might actually get us killed. Reluctantly, we followed.

As Jackson passed the dog burst into a violent fit of barking and snarling. Kid damn near leapt out of his skin; he stumbled and fell against the chicken-wire fence that ran around the building's circumference. The gang laughed obnoxiously as he hurriedly jumped back to his feet.

"Go on, get 'im," the one holding the leash ordered, and the dog dove forward, teeth bared. Jackson cried out in fear as the feral beast stopped dead just out of reach, snapping its jaws violently. It was up on its hind legs, pulling its bonds tight in an attempt to get close enough to take a bite out of him. The thug beamed. "Don't move, kid."

The three of us stood open-mouthed, too terrified to get involved, until Damian plucked up the courage to step forward. Another of the assholes spun around and shoved Damian, taking him clean off his feet. He landed heavily on the concrete with a thud and his brief moment of heroic intention ended.

"Stay the fuck down if you know what's good for you." The waster pointed a finger aggressively.

"You will leave these grounds, NOW!" A female voice cried. It was Miss Clarke, our usually droning geography teacher. Her head hung out of a second story window, thin glasses threatening to fall from her weathered face.

"Relax you old bitch." The dog was pulled back.

"Go, or I'll have the police here so fast it'll make your head spin!" Her short, sweepy hair flapped furiously.

"Whatever." The youth stated. He and his fellow fuckwits began to stalk slowly past. They stared intently at us whilst we all examined the floor. A girl with greasy black hair barged into me as they went, throwing me off balance.

"Zachary, you and your friends shouldn't be here after hours either." Clarke reminded us. I winced in genuine physical pain when she called me *Zachary*.

"But Miss, school is such a thrill. I find the force of this place almost magnetic." I groaned sarcastically. I hauled Damian to his feet. Jackson stood tall now that the dog was gone.

"Archer," She snapped "remove yourself from the premises. *Immediately.*" I huffed and gave her a weary salute. Being called 'Archer' was better than Zachary at least. The window slammed shut.

"Fuckers need to get a job. If I were in charge I'd execute every one of 'em." Jackson said brushing himself off, still a little shaken.

"Whatever, let's get going." Damian snapped, frustrated with the turn of events.

■■■

With that we continued onwards, rounding the school, crossing the field and breaching the treeline. All of us were completely oblivious as to the horrors that lay ahead. We walked for God knows how long, Damian and Jackson caught up in a deep and philosophical debate (that just happened to be about superheroes). They bickered relentlessly as we hiked our way deep into the wilderness, leaping over fallen logs and crashing our way through decaying leaves. It was only when I noticed that the sun had almost disappeared that I realised just how far we had gone.

"You two, shut up for a second." I spoke harshly to the squabbling pair. "We should probably put this stupid fucking tent up before it gets dark right?"

"I've been saying that for a while." Venn grumbled.

"Yeah, yeah you're probably right." Damian agreed.

We set to work and after a few frustrating minutes our campsite was completely constructed. The tent was a sorry sight. It was going to be one cramped night for us. The thing looked more like a crack den than anything else. Come morning, I was half expecting to wake up wrapped in whatever was left of it.

The trees, standing tall like ancient, organic columns, seemed to enclose us. As we stood in the dying light, surrounded by deathly silence, something became apparent. We were deep, deep in the woods and a long way from home. That was when the expert conversationalist in our group, Venn, decided to chime in with:

"This reminds me of The Blair Witch Project..."

Probably not the best thing to say just as all luminosity disappeared from the world around us, but hey, it was a shit movie anyway.

A Few Reasons Why No One Should Go Camping, Ever

So, it got dark. Looking back I can see that I was in a state of blissful ignorance, having no indication of the horrors that lay ahead. Now I know you're probably thinking, "What the hell, when does shit start to happen?" Well it's coming, you bloodthirsty bastards, so chill out.

We decided to retreat into our insubstantial shelter, although pretty quickly I was considering taking my chances outside. We had no sleeping bags and no personal space. Ill thought out would be an understatement when describing our epic journey into the forest, but maybe that was supposed to be a part of the fun. The tent pretty much just bowed down to the elements, doing little to protect our fragile human forms from Mother Nature's bitter night. We did, however, have light. Venn had packed one of those big handheld torches, like the kind you might expect a SEAL team to lug around on a rescue mission. That, combined with an other-worldly full moon, gave us just enough light to see by.

It's hard to judge time when you're just sat there with no TV, watch, or anything to keep track of its passing; we didn't even have phones with us, because the others had agreed that it would be more authentic in a survival expert sort of way if we didn't take them. I guess in the same way Bear Grylls, rather than taking enough water with him to the desert, decides to drink his own piss from a snakeskin. Thankfully we weren't taking it to that extreme.

I hadn't settled on the whole not-bringing-a-phone thing personally. However being a somewhat forgetful soul, I neglected to pick mine up when I rushed out of the door. We really did make all those horror movie errors, alone and isolated, no way to contact anyone. If there were any cheerleaders there, I'm pretty sure Jason Voorhees would have gone well out of his way to crash our little party, hockey mask and all. Just to really set the mood, Damian was teaching us all about a delightful guy known as 'The Camden Ripper'.

"I can't remember the guy's real name, but trust me he was he *fucked up*. He was killing all these prostitutes where he lived, cutting them up and dumping them in the river. People passing by, walking dogs or something, saw the bags floating and fished them out. Bits of his victims have still never been found." It was hard to tell if he admired or loathed the guy from his tone; all I know is that he was well into all that kind of stuff.

"But that's not the weirdest thing; loads of people have murdered prostitutes and all that, it's pretty standard for a serial killer. No, what makes it really weird was when the police searched his house they found this devil mask. They didn't think much of it until they discovered the pictures..."

"Dude, this is just sick!" Jackson interrupted "We need to make an example of psychos like that. What gives them the right to live when they do that to people? This is why we need public executions."

I doubt this country would be any better off with a guy like him making the big decisions; the capital punishment thing is up for debate, sure, but some of his solutions to problems are truly bat-shit crazy, trust me. I told him to shut up and let Damian finish, intrigued as I was by the story of the London-based lunatic.

"Yeah as you've probably already clocked, they found pictures of the victims with that mask on. I think they were in a box in his wardrobe or something. It gets a little bit worse though; supposedly he had sent them to other people."

"Who the hell would even want those sorts of pictures?" Jackson sounded sickened.

"Yeah and how the hell would you find other people who were into that shit? Like when would you even drop the question? I can't imagine having a quiet drink and someone coming out with 'Hey we've known each other a while now and we really get along, but answer me this... what's your stance on dead prostitutes?' The world is insane."

It is something that I'd always wondered. Are those fascinated with such things attracted to each other by some kind of magnetic force, some kind of invisible tether pulling like-minded individuals ever closer? It always seemed impossible to me that subjects such as that would just crop up in conversation, although I suppose it had in our very own that evening. Maybe it was more common than I thought.

"It's all about the Internet; all the freaks can find each other on there." Jackson added.

"Guys, can we not talk about this while we're alone in the woods… or ever please?" Venn said. I decided to give him some stick for it, because I was an awesome friend, naturally.

"Aww what's the matter Venny-boy?" there was mock sincerity in my voice and I held the torch below my face as though telling a campfire ghost story. "You scared Freddy Krueger is gonna pop out of the ground? He only gets you in your dreams, dude. Better not sleep." I grinned a menacing grin, winked at him then put the torch back down.

He didn't say anything, but he rarely did. That's just what he was like. He shot me a dirty look but he knew I was only screwing around.

Unbeknownst to us all though, whilst we were chatting obliviously, a very real monster lurked not so far away.

■■■

More uncounted minutes passed. Wallet-friendly Vodka was out and had been for some time. The others had been steadily getting tipsier as the night progressed. I didn't drink, which meant as a teenager, I was a failure. My reason always was that I prefer to stay in control of myself. You will understand the sweet, delicious irony of that before long. Speaking of sweet and delicious, I was elbow-deep in a box of Oreos. They were my substitute for alcohol as the others passed the bottle around again. Jackson took a swig and then coughed and spluttered.

"I can't believe you didn't bring anything to mix this with, Venn." he spoke in a raspy growl. It sounded as if his throat was on fire.

"I brought water to drink as well..." Venn said defensively. Damian drank some vodka too; he didn't cough or splutter, but you could see him fighting the urge, even in the darkness. He patted his chest with a balled-up fist, trying to look like the bigger man I guess. Compared to Jackson he was the bigger man by a foot at least, so it can't have been overly taxing for him.

So there I was surrounded by intoxicated, bickering friends on a cold and still night, in the cheapest tent you could imagine, stuffing my face with cookies. Not exactly an awesome or heroic way to begin but hey, that's how it went. The minimal light from our torch was enough to make me feel like I hadn't gone completely blind, but I wasn't far off. The shadows surrounding us made our cramped conditions seem even more claustrophobic. I had drifted into one of my trademark wide-eyed, lights are on but nobody's home states. The conversation around me was just a dull hum; there were no words at all. Then I picked out the sound of rustling leaves and it sparked my interest. Venn heard it too.

"Guys?" he said. I remained quiet, still listening out. Damian and Jackson continued a conversation amongst themselves. "Guys, is something moving out there?" he asked meekly, and our tent became silent.

We listened intently for the smallest sound, the rustling increased and decreased in intensity. We were all holding our breath, the noise seemed to slow and then stop. Perhaps just leaves rolling with the wind.

"It's probably just the breeze." Jackson said but he sounded more concerned than he would have liked to let on. A simultaneous sharp intake of breath, the sound of a branch snapping echoed through our silent little world. It was quiet, but to us it sounded louder than explosions and gunfire, so tense were we at that moment.

That was about the second it dawned on us that we were truly isolated where we were. We had travelled far further into the vast wilderness than necessary. In that instant, in our minds, any number of demons and killers could be lurking outside our fragile fabric walls. I regretted not realising how far we had travelled sooner, not demanding that we stay closer to home.

No one needed to say anything. I knew the very same thoughts were bouncing around in the heads of my comrades. The tension became unbearable, but then cold, hard logic crept into my mind. I realised it was probably just some woodland creature, a deer or whatever. Just wandering about as they do. Yeah, it was the early hours of the morning but it's not like they have a curfew. Monsters don't exist, and serial killers aren't likely to be roaming about the middle of a forest at night, despite what the movies show you. My fear began to subside.

"Okay, I think if there's a monster we should throw Jackson out there and run like hell." I said in fake B-movie terror. Damian chuckled into his palm and I could make out Venn's wide yet nervous grin.

"That would do no good. He'd be less than a mouthful. The thing probably wouldn't even slow down to eat him. Just swallow him whole on the run." An anxious laughter passed through the tent and Jackson muttered something, no doubt condemning us to any number of unpleasant fates under his breath. I decided to share my flawless logic with the others.

"We need to chill. This is a forest remember? It's probably just a deer or som-" My sentence was cut short by a low and guttural rumbling sound. The vibrations of it ran through me and sent a chill down my spine. The night had just gotten a little colder for us all.

Silence fell again and no one moved a muscle. Eyes darted but everything else remained in a state of petrifaction. Every shadow became an enemy, and we felt like sitting ducks. To put it bluntly, we were absolutely shitting ourselves. There was a sudden click and we were plunged into total darkness. Venn had turned the torch off.

"What the fuck are you doing?!" Jackson asked in a harsh whisper.

"We don't want it to know we're here." Venn rasped back.

"We don't even know what IT is!" Jackson tried to stay quiet, but he could not stifle his frustrations. He began a seemingly endless rant directed at Venn.

This is where I got annoyed. I was sick of the tension, sick of Jackson. The icy air was giving me goosebumps and we were probably freaking out over nothing. If Godzilla himself were out there, I might as well let him eat me and get it over with. That fate would be far more bearable than what I was having to tolerate. Any animal out there would probably run away if it saw a light or heard movement anyway.

"Fuck this." I used my best action hero tone, picked up the torch and flicked it on, zipped open the tent and stepped out into the bleak and frosty night.

"No man, stay in here!" Jackson exclaimed, still whispering.

It was dark out there, but you knew that already. The branches above looked like skeletal fingers in the moonlight, reaching out towards the heavens in a futile battle to one day meet the sun. The evergreen trees blocked much of the silvery light of the moon, so hardly any reached the ground. A pool of darkness lay beneath my feet; it was a surreal feeling being stood there that night. Trunks stood like totems scattered around me. My friends crouched by the entrance to the tent looking out, probably expecting to see me decapitated by the Chupacabra or dragged into another dimension by Cthulhu. I shone the torch around on the ground. Nothing but fallen leaves and broken branches, stones and moss. That sound came again. That horrid, monstrous growl, but this time not so loud.

"Just get back in here, Zack!" Jackson urged again. The others were holding their breath, lost in the apprehension of what might come next, gripped by a fear of the unknown. I ignored him and began to walk forwards.

Whatever force drove me, it must have been the same one that pushed all those screaming victims straight towards Michael Myers blade. Shit if it were a movie I'd have been hollering at the screen, vainly telling whichever dumbass was about to get butchered to turn around and head home. If I'm honest though, I think what pushed me to head right towards the terrifying sound that night was a foolish desire. I wanted to be the one to show the others that they were all scared over nothing, that we were just chasing shadows.

Adrenaline filled me, and I was enjoying the fear in a twisted sort of way. My heart raced. Silently, first Damian, then Venn and finally even Jackson stepped out into the blackness and stood behind me. They all seemed like they'd rather be back inside, but the thing wasn't exactly Fort Knox. We'd be fucked inside or out.

As I searched the darkness something caught my eye, reflected moonlight. I wheeled around with the torch. A tell-tale shuffling of leaves underfoot came again. The torch illuminated the spot that grabbed my attention. Just beyond a vast trunk I saw steam evaporate into the air. Something was out there, and it was breathing. I walked hurriedly towards the spot. Big mistake.

"What the hell man? Just stay here!" Jackson, the voice of reason, shouted this time but I ignored him. I was on the brink of panic and at the same time, the precipice of elation. I rounded the tree, and when I did the torch fell upon a set of huge, glassy eyes. They were dead things, no trace of feeling or emotion, just the cold calculating gaze of a beast. A snarl tore through the air and echoed throughout our remote location. I turned on my heels instinctively.

"Shit, RUN!" I shouted to the others, not that they needed it. They were already disappearing into shadow. I tried fruitlessly to catch up, the torchlight darting wildly. I was attempting to navigate my way through the labyrinth of trees, barely able to see them in front of me, narrowly avoiding each trunk as it spawned from the blackness. The others were already out of sight, too far ahead. Good. Well, for them at least.

Adrenaline leaked from my every pore, pushing my body ever faster. I could hear thunderous galloping footsteps behind me, and in that moment I knew my efforts were not enough. Just as I barrelled past the freshly abandoned tent, I was swept off my feet. I careened through the air in a moment of pure silence. The creature, and even my own ragged breathing ceased to exist.

I hit the ground with a sickening crunch, and some of my ribs gave out beneath me. Hell, one whole side of me felt broken. I couldn't breathe no matter how hard I tried and the torch was long gone. Regardless, I leapt up, fighting through the pain. My instinct to survive dwarfed all other sensations. Once on my feet, I took off again. The thing was still in pursuit. It was far stronger and faster than me. Even then I knew I was fucked, but God loves those who try, and try I did. I dashed around bark and branch trying to put as much distance as I could between me and it. I didn't look back, but I could hear it effortlessly stomping its way around the trees. So the monster was agile too. It seriously wasn't a fair fight.

The chilled air whipped past me as I ran. The booming footfalls of the creature at my back got louder as it closed in. It sprinted straight past me and turned, digging its heels into the ground and sliding to a stop. It had gouged great scars into the dirt. Damn thing wasn't even trying. I slid to a stop myself. I couldn't make out any detail in the darkness, just a great hulking shape with bright eyes and equally bright fangs ahead of me. I saw its whole silhouette lower, ready to pounce. I let it happen, too exhausted from the chase to move. I gave my legs the order to run but they weren't co-operating, my muscles burned like I'd been stripped bare and doused with acid. The monster wasn't even panting.

It took a fraction of a second, and I was sure that was the end. Fearsome claws tore down my side and through my stomach. Warm blood ran free across my form and I collapsed to the ground. It's hard to describe the agony, the nausea and the shock. I wouldn't recommend it, put it that way. It bounded past me, still toying with its prey, but I knew the wound I had would be fatal. I felt pathetic acceptance wash over me. I just wanted it to end. Lying there amongst the moss and leaves I wished to die. Not to linger for long. I wished harder than I had ever wished for anything before. I stared up at the moon, defiantly staring back at me, mocking me. So weak and helpless was I.

Then suddenly my skin started to burn, like ghostly white-hot flames had enveloped me. I could not scream. I shook violently, heat built up in my chest and it felt like I was being torn apart from the inside. I thought that must have been what the end felt like. It took all my remaining strength to raise my head, only to see the shape of that creature a few hundred yards away. It threw its head back and a deafening howl shattered the silent night, then it began the run towards me once more. Coming in for the killing blow.

Acceptance, my skull dropped to the soil in surrender and I was faced with what little I could see of the forest shrouded in blackness. Then yet more galloping footsteps as two more giant creatures tore through the trees.

"Shit... there are more of those things..." I whimpered only to myself before the whole world cut to black.

29 Days Until the Next Full Moon

When the colour returned it was a garish and sickly yellow. I panicked, and in a daze I hurriedly hauled my aching bones upright to try to get my bearings. My head throbbed incessantly; my body was tender and pathetic. It was what I had always imagined a hangover would feel like, but having not experienced one, I could only assume. I clutched at my temples, but it did nothing to make sense of the world around me, or to fill in the big blank space from the night before.

Suddenly my stomach contorted, it made a sickening growl and an all encompassing feeling of nausea swept over me. Quickly I flipped over onto hands and knees as the contents of my gut shot forth enthusiastically to greet the cold ground beneath me. I was faced with a disgusting pile of viscous dark red gunk, spreading slowly outwards. There wasn't time to snatch a breath before the next onslaught came, filling my mouth with a disgusting, silky texture that I couldn't place. My eyes watered, I spluttered and coughed, heaving as more vile vomit erupted from my otherwise dry mouth. Yeah, I never said this story was gonna be glamorous.

"Hey." The words seemed distant, coming from the shadows. "Drink this, it'll help."

A clattering sound followed, I shook my head in an attempt to clear it and out of the fog something finally began to come into focus. A dented plastic bottle teetered back and forth on the ground beside me. I had to peel my hand away from the unexplainably sticky steel floor to reach for it. My movements felt unsteady, and I wavered, but managed to keep my balance. Sluggishly I removed the cap and began to drink deep from the bottle. It helped to settle my stomach somewhat, which was a relief.

"Are you with us yet?" The shadow asked me, I twisted and slumped into a sitting position in a slightly fitter state to assess the situation. Thick metal bars stood all around me, unflinching. Overhead was a dusty old bulb, showering me with that yellow light. It hung limply from its broken fixture. A figure stood outside my cage patiently, hidden in gloom.

"Who the fuck are you?" I asked wearily, trying to inject some anger into my voice but failing rather pitifully.

"Hey, take it easy. I'm Matthew, what's your name, kid?" I ignored him and took another swig from the bottle; leaving it empty I dropped it on the ground and slowly stood up, holding on to the bars for support.

Now I'll level with you, I was more than a little scared, as much as I hate to admit it. I had woken up trapped, I had no idea where I was or who was keeping me there, and I was in no fit state to defend myself. If there's one thing you learn at school though, it's that if you don't give the impression that you're not to be fucked with, people will fuck with you. I wasn't about to let that happen, not if I could help it.

"Take it easy? How about you let me the fuck out of here?" I said coldly. Foul language always helps, of course. I took a step back and kicked as hard as I could at the bars. It was in that precise moment I realised my feet were bare. It hurt like a bitch. Score one to Matthew. I kept my face expressionless as my freshly damaged foot pulsated in sync with my heartbeat, and tried to grab ahold of the cage again as casually as I could manage. My head was still swimming, but it was finally beginning to clear.

"Whoa, calm down, I know this must be a little strange for you, but please give me a chance to explain..." He pleaded far more rationally than I was willing to accept.

"Hell yeah it's a little strange, how often do you wake up in a fetish dungeon? Judging by this, I'd guess a lot more often than I do." I spat the words at him defiantly, even as my voice wavered nervously. I peered around, hoping for a way out, but the cage surrounded me on all sides. The bars at the top were spaced widely enough for me to easily get through, slim and nimble as I was, but immediately above were wooden beams and thick oak planks. Not a chance of escaping that way. Beyond my prison, all that was visible was the silhouette of the man calling himself Matthew. The dim bulb was a spotlight on the world's worst one-man show, starring yours truly.

It was then that Matthew decided to join the act; he stepped into the light revealing his features for the first time. A man of around average height, he was barely taller than me and looked to be in his early forties. Soft lines adorned his face, making him look sort of wizened; from what I could make out he had brown eyes and short hair that matched them in hue. He appeared doughy and malleable; all curves rather than harsh lines and suddenly I didn't feel nearly as threatened. His attire made him look professional; a white collar with a loose tie. Although just how professional one can be at holding minors against their will is questionable. Unless he had gotten an apprenticeship with Joseph

Fritzl, I couldn't see how he could possibly have gained the experience required for such a title.

"What? No it's nothing like that." His mouth contorted uneasily. "I'll take that as the result of a vivid imagination. No, this place has it's uses, but it's nothing as sordid as all that." he assured me, but decided to stop his sorry excuse for an explanation there.

"This place? Well where exactly am I? If you could be just a little more vague in your answer this time that would be great, thanks." Back to my old self in no time, even under the circumstances. Backchat was another skill of mine, along with the perpetual lateness.

"Kid, you're asking all the wrong questions. How about the really obvious one, how are you still alive?" That moment was one of realisation. The previous night's events came flooding back in an unavoidable torrent... the bickering friends, the shining moon, the searing pain. Those things...

I glanced down instinctively, to the place where claws had met flesh. I wasn't wearing my own clothes anymore. I was dressed in a white button-up shirt and a pair of slacks a lost property box would be ashamed to be seen with. Both garments were too big for me, but I was far more concerned with what lay beneath. I lifted the shirt, heart rate picking up, nerves returning in full force. As I peeled it back what was hidden became unveiled, a quartet of scars running down my side, tracing the path of the monster's savage assault.

So, you've probably heard of an 'out of body experience'. Well that was what most of my organs were having when I had blacked out. Imagine my surprise when all that remained the morning after were scars that already looked faded, like an injury from years ago, lacerations that had long since recovered. That was enough to make me drop the attitude.

"Alright... so how *am* I still alive?" I said the words softly, eyes still fixated on my wound.

In that moment, I was half expecting the marks to disappear, to fade from existence before my eyes, or to wake up in that tent with various profanities scrawled across my forehead in bold black ink. Matthew's voice snapped me back into reality.

"See, this is going to sound kind of crazy to you. This is how it is though. Had it not been a full moon, you wouldn't have survived last night." He told me solemnly.

"Well, if this is the alternative I wish I hadn't." I said, without ever giving my brain the order to march those words out of my gormless face. Call it force of habit.

Matthew let out a short bark of laughter at whatever chemical imbalance in my brain caused sarcasm to leak free, even when in the back of my mind I was considering the possibility I might be sliced thin and served on bread before the day was out.

"Understandable I suppose. Sorry, I probably should have asked this sooner, but what is your name?" When he asked this, I considered lying, but realised instantly it would do no good. I chose to give him my name, thinking perhaps it would be like him getting a pet. Once your pet has a name you form an attachment, and then you can't dismember it in the basement right?

"It's Zack."

"Okay then, Zack, I think it's about time I cleared things up a little. Through an unhappy accident, you've become involved in something beyond what most people are aware of..." He took a deep breath and then sighed to himself, stalling. "You remember that thing that attacked you last night?"

"You mean that thing that chased me, that thing that made my insides my outsides? Vaguely, yeah." Curiosity was evident in my voice.

"Well that thing was one of us." Disbelief was my immediate reaction. It wasn't possible, that creature was like six feet tall on all fours with fangs and claws. How could that become a man? I snorted derisively.

"Yeah right, you expect me to believe that shit? Let me out of here you fucking freak, and give me my clothes back." My body was sore in its entirety and my head still buzzed with a continuous ache.

"I can't let you out, and you can't have your clothes back I'm afraid, they were destroyed in the transformation. Look, just hear me out." He was calm and measured when he spoke, unlike me.

"Transformation, what the hell are you talking about? Open this damn cage!" My voice shook as panic began to build, I was trapped and alone with no way of contacting the outside world. I slammed the bars with an open palm and proceeded to throw myself against the locked gate; it bounced in place but easily repelled my feeble attack.

"If you'll just calm down and let me explain..." Matthew requested, still remaining prim and proper.

"Fuck your explanations, just open the goddamn door!" I shouted at the top of my lungs, creating a racket with my futile attempts to break free.

"Enough." A growling voice came through the blackness and I stopped dead. Matthew's eyes widened, fear reflected in the low light. They mirrored my own. I heard the flick of a switch and a long fluorescent bulb began the stutter into life, casting light on the rest of the room. It looked to be a cellar; dusty bottles of wine lay dormant on carefully arranged shelving. There were boxes neatly stacked and other cages, smaller than my own.

The scariest thing there though, more fear inducing than the cages, and the now clearly-visible coppery stains beneath my feet, was the towering figure of a man. He strode across the cellar towards me. My resolve disappeared. The man stopped still. He dwarfed any human being I had ever seen. I took a step back from the cage door in an effort to put some space between me and him. In that lingering moment of silence the stench of my own vomit flooded my nostrils and I felt like puking all over again.

He had slicked-back silvery hair, deep, harsh wrinkles, and wore an expression that could curdle milk. The guy looked like he'd been carved from stone and wrapped in leather. His broad features were spread wide across his face and his nose looked like it had been broken on several occasions. He peered at me through narrow eyes with utter disdain.

"You are alive because of him. You will listen." His voice resonated to my very core and something within me submitted. I was terrified; it wasn't fear of harm, it was as though he emanated some kind of dominant force. The fact that he could probably kill me with one gigantic hand didn't do much to comfort me, either.

Matthew's posture had stiffened up. He looked as tense as I felt when he spoke again.

"Okay. So Zack, we are Lycans. You've probably never heard of the term, it's not widely known. You may be more familiar with the term 'werewolves'..." He spoke like he was in a rush, like he wanted the conversation to be over as badly as I did. I just stared blankly at him, trying to redirect my focus in his direction and ignore the looming giant beyond the gate.

"You saw us last night, you know what I'm saying is true. You were saved by the moon, all Lycans are born when the moon is full... you don't remember everything from last night, I'm sure. But you can feel that something has changed within yourself, can't you?"

When he asked me that, I knew he was right. That white-hot burning sensation, the intense pain and the fact that I had survived injuries that should have been fatal. Something did feel different. I felt alien, less than comfortable in my own skin. I nodded slowly.

"So when you came along, you left us in a bit of a predicament. Obviously we can't allow you to go free without knowing what you are. You would be a danger to our secret and to all those around you. We cannot be discovered, Zack. That is of the utmost importance. Some of us had a solution to this problem that I found to be... distasteful, to say the least. You seem intelligent enough, so I'm sure you understand."

I knew what he meant alright – they wanted to kill me, make me disappear to keep their little cult a secret. My eyes flashed to the silver-haired man, his face unchanged. So that was how it was. These people were serious.

"Thankfully I managed to convince them otherwise. This was not of your own doing and because of that, you deserve a chance." Matthew's face was grave. I didn't speak. Honestly, I couldn't speak. The soundless seconds passed.

"You've been given another shot at life, think of it that way. You will have to return to us, though. We have to teach you to control what you are. It's the only way." It was hard to think of my second chance as a gift from these Lycans when I only lay dying in the first place because of one of them. He said I would have to return to them though, which gave me hope of being freed.

"Alright Matthew, if that's what I have to do." It was insane, completely ludicrous to be agreeing. When had creatures of myth and legend stepped from fable into reality? Regardless, knowing what they were willing to do if I did not comply, I had no real choice. I was getting out of there as soon as possible, preferably before those lunatics realised how insane an idea it was to let me go.

"I'm very glad to hear that." He said, smiling weakly. "It's time to get you home, before people wonder where you are." Immediately the giant spectre pulled a large key from his pocket, rattled it into the lock and swung the cage door open. I didn't have time to react; he brazenly kicked the back of my legs with a lazy swing of one gargantuan boot, causing me to drop to my knees. He took a piece of fabric from his pocket and used it as a makeshift blindfold; the musty cellar disappeared from view.

Being blind was further pressure on my already battered nerves. An instant hatred had formed for the anonymous asshole who took it upon himself to drag me back to my feet and bind my hands. I was scared of him, sure, but deep within my very soul I also loathed him intensely.

"Sorry about the blindfold Zack, it's just a precaution." Matthew said. I ignored him as I was dragged forwards. Shuffling sightless I felt myself being handed over. "Thank you for giving him this chance."

"This kid is your problem. He causes us any trouble, or he blabs, it's your head." The rough voice spoke joylessly.

"I know, I understand." Matthew replied submissively.

Our steps echoed across the cellar floor. I heard creaking hinges and an obtuse clattering of wood on stone. I was then pulled upwards, slipping on hard steps my shin connected painfully with a solid edge. I resented my blindfold even more so then. My progress didn't slow when I fell and moments later I felt the piercing crunch of gravel under bare feet. Then I was released to the unmistakeable sound of a car door opening, it slammed shut.

Matthew took ahold of my arm and began to lead me. The metallic clunk of a door could be heard again. I was threaded carefully into a soft leather seat. My aching muscles were given some relief as the weight was taken from my legs. The carpeted interior was also much kinder on my little toes than the piles of pointy rocks were.

Aside from the tell-tale sound of rubber on gravel as we pulled away, the tyres meeting the road and a clinking sound of unknown origin the drive was mostly in silence. They asked for a phone number, which I begrudgingly gave them. I was informed with dead certainty that had I lied about the number they could find me anyway. I believed them without a shadow of a doubt.

They asked me where my unfortunate excursion into the forest had begun. I told them that we had crossed the school athletic field and Matthew suggested that I be dropped near the grounds. That was fine by me. It was close to home, but I'd rather not show them exactly where I lived. Even if it would make no difference, there was a small degree of comfort to be found in any tiny amount of anonymity I could manage.

The minutes slipped by. It felt like a great length of time but when sight is taken from you, seconds seem to stretch. All the while, thoughts of just how ridiculous my predicament was bounced around in my head.

When the vehicle finally came to rest and my blindfold was removed, I saw that I was sat in the back of a worn out old Range Rover, dark green and mud spattered. The leather seats were battered and faded, cracks were abundant throughout and odd lengths of rope and random tools were scattered on the floor. The old giant spun around in his position in the passenger's seat, large knife in hand and for a second I expected him to bury it in my neck. He cut the rope and I rubbed my sore wrists.

"I'm sorry this is all so rushed, but you'll be hearing from us very soon." Matthew stated.

"Get out." Yeah, that other guy really had a way with words. I was more than happy to oblige. I dropped heavily out of the huge 4x4 and landed in a heap on the concrete outside the school gates. I stayed sitting on the ground until the filthy Range Rover pulled away and rounded the corner out of sight.

It had blacked-out windows so no one would have seen me perched in the back seat like Planet Earth's least valuable hostage. I dragged my fragile frame up from the floor; it was ice cold on my bare feet. With a last glance in all directions, paranoid that I was being watched, I hurriedly staggered home.

27 Days Until the Next Full Moon

When I finally got back to where I belonged, I had a text from Damian. 'Still alive?' I replied with a single word, 'Barely.' I spent my weekend hidden away, veiled by perpetual darkness. It was always night in my room, the blind always down. I found comfort in the gloom with one exception. The flickering box that kept me sane. My head buzzed for the entire weekend. I thought about werewolves and how damn crazy the whole deal sounded. I had no idea what lay in my future, or how much of what I had been told was even true. All I knew for sure was that things would never be the same. Finally, through some miracle, or maybe out of self-protection, I just managed to switch off. I became numb and unconcerned; the whole thing began to seem like some fever dream.

Monday morning arrived and my mom, who had been periodically checking I wasn't dead, (which was sweet of her) told me it was time to leave the safety of my cave. Education beckoned. As you can imagine I was thrilled at the thought. Reluctantly, I hauled myself free from the bed's tender grasp. I promised it I would call.

Jumping in the shower was like being born anew. The water woke me from my stupor and re-established some order in my scattered brain. That is, until I looked down and saw the scars. Suddenly, it all became very real again. I felt sick to my stomach.

I threw on my uniform in a hurry. Black pants, white shirt, black blazer. I wasn't in any hurry to head to class (Come on, you should know me better than that by now.) I was however just a little concerned my mother might see the mess the giant dog had made of me. Thankfully once I was dressed it was like my hideous disfigurement didn't even exist. I wouldn't have looked out of place at a bank, or even a funeral. Perhaps if Jackson actually died of one of his imaginary ailments I'd wear this get-up to the service. I wolfed down a heaping bowl of cereal and then headed to class. A mere five minutes late – a personal best.

When I entered the form room, which was in the maths department, math teacher *cume* form tutor Mr Osborne sat perched behind his desk. He decided to make a scene out of my entrance.

"Ahh Zack! What a privilege to see you so early in the morning. To what do we owe such an honour?" he said cheerfully with his arms outstretched. His sarcasm brought grins to the faces of the class.

"I'm eager to learn obviously, as if you even had to ask." I mumbled in return.

He was a good guy really, one of the few teachers in the school who wasn't, to put it politely, a massive twat. He really knew his stuff as well; when it came to math he could give a calculator a run for its money. That's probably why I actually had respect for him; he wasn't one of those slacking, clueless, textbook teachers, whose lessons boiled down to planting our posteriors and reading a book on the subject in silence for sixty minutes. That, and the fact that he didn't seem to have a stick up his ass about every little thing, like my lateness for example.

"Well, take a seat." he said, and smiled. I gave him a polite nod and the class went back to their usual murmurings and mutterings. I scanned the room for somewhere to park my button. Damian and Venn were sat in the back corner of the classroom next to each other, and parallel to them was an empty table. I sauntered between the rows of matching desks and matching chairs filled with matching classmates and took my spot next to my fellow former campers.

"Well, look who's back from the dead." Damian leaned over. "We didn't think we'd be seein' you again." he said enthusiastically. He'd obviously been itching to talk to someone about the events of that fateful Friday night. You know, someone more talkative than Venn, who just chuckled wheezily at his comment.

"Well you didn't seem too fussed about seeing me again when you were legging it as fast as you could in the opposite direction. I like how you abandoned me and left me for dead, cheers for that one." I replied sardonically. In all fairness though, if I were ahead of him when we were running for our lives, I'd have left him too. Fuck playing the hero.

"Hey, you gotta look out for number one." He gave the cheesiest wink of all time. "What the hell was that thing anyway?"

I feigned ignorance. "I dunno, maybe a bear or something. It was too dark to tell. It may surprise you to learn that getting a closer look wasn't exactly high up on my agenda. I just ran for it." I rambled quickly. For some reason I expected them to call me out, to know that I was hiding something. Call it my guilty conscience.

"I'm not sure it was a bear. Whatever it was, it was shit scary. I wasn't hanging around. Me and Venn got out of there

ASAP when we heard it." His eyes were unfocussed, as if reliving the fear.

"Yeah, I noticed. There was me, wasting precious breath on telling you guys to run, and before I could utter a word you were long gone. Thanks again, by the way."

"Don't mention it." He replied casually.

"We managed to stay together, but we lost Jackson." Venn said in his monotone voice. I was surprised he had managed a full sentence without any support or encouragement. Perhaps this was the beginning of a whole new era of Venn the conversationalist. Then again, perhaps not.

"You lost Jackson? Have you talked to him since?"

"Nah, I thought I'd text you to see if you had made it out alright. Fuck Jackson." Damian's tone was joking, but he seriously hadn't called him or anything. Damian and Jackson really did amuse me with their inability to get along; it was a source of near infinite entertainment. Watching them argue for hours on end, those were simpler times and in a way, I almost miss it now.

"Oh, by the way, you didn't happen to pick up Venn's bag did you?" Damian asked me.

"No. Why?"

"Because I could really do with that back." Venn interjected weakly. He meekly lifted a supermarket plastic bag with all of his school stuff in. The lack of expression in his voice only served to make that even more hilarious to me. I burst into a fit of laughter; he was so pathetic at times it was practically adorable. It helped to make me feel a little more at ease, like normality was returning. Damian reliably informed me that despite the loss of the bag, the tent would not be missed. It could stay there lost and forgotten for the rest of time for all any of us cared.

Mr Osborne didn't call out the register like most teachers, he knew every person in his form by name and he would mark them silently on his list as they came through the door. It doesn't sound like a major thing but it does serve to make the fifteen minutes of form time more relaxed. He was like a Zen master. He never seemed to stress about anything. Not long before the end of form he beckoned me to the front desk.

As I approached him I took in his features. His bushy dark brown beard and thick, wavy hair that linked so seamlessly you couldn't tell where one ended and the other began. The crow's feet around his eyes that made him look distinguished and world-weary, the tie that made it seem like he was making an effort to look professional. He was a short man, which made him appear almost gnome-like. Still, I couldn't give him a hard time for that, since he was one of the few authority figures who didn't default to hating me.

"Zack I notice you're wearing trainers, as usual. They look new." He said glancing down at my feet, perfectly calm. They were, my mom had thankfully saw fit to replace what I had lost when I told her I threw the others away after stepping in the worlds biggest turd.

"Yeah, they are sir, is that why you called me up here?" I always wore trainers because fuck shoes.

"Yes, all I'll say is they stand out, so try to avoid unwanted attention. You know how some of the staff here can get." Mr Osborne seemed like a prime example of an enlightened man.

Forget Buddha -- he was what someone who was truly content was like.

"Will do sir, thanks." I gave him a nod again. Why can't all teachers be so lenient? Some would send you home for stuff like that, or threaten you with all sorts of crap. Detentions and maybe even suspension, all to show their authority. It's amazing what the smallest amount of power can do to someone in their middle age. He then peered around me to tell the class it was time to head off to lesson, so I bid him farewell, left the room and descended the three flights of stairs necessary to reach the bottom floor. Then I had to head for the upper part of the school towards the IT department. It was quite the trek.

I drifted through that lesson and the two others I had before lunchtime in my usual way, head down for the duration, failing to even feign interest. Computer studies makes my style of learning so much easier to pursue, as there's a great lump of plastic, glass and circuitry between the student and the interfering enemy. The return to mundane routine made my experience in the forest seem like a far off fantasy. It would all become very real again, soon enough.

When lunchtime arrived I found that Jackson had returned and my trio of friends were quarrelling as usual. That is to say that Damian and Jackson were, and Venn was an awkwardly-positioned bystander.

"You just left me out there, ran for it and left me!" Jackson was livid; his eye even twitched a little. Venn was trying his very best not to laugh, bless his heart.

"Every man for himself..." Damian said and grinned with shark-like teeth.

"I'll remember that. Oh and you Zack, thanks for trying to help me! No one called all weekend; I'm fine by the way!" he spat. He was so frustrated, but it was difficult not to find it comical.

"Well that makes a fucking change," I replied wryly, calling attention to his hypochondria. "I was at the back, you tit. If anything you left me." Which was a fair point, considering I was the one being spread about the forest like some sort of human fertilizer, while the rest of them escaped unscathed.

"Anyway," Damian cut in. "forget that, where have you been all morning?" He asked Jackson.

"If you must know, I had an allergic reaction to something I ate and my throat was closing up. I had to go to the hospital. Yeah, like I said, I'm fine!" Jackson repeated, obviously hoping for more sympathy than he was ever going to get.

Venn accidentally let a quick chuckle escape, which was a shame after all the effort he put into keeping his laughs in. He was met by a ferocious glare from Jackson, whose eyes narrowed menacingly. Venn looked a little embarrassed and even went slightly red, which I found to be quite amusing. Jackson got terrorised all day about his possibly true, probably false allergic episode. Damian even went as far as to tell him he wished his throat *had* closed up because at least then he couldn't chat so much shit.

We wandered from lesson to lesson, and I slouched through each one in a daze, paying little attention to anything any teacher said or did. I was glad when it was over; I had regained a sense of normality that had been distinctly lacking. Being in familiar halls and seeing familiar faces, even just being bored out of my mind, made me feel at ease. All that was shattered, though, when I returned home to find I had a text from Matthew. It simply read, 'We'll pick you up Wednesday at 6:00pm.' but behind those seemingly innocent words were secrets that no one was to know.

The thought of having to step back into the world of wolves sent a chill down my spine, and of course I could tell nobody. Forget school… Wednesday, 6:00pm. That was when the real lessons would start.

25 Days Until the Next Full Moon

Over the following days, I was constantly on edge. The hours just seemed to drag. You know what people say… the waiting is always the worst part. The building apprehension became damn near unbearable. How would anyone even go about training a werewolf anyway? I had a terrifying vision of being savagely beaten with a rolled up newspaper. My situation wasn't exactly a common one, but all the standard rules apply when it comes to bricking yourself over the unknown. Creeping towards that deadline was agony. Then, the time finally came.

I was stood on exactly the same spot where they left me on that brisk Saturday morning when I was dumped back into reality. The seconds felt like minutes, and the minutes like hours as I loitered, waiting for fate to play its hand.

I stared down at my feet and the new running shoes didn't look so new anymore. They were more grey than white already. To me it seemed like the perfect time to analyse them in agonizing detail. Anything to take my mind off my nerves. I counted the lace holes, crouched on the curb and traced the pattern the laces made with my finger, admired the small scuffs and scratches they had picked up in my short time spent wearing them. Interesting things, aren't they? Well, no, but at the time I would have drank paint to get out of what I had to do. Forget watching it dry, that would have been a goddamn pleasure in comparison.

Sadly, the world kept on spinning and time continued passing in the same selfish manner it always does. My attempts to avoid the inevitable by admiring my footwear failed miserably as the familiar grubby Range Rover pulled up in front of me. It was in far worse shape than my footwear, cosmetically at least.

I swallowed hard, a cartoonish gulp, as though I were momentarily suspended in mid-air after running clean off of the edge of a cliff. It's embarrassing to say, but I actually began to tremble. I had all this adrenaline from nowhere and nothing to use it on. It was a dreadful feeling. My fight-or-flight response was working overtime, and I silently cursed Walter Cannon.

I saw through the window that there was a passenger; I could immediately tell who it was. Reluctantly, I stepped closer to one of the grimy rear doors and with a sweaty palm I tugged it open. The metallic, mechanical clunk was my cue. Gingerly, I climbed inside. My cocky, sarcastic attitude had evaporated again, dispersed and re-joined the ether.

I felt just like a little kid, lost somewhere unfamiliar, helpless. It had dawned on me that I was heading back into the world of monsters, a world that continued to exist despite the misleadingly average few days I had experienced since my first brush with it. A world I had become a part of, whether I liked it or not. What really shifted my anxiety into overdrive, though, was that silver-haired guy. Something about him set my teeth on edge.

No one breathed a word when I got on board; it didn't feel right for me to disturb the soundless air. The silence was harsh, and in my head it spoke volumes. Bad shit was about to go down. I was convinced of it.

The stranger's silvery-white hair was swept back in the way you might imagine a con-man or a member of a crime syndicate to style their own; he turned to look at me. His mouth was nothing more than a stern line upon his face, and coarse wrinkled skin did little to disguise the hard shape of his jaw, set firmly in place. His clothes looked heavy duty, like some kind of work wear, covered in pockets and big brass zips. The fading desert camo of his pants gave him the appearance of a general who'd seen more than one battle too many. A thick leather belt adorned his waist, and his long dark coat shrouded him in the kind of mystery I was pretty sure I didn't want to solve.

He tugged me forwards, applying the blindfold and binding my wrists again. Matthew, in the driver's seat, glanced over his shoulder then disappeared from view. I got the feeling I'd be speaking to a camera in the near future. Telling everyone I was fine and being treated well via a video message, with an AK pressed at my back, naturally.

We set off to no fanfare, just a soundtrack of tyre noise and the rumble of the diesel engine. Silence was normally something I embraced, but not then, not when all I could think of were worst-case scenarios. Perhaps I'm just a negative thinker. The journey seemed to stretch on. All I could think about was how I was heading deeper into their territory. There, if they wanted me gone, I wouldn't stand a chance.

I bet the suspense is killing you, just a little bit? I can tell you this for sure, the suspense was doing a pretty good job of trying to kill me. I felt on the verge of having a heart attack but I fought to hide it, to bury the fear deep where it couldn't be seen. For a moment I imagined my heart beating so fast that it exploded, showering the entire interior of the car in crimson blood. I wondered if those assholes might say something then, just a few words. I doubted it.

I already felt sure we were going back to the forest, where else could werewolf business possibly go down without being noticed? It brought back all those thoughts of serial killers, monsters and demons from the moments before my attack, during that hugely successful camping trip. This time though, it was far worse. I knew that monsters really existed out there in that organic labyrinth, it was worse than that though. They weren't just out there. They were also living among us. I knew what these things could do, because they had done it to me before. I was headed straight for the core of it, their territory.

Silence persisted, soundless moments dog-piling on top of one another, each more intolerable than the last. I tried to keep my mind off my hopeless situation, thinking of anything and everything that didn't involve me being eviscerated. Of course, by making this my goal, my imagination became filled to the brim with nothing but my own severed limbs.

Lacking sight and hearing only my own ragged breathing gave me a feeling of being a part of the surreal. Something felt wrong, like all the pieces of reality weren't quite fitting together. Almost connecting, but not quite. I existed in the gaps where the laws of nature could bend or even break. Then the silence was briefly broken by Matthew's voice.

"We're almost the-" He said with no expression. The silver haired speech assassin next to him must have cut him off; obviously he wasn't supposed to be talking. I kept my mouth shut, hearing another human voice did little to ease the ever-increasing tension. 'He's on my side, Matthew's on my side.' I thought to myself. I had no idea what was going on, why no one was speaking, all I knew is I didn't like that old guy and I wasn't enjoying the whole experience in the slightest. 'He's on my side.' That became my internal mantra while I just sat waiting; being dragged towards destiny in a diesel wagon. 'He's on my side'.

■■

The 4x4 shuddered to a halt. My blindfold was swiftly removed. Matthew and the silver-haired man got out of the car in perfect synchronicity; my door was opened for me. I know, how polite of them to do such a thing. I stepped out, hands bound, still poked and prodded by a feeling that something horrific was about to occur. It wasn't like that feeling you get when you think you're being watched. It was a completely different sensation. More like the sort of feeling someone stood in the road might get in the moments before a frantic drunk driver tore the world out from beneath their feet. Perhaps it is the feeling of meeting fate, or maybe it's just that your instincts know you're fucked before the rest of you does. It felt like the car was coming, to strip flesh and shatter bone, leaving me as nothing more than an unrecognisable smear on concrete.

The old timer grabbed the dangling length of rope tying my hands and began to lead me forwards. As he did so I attempted to speak to Matthew.

"What the he-" I started, but was cut off.

"Please, stay quiet Zack." He said calmly, but there was something else in his voice. An element of regret. Or maybe it was guilt. He wouldn't make eye contact; he just beckoned me to follow. It was as if I had done something wrong in breaking the silence, as though there were something sacred about it and I had sullied it with my heathen's words. I considered trying to run, then realised how futile it would be, considering I was tied up. That, and should I try to flee, the man-mountain was my opposition. No choice but to play nice.

I did as I was ordered, shuffling behind Matt. The old guy was at his side. I couldn't shake dark thoughts from my mind. I tried desperately not to think of words like murder... execution... but naturally in trying not to bring those words to mind, that was all that bounced around in my head as I trudged my metaphorical green mile. I was being led deeper into the forest in a direction unfamiliar to me, and I could almost hear the news reports already. 'A young boy went missing today... sixteen years old... a student at... human remains discovered, suspected to be that of the missing boy...'

I wondered for a moment just what the forensics team would find. Would my remains even be considered human anymore, or would they discover something all together different? A twist to the formula - A change in the DNA. I couldn't help but ponder how much of me was something other than what I used to be.

Something finally broke the pattern of brown and green; a cage that revealed itself through the veil of bark and branches. Yet another fucking cage. This one was bigger than the one I had been in before, though... the same height but bigger in every other dimension. It looked to have identical features. The matching thick and heavy bars all waiting obediently, just as they had been during my last incarceration. What stood out the most, though, was what was inside it. It only added to the dream-like quality of my fucked-up situation. There was a deer shackled and chained within. Its restraints were cruelly short so it had almost no ability to move. The thing seemed incredibly distressed. It shook its head violently and struggled to separate fragile looking legs from its bonds, its efforts were fruitless.

I wanted to ask questions, but I knew they wouldn't be answered; I wanted to at least look into Matthew's eyes hoping for a glimpse into his soul, to see if good or evil lay within him. All I was faced with was his shirt covered back. You can't tell a lot about a man from his shirt, no matter what fashionistas tell you.

Then there was the other guy; I trusted my instincts on that one. He was dangerous, no question. I could just tell he hated me, resented me or something. Maybe it was a sense I didn't know I had that told me so. Maybe it was the expressions – or lack thereof – on his face. Either way I knew it for sure. That guy detested me.

We reached the cage; its door was wide open already. It was obvious what they wanted me to do. I looked up at Matthew who was positioned next to the deer's prison.

"Are you serious?" I asked him with a little anger, as my hands were cut free. My usual fire was far from returning, but beginning to rekindle.

"Just get in, Zack." He said in that same way, the sound of a man defeated. He still wouldn't look me in the eye, staring into the distance, no focus whatsoever. I hesitated at the threshold, not wanting to move any further. Suddenly I was met by some gentle persuasion as the stranger planted a hand like a stone slab between my shoulder blades and pushed me forwards, taking the choice out of my grasp.

The sight of the distressed deer made me feel incredibly uncomfortable. It stomped and shook. Obviously it wasn't enjoying itself in there, but who would? I know I wasn't. I felt really quite bad for it, and I empathized with its position. Both of us were trapped against our will; it was bound by chains, and I was forced into place by the two guys stood at my back. It made pained noises, sounds of desperation in its own tongue. We were both helpless animals when it came down to it.

What happened next I wasn't expecting, the silver haired guy stepped into the cage with me and closed the door. Matthew locked it hastily with a large metal key. The old-timer took off his belt, that formidable looking belt that I had noticed earlier.

"Wait, what the fuck?" That was all I could say before a huge brass buckle struck the side of my face with a deafening crack and I dropped to the ground with no resistance at all. Light spots flashed, blinding me. Dazed and in shock. lying face down on the sticky floor I coughed a little, choking on my own spit and blood. Gross, I know. I writhed around and attempted to turn over, the belt came down on me again this time striking me in the side. I wailed as it painfully connected with my ribs. This cleared my head and I scrambled as fast as I could away from my attacker and towards my fellow captive. What a fucking bizarre scene. Imagine an outsider looking in.

"Matthew, what the hell's going on?!" I bellowed, fear painting my expression. He didn't say a word though; he just stood by the door, key in hand, and stared at his feet. My side stung like a bitch, and I found it hard to breathe. Air felt like it was coming in solid lumps. The deer tried to kick out beside me but could scarcely move. I was ready to run, poised to make an escape but there was no way out.

So there I was stood next to the deer that looked, if anything, even more stressed out by the whole state of affairs than I did, when the guy stepped forward and swung the belt again. All I could do was crouch down and cover my head, trying to go into defence mode, and ending up in the foetal position on the icy metal surface. How pathetic, right?

The silver haired man kept raining blows down upon me with that belt; it slashed its way through the air with sickening force. The way he did so was almost clinical. This wasn't movie violence. This was real. A slow and sustained attack, genuine flesh and bone being twisted, distorted in unnatural ways. There was nothing glamorous or cinematic about it, and the pain was a close second to my Lycan attack, only this new suffering didn't seem to have an end.

Wrapped in weak, tender tissue and begging for it to stop, I lay there. I couldn't even cover my head anymore, so ruined were my arms from the brutal onslaught. It was total and utter surrender on my part, I took the blows as silent tears ran free. Finally it stopped. I could taste a mixture of salt and copper. Limply I rolled over to see that guy, still stood there. I hated that man with every fibre of my being as my eyes met his dead glassy orbs, he passed his belt through the bars and it dropped into the rustling leaves that carpeted the ground around my torture chamber. He turned back to face me.

"Looks like its game over, kid." He stated coldly, reaching into his long coat and removing a gun from an inside pocket. I don't know much about guns, but it was jet black and it was pointed right at me. What else did I need to know? It was then that my rage began to boil up. I was going to die, shot like a dog out in the woods by some cunt I didn't even know.

Something deep inside me stirred. It felt like it was alive in and of itself, a powerful force, trying to claw its way free. An immense heat began to build in my chest. I slowly began to raise myself to my feet, battered and bruised limbs being lifted from the cold hard ground. Every inch of my skin burned white hot. Some unknown entity was tearing away at me from the inside but I didn't care.

Rage consumed me, eliminating all pain and fear. In those moments it was like I was a completely different person, transformed. Gone was the feeling of weakness, replaced by the sensation of power. It was intoxicating.

"You better pray the first shot kills me." I spoke words that were not entirely my own. Suddenly it felt like invisible claws from within had burst from my chest, pain returned at lightning speed and I screamed in agony but the anger consumed it all.

"Shit! Open the do-" was all I heard before I was lost to the darkness.

Better Off Forgotten

There's something truly harrowing about waking face down in a pool of blood. I had been Lycan again.

That second time wasn't exactly like the first though; there was the fact that it wasn't a completely blank space in my memory. I had fleeting moments of something there. Brief flashes of bars and blood, steel, leaves and that poor eviscerated deer. I really felt for the damn thing. It was only a few fragments of something remembered, snapshots of single moments in the hours where I was a monster once more. Still, I suppose that was progress. There was no amount of control, I could recall those ephemeral images but that was all they were, still shots. It didn't feel like I played any part in creating them, yet there they were, sat in my memory amongst all that other shit in my head that makes me the person I am.

My vision was filled with liquid crimson. It rippled as I breathed. My body ached just like before. My stomach was churning and I could have easily slept right there and then, but despite feeling broken, I planted my hands into the fleshy pulp and raised myself from the ground. It rained red beneath me.

"Are you okay?" A familiar voice asked.

I swept sticky hair from my face and tried to stand but the most I could manage was to collapse weakly onto my side with a splash. I looked down seeing my own stained and naked flesh.

"Yeah I'm fine, just that time of the month." I groaned, taking in the scale of the gloopy mess around me.

The symptoms were the same as before, the severe headache and the distinct feeling that someone had ran me over, then decided to reverse. I looked up, bleary-eyed, to see a blurry Matthew stood by the open cage door clutching a towel and a bucket of water. His attire was formal and his expression, gloomy.

"I'll give you some privacy, to clean yourself up." He stated politely. He placed the towel on the ground next to a fresh set of neatly folded clothes and yet another new pair of running shoes. He then turned and walked away, giving me some space.

It took considerable effort to drag myself the few feet necessary to reach my makeshift shower, but I managed. All the while covering my more intimate areas as much as possible to preserve the little dignity I had left.

I stooped low and began to rinse the blood from anywhere I could see it; the wind spitefully lashed at my wet skin, so I washed in a hurry and grabbed the towel. It bore revealing signs of previous use. Dark stains in permanent residence. For a moment I wondered how many had used it before me, but I immediately stopped caring when the breeze hit again and I began to shiver.

After dressing faster than I'd ever cared to before, in an outfit that made me look like a tribute act for a member of the world's shittiest boy band, I staggered through falling leaves to greet Matthew's back. The first thing that came to mind – when the mind in question finally kicked into gear – was the cause of my cage-based misery.

"Hey," I called, and Matthew turned. "where's the other guy?" I questioned nervously, glancing over my shoulder and seeing no trace of him.

"Locke." His eyes were on the ground.

"Huh?"

"His name is Locke." So, now I had a name to put to the face I'd have gladly taken a shovel to.

"Spare me the details man, is he here or not?" The apprehension I felt was evident, given away by a slight tremble in my words.

"No, he left... he's hunting."

My four-legged friend invaded my thoughts again, now nothing more than a runny puree spread on the ground. My stomach lurched, gurgling queasily. Despite the horrific fate the deer had suffered, I thought it must have had it easy compared to whatever was in Locke's line of sight. Hell, I'd had a pretty rough time myself. I'd have been almost grateful to be brought to a swift end rather than endure what I did.

Knowing that the hulking old behemoth wasn't around brought some of my usual attitude back, and it made me see more clearly. Reliving the events before I blacked out in a single instant, anger started to flood my system.

"That asshole beat me half to death; he pulled a gun on me and you let him do it. Why?" I'd consider my slight profanity justified.

"Because Zack, it was either do this his way or he'd kill you. That was the choice, and it's not really a choice at all is it?" He told me, every note in his speech in a minor key. He looked utterly downtrodden; this dulled my rage rather swiftly. There was a drawn out silence where I hoped he would elaborate but I got nothing.

"But I don't understand. Why is he doing this to me? This can't be normal?" The use of the word 'normal' seemed somewhat out-of-place, given the state of affairs.

"No, you're right, this is far from normal. Ordinarily the process of training a new-born is slow, it's a gradual thing. This is not natural." Matthew sounded disgusted, repulsed by what was happening to me, and for that reason my respect for him grew.

"So why is he doing this to me, what the fuck did I do?" I asked, aggravated.

"Call it resentment. You're a hindrance and a risk, so believe me; he'll look for any excuse to take you out. You didn't do anything, Zack. Wrong place, wrong time, that's all." The words were so sharp I was surprised they didn't sever his tongue.

I wasn't sure how to react. Icy tendrils ran up my spine. I wondered what the hell I had gotten myself into. The words 'He'll look for any excuse to take you out' rattled around in my head. I tried to swallow but my mouth was bone dry, filled with the lingering taste of a meal I'd rather forget.

"So that gun..." I began but was interrupted.

"It was loaded. He would have shot you." He said each syllable with a conviction that left me in no doubt. For the first time in my life, I truly feared for humanity, which at the time I still considered myself a member of. If there were people that could be so cold, who could take the life of another with no ounce of emotion in them, then what chance did anyone stand in a world so unfair? His face appeared in my mind's eye, the moment where that gun was pointed in my direction. No trace of movement... he didn't even blink, fully prepared to end my existence without a second thought.

"I still don't get it though, what was the point of bringing me here if he wanted to kill me? He could have just killed me the first time I met you." The pieces just didn't add up.

"Look, here's how it is. Locke is the Alpha. That fear you have of him, that's inherent in all of us. When you got caught up in all this, his solution was to put you down, but I convinced him to let you live. Honestly though, I doubt what I said did much to sway him. You're alive because he allows you to be, and he allows you to be for his own reasons." Matthew explained.

"So basically what you're telling me is, I owe my life to a fucking masochist." I guess that was my Eureka moment.

"Yes, sadly that seems to be the case." His eyes locked on to mine. "Don't let him break you. He may try, but fight it. Never give in. Some of the others may kiss his ass, but I know he's more beast than man." That was the first time I'd heard Matthew's prim and proper mannerisms break down, a lapse in his robotic facade.

"You hate him, don't you?" I felt less alone already, knowing the answer.

"Of course I do, but what can I do? He makes us strong, keeps us safe. He sees the kind of things he does as necessary. I will never agree with that. There's no way out, Zack. I just try to limit the damage he can do as best I can. What he has done with you though, it's insane even for him." I could see the pain in his expression. Controlled fury dwelled within.

"What do you mean?" I asked growing fearful. He let out a sigh.

"Well normally a new-born wouldn't become Lycan again until the next full moon, or close to it at the very least. He forced it out of you the only way he knew how. He played on your base instincts, the instinct to survive." He shook his head "Even disregarding that you're too young, this is not how it's supposed to be done." He told me frantically, gesturing with his hands.

"Too young?" Matthew opened his mouth but before he had the chance to clarify his eyes widened. He inhaled sharply.

"He's coming back. Listen, no matter what, you have to keep composed." I must have looked as confused as I felt because he grabbed my face roughly in one hand. "Look at me. Regardless of what you have to do, don't let yourself change. You cannot control yourself yet. If you feel it beginning to happen you have to vent your emotions, do you understand?" He questioned me, his nose only a couple of inches from mine. I nodded quickly.

"Good, now stay quiet." He quickly spun me around and placed the blindfold around my eyes. So I was both blind and bemused. Looks like shit just got serious.

24 Days Until the Next Full Moon

After being dumped nearby home I spent the remainder of that evening rattled by confusion; it kept me from sleep and forced me to enter a never-ending cycle of insubstantial information. I was yet to meet any other Lycans aside from Matthew and Locke, but I saw three of them that night which made me curious. Who was the other, and were there more?

I didn't really know where I stood as a part of their fucked up little posse, but what I had to go on gave me the clear indication that the old bastard was the biggest threat to my personal well being. There was nothing I could do to alleviate the stress. This coupled with the sensation that there was a party in my stomach, and everyone was shitting themselves profusely, meant that I only got a few fleeting moments of reprieve. As a result, I felt like death walking when the sun rose.

Birds tweeted incessantly, which I found to be rather distasteful. I stared blankly at the discoloured cream ceiling of my bedroom. I was finally coming to terms with the fact that I wouldn't manage to snatch another second of sweet sleep before having to head off to school. My mom strolled in and brazenly confirmed my worst fears as I lay, scars hidden by the covers.

I forced myself out of bed in a state that fell somewhere between a hypnotic trance and severe brain damage. My stomach cramped painfully, twisting itself into knots and remaining there.

I guess that deer wasn't agreeing with me, and hadn't been all night. I felt a little less sorry for it.

I was offered breakfast but my gut protested. The thought of eating gave me a sensation like I'd fallen awkwardly on a broom handle and it was lodged somewhere deep within my digestive tract, never to be seen again. I turned down the kind offer, stepped out into the glaring light of a new-born day and made the marathon journey a few yards from my home to the school grounds.

I entered through the main doors to the lower building, ignoring the desk immediately in front of me, where the frumpy looking secretary wasted her life doing crossword puzzles and picking her teeth. I headed to the right for the ancient looking wooden staircase. For some bizarre reason, only staff members were allowed to use it. Us lesser beings were supposed to cross the length of the building to use the paupers' staircase, lest we get ideas above our station. I was one such pauper who dreamed of greater status though, so I damned the rules and ambitiously made my way up the creaking steps.

I got about halfway when Miss Clarke appeared at the top of them, hands on hips. Seeing her made my stomach turn some more.

"And where do you think you're going?" She asked in her usual totalitarian fashion.

"To form? Oh my God, if this is about the stairs..." I spoke through gritted teeth.

"It's assembly Zachary! The head will be here any second, so get in there." Her eyes were narrowed behind her thin spectacles, indicating that either she meant business or was constipated and attempting to hide her discomfort. I always assumed she was in a state of constant constipation and that was what made her so uptight.

Regardless of whether that was the case, my contorted gut had taken all the fight out of me. So I hopped uncomfortably back down the stairs, immediately regretting it as the heavy landing jostled me violently, exacerbating things further. I strolled past the pointless secretary, absentmindedly clutching at my abdomen, and pushed my way through the heavy swinging doors into the main hall.

The room was packed with students already, chatting noisily amongst themselves. Grey plastic chairs were abundant, all evenly spaced in large blocks with a runway down the middle. Most of them were already occupied, so I was left with an aisle seat next to a meek, dark haired girl I didn't know from the year below. She glanced at me uneasily as my poorly tum made a noise like it was considering making a break for it. I didn't return her look, I was too preoccupied trying to keep my insides in. It was only a matter of seconds before the door behind us opened, and a deathly silence filled the room.

Mr Starkey entered with all the presence of Kim Jong Il on a golf course. He was our head teacher, he was five-foot-nothing, and he didn't half compensate for it. It was compulsory that everyone stand as he entered and goose-stepped down his very own runway. I stood weakly along with the rest of the room, and my stomach began to bubble sickeningly. I considered the fact that making it to my feet hadn't caused my bowels to empty, a victory.

Starkey began his imperial march, crooked beak pointed firmly at the heavens. I began to sway uncomfortably, being overcome by a rather inconvenient nausea.

"Hey, are you okay?" The considerate raven haired girl next to me whispered. I felt the surge of oncoming sickness as I went to answer. I covered my mouth instinctively and held it there, pausing to regain my composure. General Starkey continued his stroll of self-gratification and the rising bile retreated.

"Yeah I'm fi-" I began but I never got to finish. The vile soup that existed within my putrid belly returned with an almost admirable quickness, and this time I was powerless to stop it. The best I could do was turn my head away from the thoughtful girl and towards what I hoped was nothing more than empty space. Yeah I know what you're thinking, of course it fucking wasn't. Headmaster Starkey had just stomped his merry way right into the line of fire and I can safely call what occurred, a direct hit.

An unbelievable amount of slimy red vomit lurched forth, covering Kim Jong Starkey from head to toe, completely destroying his ashen coloured suit. I guess that'll teach him for being so short. The room (which I thought was silent before) got infinitely quieter, no one dared to breathe as he stopped dead in his tracks. No one that is apart from me, I was breathing rather heavily after my belly decided its residents should jump ship; my head was low as I tried to fill my lungs with much needed fresh oxygen. The gravity of the situation hadn't yet hit me, which is odd considering gravity played such a pivotal role in my predicament.

His eyes bulged, horrified. In a flash, that freeze-frame moment ended as the entire school erupted into fits of raucous laughter. Staff members posted around the perimeter of the hall rushed in and ushered Starkey away in a hurry, like a politician who had narrowly avoided an assassination attempt. He left a slimy trail in his wake. I went entirely red, flushed with embarrassment. Miss Clarke bound towards me, and for an instant I wished I had more in the tank for a secondary assault.

"Zachary!" I stood in a state of gormless disbelief "Get out of here now!" She bellowed right in my face, and with that my gaping mouth closed and my body returned to working order. To the sound of uncountable heckles and copious amounts of giggling, I lightly hopped over the pool of doe smoothie and power walked my way from the hall.

20 Days Until the Next Full Moon

Well if there's one thing I learned from my act of social suicide, it's that there's no better way to guarantee a day off than to violently vomit over the head of your school. I actually felt better instantly, in the sense that I didn't feel sick anymore. However the sheer embarrassment of it all made me want to hide away forever. To never have human eyes set their gaze upon me again, so long as I should live. It's amazing how you can go from off the radar to the only thing people are talking about in as long as it takes for your puke to reach the ground, destroying a suit and a pair of expensive looking leather shoes in the process. Still, I got the Friday off, so every cloud I guess.

I spent my weekend in voluntary solitary confinement. My mom assured me people would forget about my little mishap in no time, and I assured her in no uncertain terms that that shit would go down in legend as far as the school was concerned. Not the good kind of legend though where heroes slay demons, the kind of legend where I'd be working for minimum wage at a supermarket checkout twenty years later and some asshole from back in the day would recognise me. Recognise me, and then laugh right in my drug addled face for it.

I received more than a few texts from my caring cohorts over the following days, mostly regarding just how much people were snickering about me. They revelled in it, the selfish bastards; all apart from Venn who maintained his usual radio silence. As for the other two though, I silently vowed to get my revenge some day. I also received an invite to a pointless bout of drinking in a field known for hosting inebriated teenagers. Obviously I declined. The invite was from Damian; he told me Venn was going too. I guess both of them hoped that if they stood near some popular people for long enough, they would become one with the hive mind through some sort of osmosis and find their rightful place high up in the social hierarchy.

Needless to say when Monday rolled around, I was dreading going back to school; I'd have done almost anything to get out of it. Honestly it turned out worse than even I was expecting. I ate my cereal slowly, having only recently managed to get my appetite back. Its sweetness did nothing to ease my suffering. Getting through the gates, into the main building and up all those stairs was a chore as I shuffled reluctantly towards my end goal of further public humiliation. I clung on to the strap of my backpack but I'm not sure why, perhaps I was planning to throw it at the first person who made a wise crack.

I entered the form room late, my head low. Some of the rowdier classmates of mine cheered mockingly and clapped my arrival. I ignored them and stalked my way as menacingly as possible to the back of the class, dropping heavily into the seat next to Jackson, who I will openly admit was my least favourite.

"What's up vomit comet?" He said sounding positively thrilled with himself.

"Vomit comet? You've had days, personally if that's the best you've come up with then I'm ashamed, and more than a little disappointed." Every syllable emanated gloom.

"Oh, don't you worry. I'm sure you'll hear plenty more before this is over my friend." His smug grin made me want to separate his head from his neck.

"I don't fucking doubt that."

"Well good for you, there's at least *something* else for people to talk about today." Damian spoke from the adjacent table and gestured towards a figure I didn't recognise. A blonde girl sat chatting to one of our classes stuck up bitches, Briana. Briana was a skinny brunette with a tiny nose. She honestly couldn't think more of herself if it turned out she was fired directly from God's ball sack, across time and space whereupon she crash landed here on earth to save us all from the impending nuclear holocaust. It is a shame that wasn't the case though, because at least if it were she might have something remotely interesting to say.

"The new girl's name is Lexey, cute right?" Jackson spoke. His eyebrows danced, and it was truly disturbing. I ignored him and addressed Damian.

"So, how was your time on the field with Venn and that bunch of people you don't really know or speak to but just stand near to feel included. Did you make any fwends?" My mock toddler voice was especially accurate.

"Nah, not really," Damian said "ended up getting drunk pretty much on our own, it was boring. Forget that though, Jackson wants to make 'fwends' with the new girl." He made quotations in the air. His tone making it obvious he thought the odds of that were pretty damn slim.

"Fuck off, it could happen!" Jackson - as irritant as ever.

"Do you really think after being here for like half an hour she's going to want some scrawny little tit asking her out?" I asked him, then added "No offense."

"Jackson, there's more chance of Eva Longoria showing up naked astride a *dragon* to give you a ride home tonight." Damian rolled his eyes at Jackson's entirely unwarranted confidence. The little shit was just a short, pasty, bespectacled teen with every medical condition under the sun after all. Not what you'd call a prize catch.

"I'll prove you all wrong. I'm actually pretty good looking you know!" Jackson retorted, sounding somewhat offended that the rest of us had the cheek to doubt him. We all burst into laughter, and watched as he launched into the least intimidating fit of rage I've ever seen. He told us all where to shove inanimate objects, and where we could go for disagreeing with him. We were enjoying having fun at his expense, but it would be short lived because math class was looming. At least having math meant I didn't have far to walk, my room being opposite the one I was already sat in.

Once there though, the lesson for me consisted exclusively of trying to scribble on the last page of my math book until it was entirely covered in black ink, and none of the white of the page was visible. It took a lot of effort, but I'm nothing if not determined to achieve my goals. By the end of the hour I had almost done it. I was going to have to wait until my next maths lesson to add the finishing touches to my magnum opus.

Nearer the front of my book the day's date stood proud and alone above no work. Almost all the pages before it followed the same pattern. Date after date with nothing beneath them, accurate depictions of all I had achieved. Anyway, the lesson was pretty standard, aside from getting verbally abused because of the events of that assembly. It was the class after that was interesting, for all the worst reasons.

IT was up next; we wandered out of the lower school, over to upper. Slaloming between all our other uniformed comrades until we finally reached the building, walked around its circumference until at last the door to IT-2 was in sight. When we entered our usual teacher wasn't there, instead there was some short, greasy looking guy wearing a polo shirt and sweat pants.

"Everybody, sit down please." He said in a manner that suggested he didn't really give a shit whether you sat or not. We were all a little confused but we did it anyway, wanting to see where this unusual excursion into the world of information technology would take us. My group of cohorts and I took up the best part of a row at the back of the classroom; each row consisted of five computers all neatly in a line. We were in the blind spot, the place to be if you felt like slacking. I got the immediate and distinct impression there wouldn't be much learning going on for the next sixty minutes though, regardless of where we positioned ourselves.

"Your teacher is off sick today, so I'm the one covering. I'm Mr Woods." Maybe he was hoping for a round of applause or something, but what followed his mumbled introduction was an awkward silence. "Now I'm going to pass this sheet of paper around, please sign your names on it, as this is the register for today." He scratched at his short, oily, dark brown hair as he spoke; a repulsive example of the human race.

"Who the hell is this guy?" Damian leaned over and whispered.

"I dunno," I replied "he looks like they found him sleeping in a bus stop." I had an expression on my face, which seemed to effectively indicate my distaste for the guy's lack of personal hygiene. Damian snickered quietly.

When the paper reached us there were many ridiculous names that I didn't recognise written on it. Mike Hunt, Ivor Biggun, you get the idea. There were some real names on there too. I suppose they were written by the people who were scared of being trapped inside the school during a fire as teachers frantically read out a bunch of fake names, desperately trying to make sure everyone was safely out of the building. My chosen alias was 'Jack Russell' and I don't care what you say, under the circumstances that was freaking hilarious. I even smirked a little at my own inside joke.

Once the paperwork was completed, Mr Woods piped up again.

"Now if you go into the worksheet folder, I want you to do worksheet four please." His voice was monotonous, like the boorish whir of an extractor fan; just listening to him was enough to put me to sleep. He then proceeded to sit at the front desk with his feet up and pulled out a McDonald's bag. We sat there in disbelief as he began to tuck into a Big Mac.

"What the fuck? This guy isn't even pretending to care." Jackson said with a short bark of humourless laughter. The whole room was engaged in conversation; no one had opened the worksheet he had mentioned.

"This guy's a real clown." I heard someone say. I don't know who it was, but I agreed with the sentiment entirely.

About fifteen minutes elapsed, in which time I became the target for numerous nicknames. I'm sure they were hysterical. Everyone chatted amongst themselves as our slimy supply teacher stuffed his face with fast food. Once he was done he stood, squashing the grimy bag into a tight paper ball in his hands and said

"Okay, I'll be one minute, get on with that work sheet. If anyone has finished it already, do the next one." Then he left the room. No one had even started, let alone finished the worksheet, and it looked as though nobody had any intention of changing that. So we were all just left to our own devices. Some took that phrase more literally than others, pulling out their phones and furiously hammering away at buttons and screens with an incessant clicking.

When the authority (not that you could call Mr Woods that) leaves the class alone, that is ordinarily when the worst amongst its members will try to take advantage of the situation. Even the smallest room can temporarily become an anarchic republic, devoid of all law and order. I don't consider myself amongst the worst because I never tried to cause trouble for fellow students, only for the teachers that deserved it. That's fair enough right? It's not like I was even as bad in that regard as I was made about to be.

Someone who was amongst the lowest of the low, however, was this kid Charlie. He was tall, doughy and blonde, with narrow eyes and a podgy face. He looked as though if you squeezed him he'd leak pus like a gargantuan zit. A zit that had sprouted legs and developed the ability to exude arrogance. Charlie was the sort of person who had the misinterpretation that everyone liked him, and who acted like a dick for his own amusement. What didn't help is that people wouldn't oppose him just because of his size, the fat lump.

They were scared to get on his bad side because he was prone to violence and as dumb as a post. No one wanted any trouble, so they just laughed along with whatever he was doing. This helped to reinforce the positive self-image his two brain cells working in tandem had managed to manufacture. In his eyes he was the class clown, and everything he did was side-splittingly funny for us all.

"Looks like it's time for a kick about then!" Charlie exclaimed, getting to his feet. He unzipped his school bag and pulled out a football.

"I really hate that kid." Venn said quietly to himself.

"Don't we all man." Jackson responded with a groan.

I saw all the faces in the room drop as he kicked the ball as hard as he could towards the ceiling. It bounced around erratically, hitting computers and random individuals. I saw Lexey, the new girl, in the corner with Briana, the same girl she was with in form. 'What a great first impression of our fine institution' I thought to myself.

They both ducked low behind their monitors, trying not to get hit. When the ball finally came to a stop, Charlie in a fit of laughter walked over to it, picked it up and did exactly the same again. It was amazing how people tried to look like they didn't mind, or didn't care. Even trying not to obviously defend themselves when the ball was bouncing unpredictably. The room collectively winced every time it ricocheted off a screen, a desk, or the roof again, displacing flimsy foam ceiling tiles. I guess no one wanted to display weakness in school. Canis Canem Edit, show no fear and all that. That kind of stuff really pisses me off.

That was when I started to feel different; I immediately recognised the sensation and began to panic. It was that creeping sensation like something awaking within me. The heat building in my chest, just like it had before. 'Shit, what do I do?!' I thought to myself, synapses frantically firing. My frustration building, becoming closer to rage, I placed a restraining hand on my torso knowing it would do no good. I just hoped Charlie would stop soon, or that something would make my rising anger subside. He kicked the ball again, then guffawed obnoxiously and it infuriated me. Some even laughed weakly along with him. Perhaps hoping if they did he might aim his next shot in the other direction.

The fire behind my ribs grew in intensity, the stirring from within my very core becoming more vicious as my anger increased; it was physically painful attempting to hold it back, it felt like something was trying to break free. The shaking started, my stomach clenched with the anxiety of it all. I couldn't allow myself to change right there in that classroom, I would kill everyone. An entire class of students eviscerated, and I am the only survivor? That's what you call unwanted attention. To top it all off, I'd have been found naked, and probably in a puddle of entrails. It doesn't really scream innocence, being discovered in that state.

As my heartbeat intensified, I hoped and wished for that greasy useless bastard Mr Woods to come back. To return and put a stop what was going on, but he was nowhere to be seen. The ball hit a girl on the back of the head and she just sat there lifelessly. I put all my efforts into remaining still as Charlie kept on laughing. It became too much, with a trembling hand I clutched the side of my desk and heard the sound of the wood splintering beneath my fingertips.

"Hey, are you alright?" Venn said softly with honest concern.

"I'm fine." I struggled to say through gritted teeth, the pain made my voice break a little.

The ball had come to a stop, and Charlie was walking across the room to retrieve it. My head was filled with the words 'I swear to God, if he kicks that ball again...' but I had no real end to that sentence, no plan. He took it in his hands and was gearing up to take another shot. That was when I recalled what Matthew had told me, to remain composed no matter what. I had to find an outlet. Fast.

The throbbing in my torso was close to unbearable; I sprang to my feet and took up a nearby empty chair. I wheeled it back and hurled it forwards with as much power as I could muster. Silence filled the room as it sailed through the air. In slow motion you could probably have seen Charlie's stunned expression as my four-legged gift flew at high speed towards his face. It was far too rapid for him to react.

The plastic and steel connected with his features at a blistering pace; there was a loud crack as it made contact, and the sickening sound of sinew splitting in two. It struck with such force that his legs flew up in the air, like the very earth itself had been pulled out from beneath his feet. He arced backwards, leaving a crimson rainbow in his wake. The useless turd came straight down on his colossal back with a thud. His face looked like a piece of impressionist art to me.

Instantly I felt calmer, the heat was fading away. I breathed a sigh of relief. Still in perfect quiet, I made my way back to my seat without the slightest sound passing through my lips, inhaling deeply and exhaling slowly. Air in through the nose and out through the mouth. I sat back down, with all eyes following my every minute motion. There were a few seconds of stillness in which my friends just stared.

"That was fucking awesome." Damian said, awestruck. Other faces perched behind the various scattered desks displayed a mixture of emotions, from fascination to disgust. Then the door flew open and Mr Woods, the man with about as much charisma as a rice pudding, re-entered the room. Disbelief washed over him as he surveyed the class.

"What the hell is going on in here!?" He bellowed. No one uttered a word as he stood there in the doorway and took in the sight of the unconscious mass that lay before him.

JACKSON AND THE NEW GIRL

Yeah, that was one crazy morning. The possible consequences of my actions weren't immediately evident to me. I was just relieved that I hadn't done something far worse than minor assault with an article of furniture. There was a certain buzz surrounding me that day. It's funny how all mention of my vomiting on the headmaster seemed to disappear as quickly as it had began, who says violence never solves anything?

An ambulance came for Charlie and took him to whatever hospital would deal with that gelatinous accumulation of flesh, and I made a point of acting like nothing had happened. Innocent until proven guilty, should any authority deem it necessary to pry into my business. My associates thought it was their place to inform me of just how deep in the figurative faecal matter I may be during our lunch break.

"Holy shit man, you hit him hard. What do you think is gonna happen when he comes 'round and tells people it was you?" Damian asked with a mixture of that awe from when Mrs Chair met Mr Face, and a little bit of third party apprehension.

"I don't know," I replied robotically "cross that bridge when I come to it." I was numb to the thought of swift justice finding me at that instance in time. I didn't want that lack of feeling on the matter to go away.

"Yeah but you could be in deep for that. If he's seriously hurt, who knows what could hap-" Damian continued, trying to take my happy ignorance away. I cut him off.

"Look, I don't know alright! I'll just deny it and we'll see what happens." I snapped at him when really I shouldn't have.

"Whoa, okay man chill, I was just saying." He sounded more offended at my outburst than anything; in retrospect he was quite right to react so. Jackson decided to add his two cents.

"Fuck Charlie anyway, he's dumb as a goddamn post. He probably won't even be able to string a coherent sentence together to accuse you, especially if that chair hit him as hard as it should have. Honestly, the Spartans would have left him in a ditch to die, I don't think you've gotta worry about it." Venn gave a crooked grin at Jackson's words but said nothing as per, he seemed to enjoy the whole chair to face episode.

People like Charlie are easy to read, the shallow sort who parade around advertising their lack of intelligence. People like Venn however, the quiet types, they're the ones to look out for. The ones who don't wear their hearts on their sleeves are often the most interesting of them all.

I sort of abandoned the conversation at that point because I really didn't want to talk about it. I did what I had to, and no one else could possibly comprehend the severity of the situation if I hadn't. I just hoped it would die down fast and of course, that no one would rat me out. My plan was to play the fool. I didn't see anything, I didn't hear anything, and I certainly didn't throw anything. Granted it wasn't the most sophisticated of plans, especially since my scheme in its entirety involved doing absolutely nothing, but I was completely at a loss when I tried to come up with alternative options.

I stood absentmindedly, daydreaming as they nattered on. So please, allow me to take this opportunity to draw attention to my sporadic thought processes. I guess all of our minds, both yours and mine, work in their own distinct ways. You might think in straight lines, like a train on track. You know, simple, effective and reliable? I on the other hand, do not. My thought patterns are more like a scatter bomb landing on a busy marketplace. There probably was logic, reason and motive in the beginning, but all of that shit just gets lost in the chaos of the aftermath. If that makes me a little hard to follow, deal with it.

I came back to the real world when I heard Damian utter the words

"Oh shit Jackson, it's the new girl." He gestured with his head towards Lexey, who was with that other human female Briana again. We were stood on the school track field amongst random smatterings of other students, all spread out across the grass. Some sat, some lay, we stood for some reason. Lexey and Briana had just passed us by. They walked far away enough that it didn't look like they were associating with the group of losers that we blatantly were, and dropped their stuff on the ground. They then proceeded to drop themselves.

I did momentarily wonder if Briana, who had been in our classes for as long as I cared to remember, had any other friends. Despite her obvious sense of self-entitlement, I guess she wasn't exactly the popular type herself to be latching on to the new kid so readily. I am willing to admit that I'm not a particularly fair judge of such things. Especially since our posse, with a little makeup and a couple of bolts through Venn's neck, could pass for Adams Family castoffs.

"Looks like this is your shot, time to put up or shut up." Damian smiled widely, a crocodile grin.

"You really don't think I stand a chance, do you?" Jackson was irate, obviously the most deluded member of our ragtag team of rejects.

"Jackson, even Venn's got more of a chance than you." I said, harshly managing to offend the pair of them.

"You think?" Venn asked quietly, in a voice that suggested it was a conscious effort to push air past his lips. As with most occasions when thoughts left the safety of his mind and headed over the top into the great wide world beyond, it was as though he had never spoken.

"Fuck all of you man, I'm going over there. I'll make you eat those words." Jackson exclaimed, a perfect example of short-man syndrome. He then checked his specs were in place, (which is just about the least cool thing someone can do anyway) turned on his heel and marched away in a fashion even the most regimented imperial storm trooper would be proud of.

A sensation of shock passed over us. We all stifled laughter, revelling in the failure that would undoubtedly come. Now perhaps this is the moment you're expecting me to tell you that against all odds, Jackson gets the girl and they live happily ever after? Oh if only we lived in such an ideal world my friends, if only. We watched in silence, all of the dialogue between our misguided chum, and the two females was lost to the breeze, but our full attention was still on them. We seemingly hoped that through body language, or perhaps clairvoyance that we might be able to decipher what was going on.

He rounded them so that he could face his prey head on, and stooped down to be closer to their eye level. If I had any ability to lip-read then I might have been able to tell you how their conversation went, but I am regrettably unaware of the exact exchange. All I do know is that there was an immensely gratifying moment about forty seconds into their chat, where the cocky smile on Jackson's face turned faster than a waltzer in the hands of the stoutest gypsy entrepreneur. He then looked a little aggressive, and said some no doubt toxic words to his (definitely not) future wife. That was before waving his arms around in that 'who needs you!?' sort of way, and beginning to stride back towards us. He shuffled with his head down somewhere near his feet, and his tail between his legs.

As you can imagine, we were there for him in his time of need. I mean, rejection is hard to deal with, so we were practically obligated to offer a comforting shoulder to cry on. And if you'll believe that, you'll believe anything.

"Well done Casanova, you just got shot down!" I helpfully informed him through cupped hands.

"What an absolute tit!" Damian bellowed, doing the same thing. Apparently we had both momentarily become a pair of beer swilling hecklers.

"Just piss off!" Jackson called back as he made his way closer. He was practically trembling with rage, and still saw only the ground beneath him. He stumbled over a blade of grass that was apparently a little tricky for the speck to surpass.

"Loooooser! Loooooser! Loooooser!" Damian chanted, and Venn did that same old breathy laugh as he stood there smiling so wide his teeth were actually showing. Trust me, that was not a common occurrence for him.

It became apparent pretty quickly that Damian's chant was a little grating for more than just Jackson though, because Briana turned around on the ground and decided to join our long distance discussion.

"Can't you retards shut your damn traps!?" It was a demand more than a question, but Damian carried on undeterred. Jackson reached us again but the chant didn't stop, or even decrease in volume. Then unexpectedly, the new girl had something to add.

"For the love of God, just grow up!" Lexey called, under the misapprehension that we were not acting our age. I must admit, it took me off guard.

"Oh, go fuck yourselves." Damian retorted. His response could have done with more intelligent and expressive prose, it's true, but sometimes you can't beat good old-fashioned cursing.

"Excuse me?" Lexey said, insulted. Then, the pair of them got up and strode towards us. Again not exactly what I was expecting to happen, and I could tell from the look on Damian's face it had come completely out of left field for him too. They barged up to our pathetic foursome and got close enough to invade our personal space.

"You know, not everyone wants to hear you running your mouth!" Briana screamed at Damian, close enough for him to smell her lunch. She was tall for a girl. Not as tall as him, but tall enough that he didn't tower over her like he did most people. Her mousey brown hair was tied back in a limp ponytail, and her sharp features were set to ferocious mode, like a tiger ready to leap at its next victim.

"Oh piss off Briana, just because you've finally found a friend." Damian sighed and rolled his eyes.

"And what gives you the right to talk to someone like that?" Lexey broke in sternly. Then, she proceeded to verbally tear us to pieces. First up was Damian.

"You're a disgusting, gangly jerk. So why don't you keep your thoughts to yourself?" then Jackson "You wouldn't have a chance with anyone blessed with the gift of sight, not in a million years. I mean, what the hell are you on?" Venn was next up "You, well you're just plain creepy!" Ouch. A bit harsh considering he hadn't said anything. I got it last.

"I don't know who *you* think you are. You show up late, you don't do a thing from what I've seen, *and* you smash some kids face in with a chair? Do you think you're better than everyone else? I've been here a few hours and I can already tell you're a hopeless waste, and to top it off, you're a fucking psychopath!" Now, I think it was highly unfair of her to verbally attack me so much more than she did anyone else, especially when you bear in mind the fact that Damian was the main offender. Can't argue with her on anything she said though. Sharp as a tack that one.

As she stood there and abused me, stripping my character down to its component parts with startling efficiency, I wasn't even mad. I was just completely shell-shocked. Her choppy blonde hair fell just short of her shoulders, and she had far softer, rounder features than Briana did. Her height was on par with Jackson, but despite her lack of size, she was seriously putting us in our places. I am slightly ashamed now, that I didn't use what I hope is my above average intellect to fight back, but at the time I was truly lost for words.

When she had finished, she just gave us the evilest of evil glares. The sort Hitler might have given, if he parked his car and returned to find it clamped. Then she stomped off towards the upper school building.

"Pricks." Briana spat, and followed off after her. Her saliva landed on Venn's shoe. All we could do was stand there as they left, heading for the school. The bell to signal the next lesson rang out across the grounds, but it took a little while for it to sink in. When it did, we sulkily began to make our way towards the building, and our next thrilling lesson.

"Well, aren't they just charming?" Jackson barked sarcastically.

"What a pair of bitches man." Damian mumbled.

"That Lexey, she really seems to hate you Zack." Venn spoke in his usual monotone. His powers of observation were far greater than his ability to hold a conversation, it seemed. We entered the upper part of the school on our way to a General Studies lesson of all things.

"Whatever." was my only response. It was flattering to know I made such a strong first impression.

I wasn't bothered that she hated us really. I wouldn't have liked to admit it, but I was sort of impressed with how she had stood up for herself. Impressed, yes, but did that mean I liked her? Hell no, not even a little bit. What kind of self-respecting monster gets put in his place by a fragile, little blonde? I had the power to unleash indiscriminate murder on my entire little town, but apparently I lacked the skill to think of a decent comeback. Still, I considered the notion that I had managed to get someone to loathe me in a few short hours, somewhat of an achievement.

Walking down the hall, flanked on all sides by wooden doors, we bumped into Mr Osborne. Displays adorned the walls, old work bordered with that cheap coloured paper you might get handed during a Sunday school crafts session. I admired them in a fashion I can only describe as 'exceedingly innocent', rather than making eye contact. It was rare that I saw him at all, what with me being so late to school every morning, so seeing him twice in one day was practically unprecedented.

"Boys." He greeted us. We all greeted him in return.

"I'm sure you know about what happened in Mr Woods' IT lesson today, no doubt you were there. You wouldn't be able to give me any details would you, perhaps tell me who hit the pupil who's been rushed to hospital?" Mr Osborne's voice was full of scepticism. He wasn't dumb, he knew that everyone must already know who did it.

"Sorry sir, I didn't see a thing." I told him, whilst perspiring aggressively beneath my shirt. I did my utmost to sound earnest, looking at him as briefly as possible.

"Yes, I thought as much. No one's seen a thing apparently." I felt a twinge of relief. I knew that it was probably just buying time rather than actually getting away with it, but still, it made me feel significantly better about my predicament.

Obviously no one liked Charlie, or felt enough empathy for him to spill the fact that it was me who did it. It's like school follows a prison mentality in some respects. No one likes a snitch, and right then I was thankful for that unwritten rule. The others denied all knowledge of events as people kept streaming around us in the rapidly emptying halls, until only a few remained.

"Well, I had best let you boys get to your lesson." Mr Osborne spoke after a long and thoughtful pause. His nostrils flared. "Zack, you have a very strong smell about you today."

"Well, thanks... I guess?" It was probably the stench of deception. My friends chuckled like sly hyenas. Hadn't I suffered enough for one day?

"Consider deodorant. Off to lesson then." Mr Osborne said sharply, and walked away with considerable haste. We headed for the door to an English room that doubled up as a room for General Studies. Clearly it wasn't important enough to get a room of its own.

Jackson took it upon himself to take a big, exaggerated sniff.

"At least now we know why the new girl hates you so much. You do *fucking* stink." Jackson said, smiling at his own joke.

"Well you didn't exactly get a glowing review yourself." I spat back, feeling a touch self-conscious. A hint of recalled emotional pain flashed across his face. We entered the room for another dull and pointless lesson. Oh, the Joy.

19 Days Until the Next Full Moon

We were all left smarting after our wholly undeserved verbal assault, but it didn't take long for those memories to fade into obscurity, and for our usual poor attitudes to return in full force. The rest of that day was as monotonous as usual, save for the odd backhanded comment towards our new found enemies. Obviously we wouldn't have said anything to their faces for fear of getting our asses handed to us again. Still, we toiled towards our secret, and near silent revenge. Revenge neither Briana nor Lexey would be aware of, but in our eyes it was revenge none the less, and helped to stitch together the fragments of our shattered egos.

There were random staring contests between Damian and Briana across the various classrooms throughout the day. Through narrowed eyes his efforts were valiant, but in the end he was no match. At least she had chosen the right opponent though, because I expect had it been Jackson, he'd have mistaken it for sexual tension.

My evening and the following day's school hours were equally average and uninteresting, as most of them are. Just a few more hours spent wandering the maze of halls. We were the rats contained within, but instead of cheese all that lay at our labyrinths end were better job prospects, opportunities for higher education, all that thrilling stuff. Even now, with all the mistakes I have made, all the pain and chaos I've caused over my relatively brief span, the idea of living a normal life still seems far too damn tedious.

I do regret what's happened, and occasionally think about how a regular existence could have played out. I would truly go back to the night that I was attacked and take it all back if I could, for the greater good so to speak. Having said that, I get the distinct impression fate would have found some other way to royally fuck me over regardless.

After yet another school day of impromptu daydreaming and a distinct lack of attention paid to the proper authorities, I returned home to find a message on my phone. It read 'tonight, six o'clock'. I remember thinking to myself that I really should start carrying the damn thing around with me. Then I wouldn't have to come home to this proverbial kick in the nuts after all my hard work was done. Still, I suppose that would have meant it spoiling all the joys of my education, so I guess ignorance is bliss sometimes. It certainly seemed to be in the case of the Lycans. If I had any real social life to speak of, it would have been left battered and unrecognisable by my intermittent trips into their world.

I had just over a couple of hours to kill before I would be whisked away once again, and absolutely nothing to fill them with. I slouched in my shambolic room, clothes strewn across every inch of carpet. Me, lying corpse-like on an unmade bed. A wardrobe with one door missing, a victim of past frustrations. All of its splendour, bathed in the glow of my small, black, portable TV, with an aerial as big as it was balanced on top of it.

So naturally I watched cartoons. You know the deal, bad guy does something bad, good guy superhero stops him and saves the day. Honestly I find them a little frustrating. Nothing in life is that simple. Given the correct amount of spandex and an ultimatum, what would you do if you had to choose between saving someone you love and a whole bunch of strangers? As a species, humans are more selfish than they would care to admit.

Now I will confess that nerves had been steadily building in the background whilst I awaited my date with the dogs. It became far more pronounced though as I walked out of my door and towards the filthy parked Range Rover, which was already stood humming on the spot when I left the house. So now they knew exactly where I lived, if they hadn't figured it out already.

Thoughts started rattling around in my mind about my previous assault, and I did worry about the potential of it happening again. Last time it was a shock tactic, and that probably wouldn't work for a second time. I wondered if that were the case, how would they remedy that? It didn't bear thinking about. All of those nerves evaporated though, when I opened the back door and climbed in to see a woman sat alone in the front.

"How's it going Zack?" She said cheerily, I could see her smile in the rear view mirror.

"Not too bad thanks." I murmured, a tad confused. A strange lump formed in my throat, making speaking a difficult task. The kind of fear I had felt evacuated my body swiftly, only to be replaced by an all too different sort. The musty interior of the 4x4 had never seemed so cheerful, and yet so daunting.

"You don't have to sit in the back, you know?" She chuckled to herself. When I was expecting to see the weathered old face of

Locke, the rounded features, strawberry-blonde hair and green eyes of the feminine stranger were a welcome replacement.

In silence I clambered back outside and jumped awkwardly into the front passenger's seat, slamming the heavy door behind me. She reached across to shake my hand.

"I'm Rita, Matthew's wife in case he hasn't told you." She informed me kindly. I took her hand in my own clammy paw and shook it because I felt obligated to do so, what with her making the effort and all.

"Erm... Zack." I replied in a manner that suggested I wasn't that sure that I was Zack at all, despite her having already called me by name.

"It's a pleasure. Oh, and don't worry, no blindfolds today." Rita beamed, threw the car into gear and set off. I stared forwards and said nothing for a little while, until the silence felt *too* awkward, even for me.

"So... how come it's you here today instead of the other two?" I asked, trying my hardest to project the unwilling words from my mouth. Buildings whizzed past us as we travelled towards the more rural roads.

"Don't get your hopes up, I'm just dropping you off." She told me with a smirk. I was very disappointed about that, I assure you.

"So I'm gonna end up with Matthew and Locke again?" I hoped against hope that this wouldn't be the case, but I already knew the answer even before I asked.

"I'm afraid so, kid." She seemed to find my disappointment somewhat humorous.

"Fuck my life." I muttered under my breath.

"You'll be fine, trust me. I understand that Locke is a pretty intimidating guy. You're scared of him right?" She asked me, turning a shade more serious. I'm sure you remember when they took me to the cage. Every fibre of my being wanted to run and I still just marched obediently. The guy's very nature is oppressive, I felt physically weighed down when he was around. I nodded in response to her question.

"Well don't let it get you down, we all feel it. He's our Alpha. You're sort of... predisposed to be scared of him now you're one of us." In a sense I liked this explanation, it meant that me acting like a complete pussy when he turned up for the first time wasn't my fault. Well, that was the story I was sticking to now at any rate.

"Wait, one of us?" I blurted out shocked "You mean you're-
"

"Yeah. Why wouldn't I be, what you think a lady can't be a Lycan too?" She seemed a touch offended.

"No, no, that's not it. It's just, I couldn't imagine you becoming... you know... that." I mumbled reluctantly. She seemed all too feminine to become a snarling beast.

"Well you better believe it. You and me, we're the same. Apart from you can't control yourself. I'd say that's pretty normal for a teenage boy though, so don't sweat it." She smirked. I felt myself turn a little red.

"He's wary of you though, you know. Locke I mean." Rita cocked her head. I was taken aback, and also more than grateful for the swift change of subject.

"Why would he be wary of me?" I practically whispered. The trees were whipping past us as we hurtled along a road that had been cut through the forest itself.

"Well, I shouldn't really be telling you but... you know when you were in the cage and he sort of encouraged you to transform?"

"Encouraged?" I snorted quietly. I was straight up beaten half to death, then threatened with a loaded gun.

"Well, you know what I mean. Anyway, getting to the point. You Phased faster than either of them has ever seen before. You've got real potential, Matthew truly thinks so." She nodded as if to validate what she had said. "Also, you kind of tried to attack Locke on his way out of the cage."

It took a moment for the words to sink in. I was a threat to him. I found a kind of morbid pleasure in this. The gruff, gargantuan wolf-man felt threatened by little old me, by my 'potential'. He certainly didn't act like he felt anything but animosity towards me. Regardless, he had no reason to feel threatened; I just hoped that it would mean I'd get treated in a more favourable manner in future. Perhaps he'd even belt me less, that wasn't too much to hope for was it?

As we made our way down the snaking roads, I tried to talk as little as possible. Rita was an easy person to get along with though. She was a calming entity in this realm of chaotic elements. She brought a sense of normality to an otherwise unbelievable situation. The way she acted gave me confidence that once I was over the whole learning stage, everything would settle down into what could be considered a consistent existence, one with less of the turbulent ups and downs. All that would have been pretty great, had I not felt the need to grip on to the seat the whole way and avert her gaze as much as possible.

■ ■

We turned away from the tarmac and down a dirt road, finally shuddering to a halt outside a wooden cabin. I had no idea where we were, but it was way the fuck out there. As soon as I had jumped out of the muddy green Range Rover and slammed the door, Rita spun it around, waved goodbye and left me stood there. It was only moments though before the cabin door swung open, and Locke swaggered out.

He was a huge guy, seriously huge compared to me. When I saw him that all encompassing fear began to take over again. Matthew followed behind wearing casual clothing, in stark contrast to Locke, whose attire looked like it could survive nuclear war. Thick, coarse materials, covered in pockets. He wore battered leather gloves over his inhumanly large hands, and around his waist was that belt again. I eyed it nervously.

"Follow us." Locke said, in a voice that was more of a growl. A row of sharp and bitter icicles formed down my spine. I did as I was told, and tried to remind myself of what Rita had said to me in the car. I have potential, he's wary of me, this fear of him is a part of being a Lycan. Still, I wasn't going to take that as fact, that I was predisposed to be scared of him as law, I was going to try to fight it.

I was literally walking in his shadow, with Matthew at my side. I already knew Matthew disagreed with Locke's methods, but he was certainly taking his orders like an obedient lapdog. I considered the idea that maybe the terror eventually turns into pathetic acceptance. I was never particularly good at the whole 'taking orders' thing though.

My somewhat scrambled thoughts were interrupted by the realisation that we were wandering deeper into the forest, leaving the cabin behind. I was curious, and a little apprehensive, about why. The thought of the unknown was utterly unpleasant when Locke was around. It always felt like he had bad intentions, no matter how hard I tried to shake the sensation. I decided to chance a whisper to Matthew, in an attempt to find out what was going on.

"We aren't going to the cage are we?" I asked, doing my best to remain quiet. As always, my best wasn't good enough.

"No cages today." Locke's voice boomed. He didn't even turn his head, just kept striding along through the leaves with his massive steps.

"You heard him, no cages." Matthew added "We have to go quite deep into the forest for today though." He spoke openly, and where I expected Locke to stop him with harsh words or a poisonous look, he didn't do either. There was a short burst of silence as we made our way through the dense trees. I decided to push my luck and talk.

"Do you mind if I ask why?" I said it so meekly it was pitiful. Locke wheeled round.

"So we don't end up with another mistake like you." He pointed his finger and jabbed it into my forehead. It hit me hard enough to shock, even though his hands were gloved. I stood wide-eyed, probably looking terrified, and remained there motionless as he turned back around and carried on walking. It took me a moment to regain my composure.

"Oh... fair enough" I responded. I didn't know what else to say to that. I suppose I should have been a bit offended, but it wasn't like I was going to call him out on it. He was far bigger, and far uglier than me - I wouldn't have stood a chance. After my fleeting paralysis ended, I quickly scurried to catch up with the two of them, who had rudely carried on without me.

We weaved our way through the enormous wooden spires for some time. The forest was lush and life-filled, not at all an unpleasant place to be if you were unaware of what could be lurking. Just as my feet started to become sore from all the rough terrain though, (my footwear being less than ideal for hiking) Matthew informed me that we weren't far from our destination. My relief was clear. We had been moving up a steady incline, which is probably why my legs were having such a rough time of it. The other two hadn't even broken a sweat. The gradient increased suddenly, and we pushed forward up the slope and through bushes. Once on the other side, the view was something else.

It was as though a meteor had hit the exact spot we stood before, in a time many moons ago, an age of creatures long dead. A huge circular recess cut into the very surface of the earth, filled with shimmering blades of grass. At its centre lay a beautiful lake, the rays of a dying sun reflected upon its surface. If there were a God, he'd probably have been pretty proud when he finished throwing that place together. I stood at the crest, drinking it all in. All anxiety was gone for that ephemeral instance.

"This is it." Matthew said calmly, and beckoned with his hand for me to follow. Locke confidently strolled down the steep decline, as though he were too busy to play gravity's little games and paid it no attention whatsoever. Matt and I shuffled our way down in a less dignified manner, but never the less we all made it down there and strode towards the lake. It was an odd feeling to be banked on all sides by a rippling sheet of green. It looked surreal, like the earth itself was breathing. The land seemed to be closing in around us, I felt like I was trapped inside a three-dimensional Dali painting.

We reached the water's edge, and Locke turned to face me.

"Alright, today you're gonna' Phase. No cages, no bullshit." His voice sounded rough and harsh, like the idle rumble of a high-powered chainsaw. My immediate thought was that no cage sounded pretty risky, the thought after that consisted of not wanting to disappoint the big mean bastard. He removed his gloves and dropped them to the ground, then his heavy-duty jacket followed.

"Whoa, wait, no cage, is that really a good idea? I mean, I dunno what I'm doing, I can't control it at all. It got so out of hand at school that I had to hit this kid in the face with a chair, and with no cage what's to sto-" I was rambling due to my nerves, but Matthew cut my incoherent speech short.

"You hit a kid in the face with a chair?" He sounded shocked as he asked, perhaps fearing the possible repercussions.

"Well... yeah, I had to let it out like you said. You know, do whatever it takes to stay in control? Don't worry, I don't think I'm in any trouble for it." I felt like I had screwed up, and was trying to soften the blow. I was anxious as to how Locke would take hearing about my actions, and immediately regretted mentioning it at all. Me and my big mouth huh? It certainly felt like another belt sandwich might be headed my way, but to my surprise, he just gave a dark chuckle.

"Must have hit him pretty damn hard." Locke seemed to find the mental image quite amusing, and it left me momentarily lost for words.

"Zack I should have told you, becoming Lycan, it affects your human body as well." Matthew began frantically "You probably hit him a hell of a lot harder than you realise..." This twist made me feel a small pang of guilt for that useless lump, Charlie. A very small one mind, and it was gone in a fraction of a second.

"Oh... well I'm sure I would have heard if he was dead, so don't sweat it." Locke gave a bark of laughter. "Anyway why the hell didn't you tell me?" I asked, realising I'd been kept in the dark. If there were side effects, especially ones that would effect me day to day, that should have been the first thing they got me up to speed on.

"'Would have heard if he was dead', pretty cold way to look at it, don't you think?" Locke growled with a devilish grin. His presence alone made me feel uneasy, but that smile did him no favours either. I just peered at him whilst deep in thought. I was sure I hadn't hit Charlie *that* hard anyway.

"I didn't mean like DEAD, dead, you know? I just meant I think I would have heard if anything serious had happened..." I was trying to convince myself just as much as Locke. Then I dropped that subject and got back to my hard-hitting interrogation.

"Anyway, spit it out, why didn't you tell me about the changes to my human body? I better not sprout a damn tail."

"Letting a kid know he's becoming freakishly strong didn't seem like the wise-" Matthew began defensively, but was shut down.

"This is not the time Matt. You'll tell him when you take him home." Matthew said nothing, just nodded, accepting his orders. "Right now we have shit to do. I suggest you get undressed." Not exactly the sort of thing you want to hear when you're far from home with two grown men. This is why context is important. Still I wasn't entirely comfortable with the idea. Sensing this, Matthew suggested I keep my underwear on. It would be lost in the transformation, and they'd see me in my birthday suit afterwards anyway, but it somehow felt a little more dignified to be semi dressed, at least for that part of the process.

I stripped down to my pair of rather unflattering white boxer shorts, and nothing else. Needless to say, I felt pretty damn exposed. And with the sun on its way out of the equation, it wasn't as warm as I would have liked. Sure, the scenery was still beautiful, but it was way harder to appreciate in my de-robed state. Locke, who was facing away so only his back was visible, stripped down to full on nakedness. It looked like he had gotten it far worse than me when he had had his first run in with the Lycans. From neck to waist was a latticework of lacerations. I dreaded to think what had actually happened to him.

"That feeling you got when you were being hit in the cage. That's the feeling you need to remember. Locke is going to call to you, it should help stir your inner wolf, so to speak. It'll make that feeling easier to grasp." Matthew explained.

I was more than confused. The idea of holding on to a feeling seemed like the sort of shit they come up with in crystal therapy, or one of those other insane, voodoo healing things. I did, on a very basic level, realise what he was getting at. I mean, I knew the feeling he was referring to which was a start. I nodded to Matthew to indicate that I understood. Well, I understood a little. Then Locke Phased in front of my very eyes.

The already huge man crouched, gargoyle-like on the ground. Then, his whole form began to stretch and twist with a painful collection of cracks and crunches. Next came the blood curdling sounds of tearing flesh. Save for some pained grunts, there was no indication Phasing was a struggle for him. His limbs morphed, and his muscles expanded. Coarse white hairs pierced every inch of his skin, and newly formed claws dug deep into the dirt, scoring the ground. He then turned to face us, the colossal, living, breathing definition of a beast.

Locke growled briefly, baring fearsome fangs. The vibrations of it reached my very core. It was a low, guttural noise, and it sent shivers all through me. I felt movement within, signalling that whatever it was in there, was waking up.

"Now, it won't be easy, we're trying to get you to learn this stuff a whole lot faster than normal but you can handle it. So don't worry if it feels like you can't manage it now, just keep trying." Matthew's words of encouragement weren't nearly as prominent in my mind as the idea of upsetting the big bad wolf opposite me. I was short one red hood, and one partially digested elderly relative, but I still felt like a helpless little girl.

I tried mentally to clutch at that invisible force, wrapping none existent hands around it and attempting to drag it to the surface. How irritating it was that when I was pissed off, I couldn't pay the damn thing to pipe down. Now, when I needed my canine side to come out to play, suddenly it had gotten all shy. I was trying, and I was failing to get this whole Phasing thing to happen. I even shut my eyes, hoping it would help me focus. I thought that then, just maybe, I'd have a slim chance of changing without the aid of life threatening situations or fat fucking bullies.

I guess I was taking too long, because Wolf-Locke snarled aggressively at me and splayed out in a ready to pounce position. I almost jumped out of my skin, and immediately regretted wearing white underwear.

"Shit. I can't fucking do it Matthew!" I bellowed in frustration. I just couldn't elevate that distant inner stirring to become the feeling I got when I was losing control. I don't know if it was made harder to do by the fact that I was on the brink of shitting my pants. The fear of what Locke might do to me should I fail really should have been enough motivation.

"It's okay. We're far from the full moon and you've never done this before. It will happen, just be-" Matthew's sentence ended prematurely as a vicious snarl tore through the still air. Apparently Locke was less patient than him. The hulking silvery-white wolf leapt forward and struck me in the chest with the back of his giant clawed hand. I was sent sailing through the air, and landed with a painful thud a few metres back. The grass felt cold and almost damp against my bare skin, as I struggled to breathe on the ground.

Quickly I rolled over and staggered back to my feet. I could feel that creature that dwelled deep in my chest making its way forward. It felt challenged. I however was not ready for conflict of any kind. I thought about asking if we could all just sit down together and calmly discuss matters, but I got the distinct impression that my suggestion would fall on deaf ears.

"Locke, give him a chance." Matthew pleaded. The Lycan began to circle me menacingly, thunderous sounds emanating from deep within. I willed myself to transform, I tried to allow that thing inside free reign to take my body. To twist it into a mirror image of what I saw before me. It seemed that even though it wanted to be free, and I wanted to Phase, something was holding it back. Maybe it was because I was a trembling mess, wearing underwear soiled (mostly) by dirt from the fall, and it felt embarrassed to exist inside such a pathetic host.

The light was fading fast, and from within the giant grass bowl the sun's disappearing act seemed all the more swift. Still Locke paced up and down like a crazed animal caged, impatiently waiting for me to turn. It was my first time trying to Phase at will and he was acting like I should be an expert, like I could just transform on a whim. The pressure was unbearable, it made every muscle in my body feel like it was wound tighter than humanly possible, causing a dull ache to spread over me.

I wondered if any other werewolves got this kind of treatment, or if it was just me because I was an accident? After all, I'm nothing more than an illegitimate mistake, one that nobody had planned for, or ever wanted to deal with. I tried constantly to bring the wolf out of me, but it was like attempting to tense a muscle I had never used. Frustration grew, and a strange cocktail of fear and frustration ran through my veins in place of blood.

"Matt, I don't fucking get it, I can't get the Lycan thing to take over!" I shouted at him. What I said was met by a derisive snort from the wolf still running a perimeter around me.

"That Lycan thing? That Lycan thing is you, Zack. That is a part of the whole now, not some separate entity. You and it are the same." Matthew's words made something click in my head, he was right. It's not like I was leaving for the night and going elsewhere whilst it was running free in my skin. I was still there somewhere, I just didn't remember it the morning after. Like some sort of drunken bar-crawl, I could only remember fragments of it. I felt like a schizophrenic who had finally figured out his personalities were split and realised who kept moving all of his shit around.

"Okay, I think I get it... sort of. I am it, so I can control it right?" Before Matthew could respond though, Locke snarled furiously again, jumped forward and struck me once more. He was more frustrated by me not Phasing than I was. A hell of a lot more, it seemed.

I tumbled down again, feeling pain rock my body. The creature inside set into motion. As I lay on the ground I tried to convince myself that the entity within, was me. I stopped trying to mentally grasp at it, like it was some sort of ghost. Instead I allowed it to spread, and to move without trying to guide it. It wanted to fight Locke because I wanted to fight Locke. We both *really* wanted to fight.

I hoisted myself back to my feet again. My ribs felt sore from the strike and the fall. Locke's teeth were bared, and he began to stalk forward. The dread was still there, he was the Alpha after all, and he was fucking huge. There has always been that part of me though that hates authority, and finally when I needed it to the most, that side of me was beginning to dominate. 'Alright,' I thought to myself, 'let's do this.'

Suddenly I couldn't understand the struggle at all, could not comprehend how I had been stood there for so long trying to make myself Phase. It was beginning to happen. My entire body felt odd, like it was more liquid than before, somehow more malleable than normal. There was a ringing in my ears that cut out all sound around me, that of the gentle breeze, and the monstrous noises from the overgrown dog dead ahead. Then the pain hit, full force as though I'd stood in the path of an oncoming train and I was swiftly becoming a streak on the tracks. Every bone and every muscle felt like it was being stretched and pulled from all angles, in unison they began to tear and break. I fell to all fours, and watched my hands grow and become covered in jet-black fur between the blinding flashes of agony. My fingertips felt white hot as the claws forced their way through my flesh, and out to the surface.

Vision blurred and my view of the world changed, becoming more defined, enhancing the beauty of the stunning location. My hearing and sense of smell became sharper, and my breathing slower as I gulped huge amounts of air into spacious lungs. I was on all fours, and the viewpoint seemed alien to me. My transformation took moments. I had no control, simply a passenger behind my own eyes. Things got a little fuzzy from there on, as the beast within gleefully took over.

Locke's whole body, still far larger than my own even though I was in wolf form, shuddered with excitement. He crouched low, I knew he wanted me to fight, it was as though I were being given a command. Through some kind of shared pack mentality, I could understand what he wanted. I had instincts guided by his will, interpreting silent orders.

I will tell you what I remember of that event. I remember pouncing towards Locke in the same instant he pounced at me. I remember claws and teeth, blood and fur. That familiar coppery taste made a return. I can recall a lot more about then than any transformation previous to that one, but there are still blanks spots. There was a definite sense of feeling overwhelmed as well, by the sheer power of the creature attacking me. There was also pain, but it never lasted long. Claws would slash and gaping wounds would form, but they would heal fast, gone within minutes. I sunk my own fangs deep into his flesh, that part is vivid. When I let go however, every puncture and tear began to heal over before my very eyes, eventually leaving only a film of liquid blood sat idly on flesh and fur.

It was dark by the time it was over. The experience was like something from a movie, but all in first person. It was both terrifying and exhilarating in equal measure. Splintered though my recollection of the episode is, I know for sure that I was losing the whole way. I was utterly dominated and most (if not all) of my efforts to fight back were entirely futile.

Eventually, as I was struck down yet again, I felt the urge to stop, the impulse to end the fight. Everything suddenly seemed calmer, and Locke ceased his relentless assault. I was exhausted, all four of my limbs felt weak from the exertion of it all. I slumped to the ground and all sound disappeared, the blurred vision and pain came back again but it ended with relief this time. It's similar to the sensation that takes over your body when you've been on your feet all day, and you make that final push to lie down in your bed. The ground came closer, and everything that had stretched out when I changed seemed to relax and sink back inwards. Before I knew it, I was laying face down in cool blades of grass.

As I lay naked on the ground, I heard the soft thud of clothes hitting the floor next to me.

"You did well Zack. Very well. A whole lot better than anyone could have expected." Matthew said reassuringly. I just wanted to sleep. I heard Locke speak then.

"He was in there. Nothing ground-breaking, but there were moments of self-awareness. That's progress." His voice was his usual gravelly tenor. The words echoed in my head. Perhaps I could become an upstanding monster after all.

18 Days Until the Next Full Moon

That night really took it out of me. On the return hike I felt like death walking, and my aching bones made me resent the fact that I had to suffer through another day. Matthew explained to me that strength wasn't the only new trick for this puppy. My sight would improve, and I had an increased sense of smell and better hearing to look forward to, even in my human form. As anyone who has ever gone through puberty will know though, development is a bumpy road.

I left my sty the following morning in a suitably foul mood, and battled valiantly against the mountainous staircase, shuffling my way down like an arthritic pensioner.

The fact that my first lesson was already underway did little to hurry me along. I was ravenous, hungrier than I had ever felt in my life, and my priority was to satiate that hunger. Priority two was destroying the entire human race in my blackened mood. I reasoned however that complete destruction of an entire species is probably more manageable on a full stomach. I filled the four slots in the toaster with thick white bread and proceeded to raid the fridge, not convinced that I'd survive long enough to consume my toast if I waited for it. It felt like I'd been caught in a stampede as I lowered myself down into a wooden dining chair at my humble little table. I was eviscerating the carcass of a defenceless chicken with considerable speed, when my mom wandered in.

"You're late." She stated bluntly.

"I'm always late." I replied equally blunt, as I dismembered yet more of my poultry. Her eyes narrowed but she stayed silent, gazing intently. I could feel her stare and it made my skin crawl. I continued eating and tried to pay her no mind.

"Where do you keep disappearing to?" She snapped at me. Her short frame did nothing to intimidate me as she demanded answers. I kept my features blank, tearing a leg from the chicken.

"I'm just hanging out with friends, Mom." I couldn't bring myself to make eye contact with her, so I kept them on the table, hoping to keep my deceit concealed.

"Friends? You're out 'til God knows what time, and you've come home in completely different clothes on more than one occasion. What exactly are you getting up to with these friends?" I began to feel hot, frustrated. She would never understand that I couldn't tell her, she would never be able to comprehend the truth, the fact that her son was something other than human.

"Nothing." I said through gritted teeth. I bit down on the leg, and bone splintered weakly between blunt fangs. She huffed in exasperation, clutching at wavy, sun-bleached hair. I reserved my right to remain silent, despite the fact that she was clearly hoping for more. Her patience was wearing thin. She paced towards the table and planted her hands like the bad cop in an interrogation.

"Listen to me Zack, I am your mother and I have a right to kn-" The words caught in her throat, I peered up to see her deep blue eyes widen. Glancing down I realised why.

"What happened, did someone hurt you?" My lackadaisical attitude to clothing myself had backfired. Open buttons had left a fraction of my disfiguring scars on show.

"What? No!" She approached me, and in a moment of overwhelming confusion I lost it.

"Get the fuck away from me!" My fingertips squeezed down hard on the table, and the thick wooden surface split under the pressure with a thunderous crack. She stopped dead in her tracks, fear present in every inch of her.

I could find no words. I lifted my weary body from the seat and stood, motionless. Those seconds seemed to last an eternity, and the woman who I'd known since my very first day on this spinning ball of rock had never looked so fragile. If I could change my life and rewrite one scene so to speak, it would be that one. Even after all that I've done, all that's happened, all the pain that I've caused and endured, at no point have I felt more terrible than then.

The toaster ended the longest moment of my miserable existence, each slice popping up in unison. I hastily fastened the traitorous button that had caused all the trouble.

"I have to go to school." My voice was weak. I swiftly called sore limbs into action, grabbing the food and striding from the room. As I passed my mother she recoiled only slightly, but the pang of guilt it caused twisted my stomach into painful knots. I couldn't leave my home fast enough.

I stomped my way across to school like a petulant child, annoyed at myself for what I had done. I only felt worse when I realised that English was the lesson in progress, it literally couldn't get any crappier than that. I've had some terrible teachers in my time, but Mrs Stonehall took the concept of shitty teaching to a whole new level. If there was a separate reality made up entirely of inadequate school staff, then she would be ruler of all she surveyed, literally the best of the worst. The fact that she had a job at all still stuns me to this day. My tainted disposition considerably worsened, I made my way to class and barged in half an hour late.

When the door burst open, everyone felt the need to look. I refused to acknowledge that the other people in the room existed.

"And what makes you think you can just storm into lesson thirty minutes late?" Mrs Stonehall snapped at me. Seriously, I was not in the mood.

"Alright whatever, I'll go." I turned to leave, but she spluttered and stopped me.

"Sit down!"

I turned back and muttered to myself about how she should make her fucking mind up. I noticed a free seat behind Jackson and Damian; they always sat towards the back of the room. Venn was nowhere to be seen.

Still being gawked at by every future college drop out in the room, I went to my chosen throne and sat down. That day, I was the self-proclaimed prince of misery. I spotted Lexey giving me a venomous look. It mattered not. I had too much other shit on my mind. When I took my place, I sat sideways on my chair with my back against the wall, because brick somehow managed to be more comfortable than the terrible seating on offer. Apparently though, even this minor detail was a cause for concern.

"Will you sit properly?" she demanded. Yet another case of trying to show dominance, to publicly embarrass a student in front of their peers. Oh, how the young must suffer.

"Will you just get on with whatever it is you class as teaching?" I retorted, and slammed my head back against the wall in frustration. She really did have pissing me off down to a fine art, the feeling of building heat and bad intentions began to rise.

"The lesson will continue when you are sat properly." She stated in a nature as blunt as a cricket bat, which coincidentally I was sort of wishing I had at the time. I was irritable and lethargic, I really wasn't up for the fight, so I sighed an over dramatic sigh. The kind of overacting you might get in a high school play. Then, I turned to sit in the conventional position. She paused and stared at me for a while, but I just blanked her. Finally she carried on.

I really do hate that woman. I watched as she yammered on, not taking any of it in, naturally. She stood at the front of the room, lank, greasy, dyed blonde hair with deep brown roots on show. Dressed like a Victorian lady of the night in stockings, brown knee high boots, a waist high skirt, and a shirt that could pass for your grannies curtains. Of all the teachers I disliked, and there were a lot of them, she was the one I loathed the most.

She continued to bang on about one thing or another, but I decided I was sick of the sight of her. I lay my head on my arms and looked at the wall, admiring the work on display. Wooden framed ensembles of previous toil. Backed with coloured sugar paper, surrounded with patterned borders and laced with extra effort, it was certainly more worthwhile to look at than my lacklustre educator. Even if only for all the pretty colours and swirly letters, or the lingering smell of those pens which are supposed to stink of various fruits, but actually don't seem to share any similarities with any odour nature has produced. The stench of them was vague and far off, but it served to annoy me further none the less.

"Zack!" Apparently my newfound seating position was just as displeasing to her as my previous one.

"Will you sit up and pay attention, please?" She was getting more irate; I didn't even argue, just sat up and stared at her, dead eyed. I took her unwavering glare as a contest, which I won when she finally remembered she had a class to teach. She continued to unleash her torrent of questionable information, but I paid her no attention because Damian, when the teacher seemed sufficiently preoccupied, turned around and spoke.

"Hey." he tried to talk quietly, so as not to gain any further attention from our wondrous figurehead for the English language "We got some news on Charlie in form this morning, I thought you should know man." That whole event seemed like so long ago now, but it really was only a matter of hours. The realisation was not a pleasant one, and I began to worry that I might be getting questioned by some real authorities before the day was out, not just a teacher with a severe case of inflated ego.

"Shit, what did they say?" I asked it as quietly as possible, without making it inaudible for Damian.

"Apparently, he's basically okay now. He'll probably be back next week. They told us he can't remember a thing though, for like that whole day. You must have hit him seriously hard." He gave one breath of laughter. I guess I really had hit him harder than either of us had known at the time.

"Good." I let out a sigh of relief.

"You aren't really in the clear yet though, they're asking if anyone knows what happened, but so far no one has ratted you out." He told me. I didn't like the addition of 'so far', but that was the best I could hope for. I was a little surprised though.

"Not even Lexey or Briana?" I asked. I gave them a glance; they were sat together, apparently attached at the hip nowadays. I couldn't think of anyone more likely to give me up than them, but they hadn't. Even though I disliked the pair of them, I appreciated that, and they moved up a single notch on my imaginary scale of acceptableness.

"Nope, not a soul. Not even those two. People really do hate Charlie." Damian smirked in a satisfied manner. I took comfort in hearing it, then wondered about Jackson's conspicuous absence from the conversation. There he was, listening and diligently taking notes in his English book. My book was still lying at the bottom of my bag, along with a half eaten chocolate bar and several decades' worth of dust.

"What's with Jackson, he taking more of an interest in bullshit recently?" I directed the question at Damian, but Jackson answered, still scrawling away without lifting his head from the page.

"If I don't listen, I'm gonna fucking fail. If I fail that just gives my parents even more of an excuse to shit on me every chance they get." He managed to say despite his inability to stop scowling.

"Oh, don't mind him, he's just pissed that his parents prefer his little brother." Damian gestured towards Jackson with his thumb. I saw Jackson's back physically tighten at the mention of his family.

"It's not goddamn fair, he gets whatever he wants and I get blamed for everything. I swear, I'm leaving that house the second I have somewhere to go." His jaw was grinding away. I remember thinking he'd wear his teeth down to nothing if he didn't lighten up, which was a bit hypocritical considering my bad temper that day.

"Fair enough." I thought I'd just close that whole avenue of conversation. I'd already heard of the supposed favouritism Jackson's parents had for his younger sibling, and to be perfectly honest, I didn't care the first time. It made me sort of glad to be an only child though, and I'm sure Damian was on a similar train of thought whenever the subject came up. I recalled my early morning outburst, and felt the need to move on from the topic of family.

"Hey, where's Venn?" His absence was less noticeable considering he never really brought a whole lot to the conversation anyway, but I had clocked on eventually. That's something to be proud of, considering only chameleons have a sporting chance when it comes to taking on Venn at blending into the scenery.

"I dunno. He'll turn up soon enough I'm sure." Damian seemed disinterested. "Anyway, have you paid for the geography trip yet? It's this Friday, and I don't wanna go on my own."

"Thanks." Jackson added sarcastically. Obviously he was going too and felt slightly offended that he wasn't classed as 'someone'. It didn't distract him from his fevered writing though. It was then that our conversation caught the attention of Mrs Stonehall, and of course a conversation involving three people was *entirely* my doing.

"Zack, you show up late, and then you start disrupting the learning of other students! Who do you think you are?" Those words reverberated in my head, exactly the words Lexey had used, 'Who do you think you are?' My eyes flicked in her direction, and sure enough she was giving me another, I felt undeserved, dirty look. I made an odd growling noise in frustration, since nothing else came to mind. I just wanted to be left alone.

Normally I would have enjoyed the argument, the chance to easily outsmart someone whose level of intelligence lies somewhere between a shrub and a house pet. That day was different though, my usual fire was doused with remorse, and I found the idea of solitude far more appealing than a one sided battle of wits.

I resigned myself to sitting statuesque for the remainder of the lesson. I had already missed a fair chunk of it, but its conclusion seemed to be far off beyond any horizon I could see. If I sit still and silent she will have no reason to bother me, that was my reasoning, and it seemed sound enough. After yet another silent stare in my direction, one where I refused to make eye contact effectively taking my ball and going home, she continued her excellent, albeit so far unheard lesson.

"So, we all know imagination is an important part of creative writing, and one way of telling how imaginative someone is, is by exploring their dreams." She paced between the desks, up and down the length of the room as she spoke, constantly moving her hands, talking with them in tandem with her mouth. She walked past Jackson who was still nose deep in his English book, but the movement distracted him and he looked up only to get a rather full on view of Mrs Stonehall's rear-end.

"God, that's an arse you could park your bike in." I heard him mutter. He shook his head as if he were trying to dislodge the very memory of it, and returned his attention to his book. I tried very hard to stifle my laughter, honestly I did. The effort took everything I had.

"A lot of people think dreams have meanings behind them. A lot of people dream of falling, or being naked in public, anyone had a dream like that?" A smattering of hands went up in response to her query.

"I thought so, dreams like that are common. Anyone had any more unusual dreams they want to share?" She asked the whole room and got no response, only vacant eyes. She looked around hopefully, but was disappointed. I highly doubted the worth of discussing dreams in English, but then again, I wasn't the one being paid to be there.

"No one?" Silence. "Okay, well I'm sure you've all had interesting dreams but maybe you're just too shy to say. I'll go first then." I could think of nothing worse than having to listen to a daft, middle-aged woman talk about her dreams, but there I was. I'm sure even the out-dated work on the walls would have peeled itself free, left its staples behind and leapt into the nearest puddle or open flame in an act of suicide, if it had the capacity to do so.

"Alright, so I have this dream, I have it quite a lot. It's a recurring dream. I'm trapped in this small white room, and there's no windows or anything, just this metal grate on the floor, and water starts rushing up through it. The water keeps on rising and I'm trying to hold my head up above it so I can breathe, but eventually it reaches the top and I'm under it. Then I start to drown, and I wake up." Considering she was talking about how dreams involved a lot of imagination, I was significantly underwhelmed by hers. A bare white room and some water, was that it? I'm sure dreams of drowning are just as common as the ones about falling, and that one where all your teeth drop out. Still the thought of her drowning did amuse me somewhat. Is that wrong? Probably.

"So, I think that dream has meaning. I tend to have it when I'm stressed about something, so I think the water is like a metaphor for all the things I have to do, and I'm drowning in them because I feel like it's all getting on top of me." I watched her as she spoke and could only think to myself, dressed the way she was, it looked like anything could get on top of her. I let out a small chuckle at my own mute joke. Unluckily for me, she heard it. She glared at me with malice in her eyes.

"Something funny?" Stonehall snorted.

"No Mrs Stonehall. Nothing at all." I think my tone must have been a little too formal, suspiciously so, because she seemed offended.

"Well then Zack, what sort of dreams do you have hmm… dreams about death?" The bitch was derisive. So because I have dark, messy hair, I must have a dark, messy mind? My nights must be filled with dreams of the macabre? She was right, but I'll be damned if I let that kind of stereotyping slide. She had no idea what I could do. A thought that seemed removed from my own told me I could tear off her head and swallow it whole. I whispered in return that she would taste vile. Heat started rising.

"Oh yeah, all the time Miss, most of them involving you." Half the room laughed at the sheer cheek of what I had said, while the others acted as though my words were aimed at them personally, like they felt hurt on her behalf.

"Zack, that's a terrible thing to say!" My dear teacher sounded like she was about to break down, but I didn't believe her whimpering voice to be anything close to genuine upset.

"You see, I'm in this dark room full of screens. You know, like CCTV? And I can see you in this tiny white room. There's a guy in an equally white coat. He tells me this big red button will pump water into said room. That I should press it every time you do something that irritates me, and well, you just don't stop breathing do you?" I wanted to make her regret pushing me so much, when all I wanted to do was sit quietly and wait out the day.

"Stop it, you are being unbelievably hurtful!" She exclaimed in her best shot at emulating a grade school play. She couldn't even manage a single crocodile tear, what a poor show. I sat glaring back at her in absolute defiance, the dog in me wanted out, but I willed it to stand down.

"Why don't you just do as you're told?"

The wolf pushed harder to get its way.

"Why don't you just listen to me?"

It hates being told what to do.

"Why don't you just do what's right for your future?"

If I didn't take care of her, it would.

"WHY DONT YOU JUST SUCK MY D-"

■■

"We will not have foul language in this school!" Deputy Headmaster Granger screamed at me.

"Between students is bad enough, but to a teacher?" Honestly, I found his outrage to be a little over the top. I mean, it's hardly unheard of. He had even stood up from his cosy looking leather chair. It was a big black old thing, worn in any spot that made contact with his scrawny body.

"Look sir, she pushed me." I tried to justify my novel approach to stifling a werewolf transformation "She kept singling me out. What was I supposed to do?" It was an utterly honest account. I wasn't the only one who spoke, or lay their head on the desk, yet I got all the flack.

His beaky nose was right in my face, an invasion of personal space if ever I had seen one. The Lycans had torn me open, and even that felt less intrusive than having Mr Granger so close. He absolutely reeked of coffee. It got right in my nose and the back of my throat. It was like he was obsessed with the stuff. He had a coffee machine right in his office, all buttons and knobs to twiddle and press.

"No teacher at this school would ever single out a student for no reason, how dare you even suggest such a thing!" Like he knew what teachers would and wouldn't do, he was never in any classes. He just sat in his office drinking his putrid brown sludge all day.

I remained soundless, that seemed to be the best way out of any situation involving teachers. My advice, just let them run their mouths and tire themselves out. He inhaled deeply and stood up straight, no longer leaning down to be at my eye level. I was tempted to check if my face was moist. Then Mr Kenco decided sitting in his chair was almost certainly more comfortable than standing on those pins he called legs. He took two large steps around his sizeable oak desk and planted his bony button within its soft leather grip.

The Deputy Head was a lanky man - a streak of piss, some might call him. He had been wearing the same black trousers and white shirt with thin, blue, vertical stripes every time I had ever seen him. The same old belt was always around his waist too. It looked to me like fake leather, and I've considered myself an expert on belts ever since one connected so lovingly with my jaw, so you can probably take my word for it. The unchanged old pixie toed black shoes he had on were even more battered than his chair was. Covered in cracks from all the wear over the years. Honestly, you'd think he had to wear a uniform like the rest of us with how strictly he stuck to his dress code. That rang true with one exception though, his ties. His tie always changed.

It was probably one of those things that boring people do to make themselves look like a bit of a character. 'Hey look at me, I have wacky ties. I'm not planning on hanging myself with one tonight, honest, because I have an interesting life.' You know, that sort of thing. This particular day's regular ensemble was topped off with a bright pink tie covered in lime green polka dots. How garish.

He reclined on his squidgy chair, (which looked far more appealing to my buttocks than the crummy old plastic thing I'd been dumped with) and drank deeply from the steaming mug on his desk. The mug confidently proclaimed he was the world's greatest dad. I'd say that was debateable, I'm sure that amongst all of the people in the world, over seven billion of them, there's one, possibly even two or three fathers more competent than him. Still if the mug said it, it must be true. Personally I think all meaningful awards should come displayed on kitchenware.

"Young man, I'll level with you. Ordinarily I would consider suspending you for something like this. Mrs Stonehall doesn't even want to teach you anymore. She says you're a constant pain." He was talking to me in that 'what would you do in my position?' kind of way.

"Well Sir, to be honest, I think she may be over reacting." Replace the words 'may' and 'be' with 'definitely fucking is'.

"Yes, I don't doubt that. It's true that Mrs Stonehall is one of the more emotionally fragile members of our staff." He said looking down at his fingers, which were drumming on the desk, mulling the situation over. Emotionally fragile... shit, maybe I should have been taking notes?

"We are getting perilously close to exams though. With that in mind, I wouldn't want to suspend you for any length of time, because that could have a detrimental effect on your grades. A fail doesn't reflect well on any of us, Mrs Stonehall included." I decided to let him continue to think I gave a shit about my grades.

"I'm sure you understand though, I can't be seen to be doing nothing about this."

"Yeah, I completely understand that." The stench of leather and coffee made my nose wrinkle, it was almost bitter to me. I wanted to be anywhere with a less repugnant odour.

"Okay, here's what we'll do." He hummed to himself, and drummed his fingers on the desk some more. "I will put you in isolation for the rest of the day. You must however, promise not to act up anymore." Act up? She fucking started it. I kept that thought to myself, just nodded in agreement.

So I got a day away from all the phony kids, always fronting and trying to be popular? A whole day where I didn't have to deal with all the noise and the teachers? A day where I could just sit quietly and mind my own business, without anyone telling me to pay attention? Hell, it sounded good to me.

"Oh, and I had better give you a detention too, just to appease Mrs Stonehall."

That part, I wasn't so thrilled about.

THE HUNT

After my long overdue release from incarceration, I shuffled my way home feeling far more relaxed than when I had started the day. As soon as I entered the door, the frosty atmosphere hit me full force. I crept into the kitchen to find my mom sat at her now damaged dinner table.

"Erm... Mom?" The word lacked any impact, barely escaping on my breath. Her eyes met mine, but her reluctance was obvious. The following silence twisted my stomach in unnatural ways. I glanced at the sizeable crack in the polished wooden surface.

"I'm really sorry about the table..." I said in an attempt to break the tension.

"I don't care about the damn table, Zack." Her voice was soft, melodic. I shuffled awkwardly in place. "I am your mother. I have every right to be concerned about you." She remained stoic, absentmindedly tracing her fingers over the split in the wood.

"I know Mom, I'm sorry." I meant it wholeheartedly.

"Are you going to tell me what happened to you?" She asked in an almost casual manner.

I looked deep into her dark blue eyes and couldn't lie. I shook my head slowly, deliberately.

She sighed to herself, and an aura of sadness surrounded her.

"Are you safe?"

"Yeah, don't worry about it, it was just an accident." I told her.

"What kind of ac-" She caught herself, and let out a deep sigh. "I'm not going to try to force you, but please, when you're ready to talk about it, come and speak to me." Her tone was so earnest, her intentions so pure that I could not refuse.

"Okay. I promise, I'll do that." I never did. She nodded and smiled weakly in my direction, her eyes looked anywhere but.

It seemed we had come to an understanding and nothing more needed to be said, so I made my way towards the sanctuary of my bedroom. The familiar chaotic mess remained intact. My patchwork floor of unwashed clothes forever bathed in gloom, a result of the ever-present blind blocking beams of light from a distant star. My comforting darkness however was being spoiled by a harsh, and unnatural glow. My phone wobbled erratically on the unmade bed, buzzing intermittently like a wounded bee. I strode across the sea of laundry and grabbed it. It became motionless in my hand. The words 'Damian - 4 missed calls' were emblazoned across the screen. Suddenly it burst into motion again, Damian calling.

"Hello?" I answered. The slurping sound of loose snot and salty tears came from the other end of the line.

"Zack! I didn't know who else to call." Damian blubbered hysterically and then mumbled something inaudible.

"Whoa, calm the hell down man, what's wrong?" I felt very uncomfortable speaking to someone who was clearly so upset, but I thought it might be considered rude to hang up.

"He came back!" He whimpered with as much force as he could muster.

"What are you talking about, who came back?" I asked, my mind a completely blank canvas on which memory was not willing to smear a brush.

"My Dad!" He bellowed "That fucking asshole, he found us!" His voice cracked under the weight of his words. Realisation hit me.

"Fuck, are you alright?" I asked one of the few people I genuinely gave a shit about.

"I'm fine," he sniffed and let out a small squeak of anguish "it's my mom..." He stopped speaking, but I could still hear his laboured breathing. I wasn't sure whether to ask, or to wait for him to tell me on his own. After a moment's hesitation, I decided to get it out of the way.

"Is she okay?" I questioned him gravely.

"No, no she's not, he stabbed her man, that bastard stabbed her!" His raw emotion was not at all diminished by its journey over the airwaves. I clutched at my head, clueless. The situation was way too heavy, what was I supposed to do? I reached for meaningful thoughts, but ultimately grasped none.

"How the hell did he find you?" I said, frustrated at myself for being too useless to come up with anything helpful to say.

"I don't know man, I don't fucking know! I'll find him though, I want him dead!" His voice was hoarse, and fraught with pure rage. Suddenly my brain kicked into gear, and an idea formed inside my thus far disappointing grey matter.

"Where is she now?" I asked hurriedly.

"The ambulance took her, hopefully she's made it to the hospital by now. I swear to God I'll make him pay for this..." fury oozed from every syllable. I didn't doubt his conviction.

"Okay, just stay at your place. I'll be there as soon as I can." I told him and hung up.

When I mentioned earlier that Damian's home life had been far more eventful than my own, his father was the sole reason why. An abusive snake of a man on a persistent power trip, he did nothing but lie, cheat, and unleash his frustrations on his wife and young son. Had it not been for him, I wouldn't have known Damian at all. They moved to my town to escape their horrid past, when Damian's mom finally realised that he would never change. They'd been around a few years, long enough to get that false sense of security, but the past has a way of catching up with you, as it did with Damian that day.

I pondered for a moment, wondering how the hell shit could go so wrong, so fast. Then, I took a deep breath, and set my ill thought out plan into action. I dialled the number that gave me my orders, the bleeping tone was shrill to my ear. Matthew answered.

"Hey Matthew, I need to speak to Locke..."

■■

"Who the hell is this guy?" Damian spoke in near whispers. I couldn't really tell him now could I? Locke was skulking around the outside of Damian's house, one of many identical houses in the cul-de-sac where he lived. Damian and I were perched on the curb. Two police officers sat in his lounge engaged in idle conversation, just another day on the job.

"Never mind that, just trust me dude." I said in blunt response. His face was red and blotchy, eyes all puffed up from the tears.

"He can't get away, if he does I don't know what I'll do. He needs to pay for what he's done." His tone was menacing.

"He wont get away." I was confident this would work.

"Damn useless cops," He muttered under his breath "they're here to protect me in case he comes back. They should be out there searching for him, not sat on a sofa chatting amongst themselves." I could taste the bitterness of his words, and my own thoughts mirrored his.

"Have you heard anything from the hospital yet?"

"No, not yet..." his head lowered, dragged down by the weight of his concern. "You know, he took her ring. Even after we ran, she wore that thing every day. I have no idea why. Maybe to remind her of what we escaped from. Sick fuck, knifed her and took that with him." Diamonds rolled silently down his face, leaving clean streaks in the dirt. I lacked the verbal skill to comfort him.

Locke turned towards us, and beckoned me with one giant hand from afar.

"Looks like that's my cue." I hauled myself to my feet.

"Wait, where are you going?" Damian sniffled.

"Just trust me." I lay a reassuring hand on his shoulder. He wiped his face with a damp sleeve. "Oh, and don't tell anyone about this, seriously."

"I don't know what the hell you're planning, but I want to come with you." He began to lift himself from the ground but I pushed him back down.

"No way man, you've gotta keep the pigs busy. You know they wont let you leave, and if you do they'll come looking for you." Damian punched the ground in frustration, but knew it was true.

"Fine. I don't understand what the hell your plan is but if it works, don't let that son of a bitch get away Zack." He sounded sceptical, but regardless his stance was clear. A clenched fist turned his sore knuckles white. Little did he know, we had an unfair advantage when it came to a manhunt.

"You have my word." I told him as I walked away.

I fell into step next to Locke, leaving the blood-spattered kitchen, the traumatized son, and the indifferent cops behind. Given my small frame next to his large one, I must have looked harmless. But to an average person, I was just as much of a threat as he was. Either one of us could tear through that entire neighbourhood, leaving nothing but blood and bone in our wake. And that thought, at that time, it made me feel alive.

"How much does he know about us?" Locke growled at me. I noticed his clothing, it was exactly the same stuff he wore that day in the cage. It was the attire in which he chose to do his dirty work.

"About me, not much. As for you, nothing, he's completely in the dark." I assured him. I was focussed on the task at hand, getting revenge on Damian's behalf.

"Good. You were right not to try to do this on your own. You still lack self-control." He stated coldly, as we walked towards that now so familiar vehicle.

"Well my sense of smell isn't as good as yours yet, right?" I replied. I kept to myself the fact that I knew, he of all people, would not be able to resist the opportunity to cause some suffering. My gradually improving sense of smell was more of an annoyance than a useful trait in the early days. It came and went as it pleased.

He chuckled darkly to himself and a shiver ran all through me, cold enough to freeze the very ground at my feet.

"Right you are. Well, consider this your first lesson in tracking." And with that we both jumped in the Range Rover and set off in search of sweet vengeance.

■■■

The wind whipped at our faces as well travelled, windows rolled down to catch the scent. To Locke it was child's play; he could home in on the stench of drying blood and cheap cologne. The specific body odour that he had picked up on at the house left a trail through the air, one that to him reeked of salty sweat, and oily skin. I wasn't quite so adept, but as we neared our final destination I began to notice more of the unique features of our targets stench. The musty fragrance of the leather that was his jacket, and the unmistakable aroma of filthy, moistened innersoles. It had begun to become more apparent that my sensitivity to smell was increasing at school, but never before had I tried to utilize it. With a little practice, focus, and the resolve to put up with taking in high doses of near toxic stink, I could probably find just about anything.

The Range Rover rumbled to a halt on the outskirts of town, near the train station. I inhaled deeply, and the very essence of revulsion filled my lungs. He was close. The key was turned and silence fell.

"The aim is to pinpoint the particular collection of elements that make up the target's scent. You do that, and you've got them." Locke had been teaching me on the job, not exactly your average apprenticeship.

"Understood. He's in the station isn't he?" I asked, already knowing the answer.

"Yeah." large intermittent raindrops started to spatter the windshield. "Good thing we found him when we did, rain would have made it near impossible." I made a mental note of that.

Locke stepped out of the vehicle with a heavy thud. I followed comparatively daintily. For the first time, I felt that pack mentality. For once it didn't seem like we were enemies, we had a common goal. We were on the hunt, and we were linked.

The sky was crimson, fittingly so. To look out past the station, and see the vast woodland that was fast becoming my natural habitat gave me confidence.

"Sort of convenient to have so much open space outside of town huh?" I mentioned off hand. Locke gave me a wry glance.

"Why do you think we live here?" He mumbled.

In the gentle rain, I followed his lead around the station. We found a vantage point near the tracks, hidden amongst the plant life. Our target was alone on the platform, pacing impatiently. I could make out his features, his resemblance to Damian was clear to see. I could even perceive the shining stud in his left ear lobe. Improved vision made the world pop, everything had a sharpness to it that wasn't there before. Through the damp air, I caught the scent of blood, Damian's mom's blood. Mine began to boil, and my dark side started to wake.

"Keep control." Locke spoke quietly, but still sounded like someone had thrown rocks into a blender.

"He's right there, and he's alone. Let's just jump him, he'll never outrun us." I was impatient, ready to set things right, to bring karmic balance to the universe.

"Stupid kid, there are cameras in that station. We have to get him to come to us." Locke's tone suggested that he thought he might have been better off unaided, and he'd probably have been right. I watched as our prey shifted uneasily from one foot to the other, wishing his carriage to freedom would arrive. It was evening though, and trains were few and far between. Perhaps if he had considered that beforehand, that night might have gone a little better for him.

"So what do we do?" I asked, frustrated that I needed to exercise patience. He reached into one of his many pockets, and pulled out a fearsome looking folding knife.

"I hope you're good at acting kid." There wasn't a hint of empathy in what Locke said. I wondered why I had to end up in some kind of pain every time I was around the Alpha of the pack. A pack I was supposed to be a part of, might I add. It seemed to happen a little too often to be mere coincidence. Never the less, I was willing to take one for the team this time.

"Acting?" I glanced at the giant crouched next to me "I can do that." He lifted the sleeve of my plain black t-shirt, and I thanked a none-existent God that I was wearing a colour that wouldn't stain. With my mom already on high alert, the last thing I needed was to come home in bloody clothes.

He raised his hand and sunk the blade into my shoulder, deeper than I thought necessary. I winced as cold steel ran through my flesh, opening vessels and spilling claret fluid down my arm. It merged and flowed with the drops of rain.

"You lure him over here, but don't get too close. Under no circumstances are you to Phase. Understood?" The general gave his orders.

"Whatever, as long as the job gets done." I rubbed dirt into my arms and face, completing my injured and dishevelled look, and after a second of regretting not studying drama, rushed out in to the open.

I sprinted forward, faked a stumble and fell into the mud.

"Help! Please, help me!" I scrambled to my feet, clutching my pouring arm. Damian's dad looked shocked and confused.

"What d'you want?" he enquired, panic stricken.

"I want fucking help! My friend's hurt bad, come quick!" I panted like a thirsty dog. He stood there, shell shocked, but I committed to the role, turned on my heel and began to limp back the way I had came. I looked over my shoulder and bellowed at him.

"Help me or he's gonna fucking die!" This set him into motion. Whether through utter bewilderment, curiosity, or an uncharacteristic intention to do some good, the knife wielding wife beater followed, and fell right into our little trap.

He reached the tree where Locke was waiting, and a gargantuan fist struck his face with a sickening blow. I ended the show and turned to follow as the silver haired titan grabbed the scumbag by his out-dated leather jacket, and threw him in amongst the trees. He begged for mercy through broken teeth, but there was none to be found. He attempted to run, faltered in a daze, and I took the opportunity to sprint around him, faster than I knew I could run. Leaves crunched beneath my feet in rapid succession. Our target tried to stand, but before he could fully elevate himself I leapt forwards, throwing a right hook as hard as I could manage. It hit his chest, and I felt a rib give way to my knuckles. The target wailed in agony and collapsed in a heap to the soil.

"Let me go! Why are you doing this?" He pleaded with a mouthful of blood, then spat it to the ground. "What did I do to you?!" His speech was garbled.

"Oh, it's not what you did to us dude. It's what you did to your son. What you did to your wife." I spoke in an intentionally eerie calm. His eyes bulged at the mention of them.

"I don't know what the hell you're talking about!" He scrambled to his feet and tried to dash past Locke, who snatched his throat with lightning speed. The abusive husband and father reached into his jacket, and limply swung a knife in the big guy's direction. Locke caught his hand with ease, twisted the weakling clockwise, and then brought a fearsome boot down on his leg. Bone pierced his calf, and came out to greet the world. His cry of anguish caused the birds perched high above to scatter. Locke dropped him callously to the earth below.

"Okay, okay I'm sorry! I'll hand myself in, just please, don't kill me!" He was pathetic, attempting to crawl to safety and getting nowhere fast. Even though the rain was falling, I could see the tears spilling from his eyes. Tears of fear no doubt, like the countless ones he'd caused himself. Locke disappeared behind an ancient looking tree, and I knew what was coming. I heard his large coat hit the fallen leaves.

"God, have some dignity." I followed the worm of a man as he inched his way through the dirt. A swift kick flipped him onto his back, and made him squeal. Monstrous noise began to emanate from beyond the old tree, beginning with pained grunts. I rooted through the pockets of his wholly unstylish leather jacket and found what I was looking for, the ring that belonged to an innocent woman who was fighting for life. The guy whimpered.

"What's going on back there?" He asked, terrified. I twirled the ring between my fingers, glancing over my shoulder.

"You don't need to worry about him." I assured him most earnestly. I stooped down low, and grabbed the so-called father's face, noticing that the river from my shoulder was still flowing down my arm. He flinched as I touched him, which the presence inside me found amusing. I took in the sight. He had the same dark hair, the same kind of pointed features, and the same eyes as the friend I had left sitting on the curb not long ago.

"He really does look like you, you know?" I examined every similarity in great detail, as the pained grunts turned to vicious snarls behind me. His eyes darted as terror enveloped him. Then I asked a question I had always wanted to ask, ever since I first heard of Damian's tragic tale. I hadn't done so because I felt it wasn't my place, but then, I had the opportunity to get the answer straight from the horse's mouth.

"What's your name?" I asked him conversationally. The falling droplets made him blink uncomfortably.

"W-what?" He groaned, apparently not understanding the question. The snarling at my back grew louder.

"It's not a trick question," I rolled my eyes "what is your name?"

"P-P-Phillip, my name is Phillip." Phillip stammered, as the snarling became a low and thunderous growl.

"Huh… don't really know why I asked that." I said absentmindedly, putting the wedding ring in my pocket as a shadow crept over me. The growl intensified, and the ground seemed to shake. "Well, looks like it's game over Phil." I smirked. For Damian, justice was being done.

I turned, knowing that Locke would finish what we had both started.

"What the hell is that?! No, someone help me ple-!" Phillip's words were lost to far more visceral sounds. I listened to the fangs and the claws as they did their work. But as I walked away, all that could be heard was the rustle of something dragged through fallen leaves, and the rhythmic patter of the crystal rain.

The Morning After

The following day I silently placed the wedding ring on Damian's desk as I passed. He looked at me through grateful eyes, ones that seemed unsure whether to be appreciative or afraid. He asked no questions in the beginning, there were too many ears to hear it. Too many intrusive forces, ready to pry into private business. Silence suited me just fine. His mom was stable, and recovering well. Luckily she received the medical attention she needed in time, and the death toll that night stopped at one. She insisted that he continue to attend school, and urged him not to worry about her, or his deadbeat dad.

Something told me he wasn't worried about old Phillip at all anymore, and rightly so. The relevant authorities assured everyone involved that they were doing all in their power to find poor, pathetic parent Phil, entirely unaware that there was nothing left to find. For those of you lacking the necessary levels of imagination and common sense, let's just say Locke has a hell of an appetite.

I did my best to coast through that day, avoiding conversation wherever possible, and limiting it to small talk when it was completely inevitable. I retreated into my own head at every opportunity, blocking out the world around me and trying to drift into a near unconscious state. Something was different though – the usual comforting solitude was gone. Sat in class, the chatter around me nothing more than formless vibration, I realised something. I was not alone. That thing lurked in the corners of my mind, shrouded in shadow, ever-present.

I got through the school hours largely unscathed, dodging having to awkwardly admit to Damian that fifty percent of his biological origins were fast becoming fertilizer. I knew though, that eventually I'd have to tell him something, he wouldn't accept being kept in the dark indefinitely.

When I returned home, I checked the knife wound on my shoulder. Locke had thoughtfully provided bandages, and even showed me how to apply them properly. They held up all day, concealing the cut from classmates and a worrisome parent. The gash was still raw and a little painful, but it bothered me not, since I knew that it would disappear completely the next time I transformed. I cleaned it up, applied new bandages and spent the rest of my time achieving absolutely nothing, until I fell in to a deep, almost coma-like sleep.

16 Days Until the Next Full Moon

So finally Friday came. The day of the geography trip. The day I was hoping would be a brief respite from my increasingly ludicrous life. Things never turn out exactly how you want them to though, do they? I woke up in high spirits, and for me, that's saying something. After cleaning myself up and eating like a man who'd never seen a meal before, I headed for school knowing full well there wouldn't be a single lesson.

Believe it or not, I was on time when I strolled up to the front entrance where two coaches, and a crowd of people were waiting. Everyone was wearing their own clothes, which to me felt like liberation from that oppressive uniform. It was always a little strange on rare occasions like that to see faces I recognised in attire I didn't. Most of those kids I had never seen outside of school hours. Everyone was talking amongst themselves, under the gaze of envious eyes. All the other students were preparing for a day of more academic pursuits than our own. It wasn't long before I spotted my usual cohorts. Well, two of them anyway.

I strode over to Damian and Jackson, who were stood at least ten feet away from anyone else, always so anti-social. I choked on an unexpected laugh when I saw what Jackson was dressed in.

"I didn't realise Columbus was leading this expedition." I said with a wry smirk. He was wearing combat trousers, a rugged looking shirt, and heavy-duty boots. The real cherry on the cake though, he had on one of those hats with a skirt on it, more suited to desert exploration than a breezy school parking lot. The biggest backpack I had ever seen was strapped to his feeble frame. It was quite a sight to behold, considering how small and fragile he appeared to be. If he had fallen backwards, he would have been left stranded and furiously kicking in the air like an upturned turtle.

"That's exactly what I thought when I saw him." Damian added, chuckling. Jackson looked pissed off, but then again, when didn't he?

"Well it looks like you've come prepared Zack. Fucking prick." He said in a display of blunt sarcasm. I didn't have a thing on me apart from the clothes on my back and my latest set of running shoes. I saw no reason to stock up on supplies. I didn't know where we were going, but I was pretty sure I could survive a day trip without kitting myself up like a Navy Seal.

"Trust, you look prepared enough for the both of us." I replied, regarding his getup and rolling my eyes.

"To be honest, you do look a little under dressed." Damian said, eyeing me up and down. This made me wonder what exactly I was supposed to be dressed for.

"Why, what are we doing?" I asked, but before he could answer, Miss Clarke called for the attention of the two geography groups scattered around in front of her.

"Okay listen up everyone, I'm sure you're all looking forward to our hike today but we need to do a quick register before we can all get on the coaches!" She raised her voice in an attempt to be heard over the people who were still deep in their own personal conversations.

"So everybody line up!" She ordered, ushering people with her hands.

"A hike, are you kidding me?" I said with a heavy dose of reluctance.

"What's wrong pal, walking a little too strenuous for ya?" Jackson patted me on the back, and left visible traces of smug behind.

As I glanced around, it finally dawned on me. Everyone was wearing boots and rucksacks. Great. I turn up expecting a leisurely stroll through the dusty halls of some dull museum, and look what I get. The other kids might call an arduous walk through the wilderness a field trip. By then I was calling it a Wednesday night. One thought, and one thought only crossed my mind – Fuck my life.

■■■

My good mood from the morning was very short lived, and my temper was equally short on the coach trip to wherever the hell it was. I was caught in a state of perpetual bitterness about the whole situation, as though it had somehow betrayed me personally. We were sat towards the middle of the coach. Damian and Jackson were in the two seats ahead of me, and I was all on my lonesome, looking sullen. The incessant nattering of the two girls at my back grated on my very soul, to the point where I grew envious of the deaf.

My miserable disposition worsened as the journey went on. We were told wherever we were headed was over an hour's drive away. I wondered why we couldn't just walk a few laps of the school instead, and then file our way back into our usual classrooms. At least then I would be sat down all day. What really irritated me though, more than anything else was this kid, Luke.

Luke was from the other class; the one I didn't have the misfortune to attend myself. I didn't really know him personally, but I knew of him. I'd heard he was the sort of person who picks on people to assert his dominance. Sadly this is pretty standard. Every school has a bunch of them. These are the ones who stand out for all the wrong reasons, whilst the rest fade into the background like well-mannered ghosts.

As we rode along, he was proving that my previously unverified intel on him was spot on. There was some scrawny little weed sat alone in the seat in front of him reading a book, and Luke obviously felt he had the right to torment him. Looking back, I realise he had probably only picked that seat to do so. I had a clear view of it from my own uncomfortable, musty perch on the coach. Gradually my mild annoyance increased to unbearable levels.

To begin with, he just kept reaching around his seat and poking the kid in the side of the face while he was reading away. The kid kept glancing back, as if a stern look would send him cowering. It didn't. Then Luke started slapping him, and everyone turned a blind eye.

Now, I'm not going to claim that I felt some sort of duty to protect a defenceless fellow pupil, that's simply not true. I did however feel a duty to make my own journey as tolerable as I could. My improved sense of smell meant that I caught the stench of every sweaty pubescent body that surrounded me, and my increasingly hypersensitive hearing meant that every screech and shrill cackle of laughter cut straight through me, like Jason's blade through a clueless cheerleader.

There was nothing I could do about the repugnant scent, and I couldn't really demand silence and expect to get it. I could do something about the bully though. The final straw was when the kid turned around and weakly asked Luke to stop it. He tried so hard to sound forceful, but he failed even harder. It was pretty pitiful. Then Luke slapped him again, this time with feeling.

"Don't be an asshole. I only wanted to ask what book you were reading." He garbled in the manner of a member of the uneducated, cider swilling community. He had one of those faces that does enough on its own to insult the senses. His dyed, bleach blonde hair, and the single coppery stud in his ear didn't help. Luke's laugh sounded like an asthmatic donkey trying to fight its way free from a tar pit. Now imagine that sound amplified to beyond human levels. I had had enough then. Of everything, of everyone, of all the damn racket.

"Don't pick on him just 'cause you don't have any books in whatever trailer you call home, you fucking pikey." The bus continued to trundle along as everyone turned to look. The silence was bliss.

"Errr! We'll have no language like that on this coach thank you!" Miss Clarke stood at the front, holding on to a vertical hand railing, peering down the length of our decrepit diesel prison. She was unaware who had spoken, but Luke knew, and so did seemingly everyone else. Then the air was soundless again for a few more precious moments. Miss Clarke sat down, and a hundred thousand conversations all sparked up at once. It was good while it lasted.

"What the fuck's it got to do with you?" Luke leaned over and asked me quietly.

"Nothing, I just found the idea of you taking interest in a book slightly offensive." I replied. His face appeared blank, like that was too many noises in a row for him to process. I leaned my head heavily into the back of the chair, wishing all the commotion around me would just end. It was like I could hear every syllable of every word, and it was infuriating. Even the tyres on the road, and the whistle of the breeze through a window that was open just a crack, managed to reach my ears.

"Well mind your own damn business." He cleverly retorted, turning back. Then he poked the kid in front of him again.

"Oh for Christ's sake. Kid just come sit over here." His head spun and he looked at me, hesitated for a moment, then finally came over. I got up to give him the window seat where Luke wouldn't be able to see him, let alone bother him. I waved him in like an usher seating a theatre patron who tips well. That put a stop to it. The bully stared at me in an attempt at intimidation. It fell flat though because what he thought was an intense look, appeared more like uncomfortable constipation.

"Faggot."

"Yep." I said, saluting him. I blew him a kiss and sat down. I hunkered down into my seat, hoping I might be absorbed by it. Then I forced my eyes shut, trying to ignore the crowd of clamorous individuals surrounding me. I wished I could just forget the world and instead drift in infinite blackness, and absolute peace.

"Thanks." The kid next to me squeaked. I sighed. I wasn't trying to strike up a dialogue.

"You're welcome." I replied moodily. He didn't say anything for a few seconds, and *I* was thankful for that.

"I'm Elton." He told me uncomfortably. I opened my eyes to look at him, whilst he inspected his footwear. He was a tiny thing, around 5ft 3, with short brown hair and a permanent vacant expression.

"Elton? Well no wonder you get fucking picked on." I let my head drop heavily, and willingly returned myself to the darkness once more.

■■■

So, Elton was not too adept when it came to the art of taking hints, he just kept on talking. The book he had stopped reading to bother me was 'The Fellowship of the Ring', and he gloatingly informed me that he had read it many times before. I just wished he would've carried on with his repeat run through of The Lord of the Rings, I was having a hard time dealing with all the noise without him speaking right down my ear. When all was said and done, it was a very unpleasant journey for yours truly.

It was with a great sense of relief that I finally stepped off of the coach and into far fresher air. I breathed in deep through flaring nostrils, trying to clear out the stench of dusty seats, stagnant air, and the combined body odour of filthy teens. It was immediately replaced with the stench of animals. I moved away from the group, and the decreasing volume was almost pleasurable. I had never longed to sit in utter silence so much in my life. Elton followed me like a lost puppy. I paid him no attention as I rubbed my ears and shook my head, trying to regain my bearings. I relaxed for a moment, alone aside from the sheep at my heels. It felt like a release of some of the tension that had built during the ride, a necessary short reprieve.

I looked around taking in my surroundings. We were on a gravel parking lot, just off of the small back road we had taken to get to our precise little portion of the middle of nowhere. There was an unimpressive concrete building situated next to the makeshift car park. Its battered sign proudly proclaimed it was the 'Shady Grove Educational Centre'. Behind the building lay rows of unimpressive looking enclosures, far less sturdy than the ones I myself had occupied, but no doubt more spacious.

"Are you okay?" Elton asked curiously. Thus ended my moment of peace. I let out an exasperated breath.

"Yeah man, I'm fine." I replied, and turned to face his fish-like, unblinking eyes. We shared an awkward moment where neither of us spoke. It was interrupted by the sound of Mr Jeffries, the other geography teacher who had come along for the trip, shouting for everybody to give him their attention. 'No need to yell' I thought to myself, rubbing my ear again. We plodded our way back over to the main group.

"Alright everybody, this is how it's going to happen! We'll be split into groups, and each group will take one of the different routes marked out on the maps we have for you here." He pointed to a small cardboard box full of folded paper.

"Now it's pretty much impossible to get lost, because we are heading for there." He pointed to an obnoxious looking lump of green off in the distance.

"I know, it's not exactly Everest but I assure you, *that* is a mountain." He chuckled at his own joke. Everyone stood stone faced and silent. Sadly, no tumbleweed rolled on by.

"Right then, everyone needs a map!" He deafeningly informed us, then began taking them from the box and handing them to everybody.

Mr Jeffries was a short, balding man. All the clothes I'd ever seen him wear looked too big for him. He had a weathered face, grey stubble revealing his age, and a voice a couple of octaves higher than you'd expect it to be. The aging educator bore all the trademarks of a prolific rambler, the hefty looking footwear, and coarse materials covering head to toe. I know little about Mr Jeffries, he disappeared from the school for a while, but I didn't really notice until the rumour that he was dead started circulating. After months away though, he returned as though he had never left without so much as an explanation.

Everyone exploded into deafening discussion as he handed out our maps. All dissolved into chaos, the way it does with students whenever the teacher is preoccupied. School kids, they're an opportunist sort. I didn't do any talking, just stood there at the back of the group, wishing I was elsewhere. Preferably at home in the familiar shade of my bedroom. Elton swayed faithfully by my side.

Mr Jeffries extended his hand, brandishing the folded paper map. I was reluctant to accept his offering.

"Come on son, look alive." He cheerfully chided, planting the thing in my chest so I was forced to take it. A patronising pat on the shoulder sealed the deal. He handed Elton his copy, and continued on his way. I carelessly folded the map up in one hand and shoved in my pocket.

"This looks pretty far..." Elton spoke, examining the various routes intently. I chose not to interrupt.

"Okay everybody, you've all got everything you'll need to make it to the top of that mountain! Now, while myself and Miss Clarke decide on your groups, please feel free to take a look around the facility's zoo, just to the rear of the main building. Meet back here in twenty minutes!" Mr Jeffries unshakeable enthusiasm continued to shine.

■■■

The grubby sign outside the so-called zoo read 'Shady Grove Animalarium'.

"Animalarium?" Elton said, puzzled, glancing around at the miserable looking animals and the chicken wire fencing. "Do you think they have to call it that because it's too crappy to be a real zoo?" He asked, one eye squinting awkwardly in a show of confusion.

"Probably." I replied, setting off to experience an animalarium for myself, the stench of faeces hanging heavy in the air. He was hot on my heels of course. The rest of the students were already scattered, observing first hand that yes, it is possible for animals to suffer from depression. We peered at some extremely bored looking meerkats, a sloth that I'm almost certain was dead, and a lone chimpanzee, which seemed on the verge of resorting to cutting itself.

"Hey, this guy looks almost as happy as you, aha..." Elton muttered smirking. I shot a menacing look in his direction and his lips tightened.

"You know, in my defence, I was expecting to be in a museum looking at shiny rocks or something. Not out here *hiking.*" I mumbled moodily.

"You're thinking of geology." Elton stated, never taking his eyes off of the pessimistic primate. Admittedly, I might have become a little flushed.

"Alright, listen up Candle in the Wind. You're not really helping my mood here." I muttered wearily.

He cleared his throat, aiming a sneaky, sideways glance in my direction. "Ahem. Sorry."

We left the chimp to contemplate suicide in his joyless box, passed some pallid parakeets who lacked the room to spread their wings, and arrived at a cage which looked a little more hard wearing than the others. Within it, a fearsome looking tiger paced back and forth, never taking its eyes off the crowd of school kids staring into its prison.

"It must be horrible, being trapped like that." I overheard Lexey speak from her place at the front of the group. She leaned forward over the rickety fence that stopped anyone getting close enough to the enclosure to poke delicious looking fingers through the bars.

"Who cares," a sharp, unknown voice "it's just a fucking animal." She glanced towards the unseen person, mouth twisting in distaste. After a moment's consideration, she returned her gaze to the caged beast.

"I can barely see the thing." Elton complained, as he tried valiantly to peer over the shoulders of those whose height was staggeringly average.

"Dude, you need to take some initiative every once in a while." I told him, hoping to instil some kind of life lesson perhaps. I pushed my way through the group, easing people aside until we had front row seats to the big cat's suffering. Elton stood on the bottom plank of the not so stable looking fence, elevating himself to near human tallness.

The tiger continued its march to nowhere, its rage evident in its piercing stare. It looked familiar to me, reminiscent of a cold night bathed in moonlight. I leaned nonchalantly against the insubstantial wooden structure, wondering exactly what was going through the fur-ball's mind.

"This guy sure looks more impressive up close, huh?" My new sidekick mentioned, incapable of keeping a single thought in his head.

Suddenly his legs disappeared from under him, and he crashed down painfully on to the gravel below. I saw Luke, and all at once the darkness within me snarled in silent, yet vicious fury. Every animal erupted in unison into frenzied cries. My vision blurred, white-hot pain pierced my skull, and all sound disappeared for a moment to be replaced with the thunderous gallop of my own beating heart. I squeezed in an effort to regain control and the fence turned to splinters in my hands. I staggered, but managed to stay on my feet. It felt as though the wolf wanted to leap free from my flesh, but I stifled it, held it back.

All sound returned in an instant, and the screeching calls of a dozen daunted creatures near deafened me. My hands clamped down on my ears instinctively, trying to cancel out the noise. Despite my efforts, I still heard Luke's smug quip over the racket.

"Guess you need a better bodyguard shorty!" He shouted through cupped hands, backing away as he did so. I shook my head and the fog began to clear, the world came into focus again. Even the animals began to calm. The crowd of students were static, Elton and I were the unwilling centre of attention. Lexey peered at me, I glanced at her for just long enough to see the confusion etched on her face. Then I decided that looking at the ground was preferable to taking in the sight of all our gawking peers.

Damian appeared from somewhere within the rabble, he hauled Elton back to his feet. Elton let out a little whimper and rubbed his grazed elbow, when he was again standing rather than involuntarily lying on his back.

"You alright?" Damian asked me sincerely, taking in the scene. The tiger, teeth bared, was at the far end of its enclosure. Adopting a defensive position.

"Yeah," I replied not all that convincingly "yeah I'm fine." I took a final look at the caged cat. Its fangs flashed threateningly, eyes locked on mine. Maybe some things are better off behind bars after all.

ROUTE B

I was relieved when the crowd finally dispersed. Truth be told, since becoming one of the Lycans, I'd done a pretty shitty job of blending in. If I were a super hero, my secret identity would have been revealed, and my mask up on eBay within a week. Luckily I wasn't out there trying to protect the innocent, so rather than seeming like a vigilante who was hiding secret super natural abilities, I was beginning to appear more like a sociopath with violent, possibly homicidal tendencies. Sadly for this sociopath, he still had a hike to endure.

"Zack, you're with Claire, John, Lexey and Graham." I let out a small groan at this news, and Miss Clarke told me to stop whining. Leaden feet slowed me down as I joined the group of brave explorers, the ones who would be facing the horrors of Route B along with me. Claire, a doughy bleach blonde who looked liked she'd been involved in an explosion at the makeup factory, subtly edged away as I approached. I couldn't really blame her. Yet again I became the recipient of dirty looks, the gangly, gaunt looking kid called Graham appeared genuinely uneasy in my presence. This cheered me up somewhat, it offered the potential for a peaceful journey.

"Oh miss, MISS!" Elton rushed over. "Can I go with group B please?" He requested with great civility.

"Well, since you asked so nicely young man. Is anyone willing to switch with Elton?" She asked my fellow B team members. Graham, the pumpkin king, could not leave fast enough, and my coach buddy dropped his shiny boots firmly at my side. I decided this called for another groan.

"Can I switch with someone?" I begged, like misery itself had found a voice to speak in.

"No, you cannot. For once you will do as you're told Zachary." I grimaced at the sound of my own name.

"Tryin' to get away from me already, huh?" Elton chuckled.

"Wouldn't dream of it." I replied, wearing a face that suggested a tantrum was imminent. I pulled the squashed up map from my pocket to see exactly what I had gotten myself into. Our path was a long and winding one, through trees, over water. There were hills, and a bridge to contend with too. All of that was before we even got to the pathetic excuse for a mountain we'd have to climb. I could hardly contain my joy at the prospect.

■■

The epic journey down Route B began. The ladies led the way, maps in hand, taking it all very seriously. I didn't really see why, as the path we were on was well trodden. Countless footfalls had left the grass sickly, and in some places it was gone altogether. It didn't take a brain surgeon, or a map to follow that. I hung at the back of the group, maintaining as much distance as possible without giving the impression that I was a wounded soldier falling behind. Elton matched my leisurely pace. John, who I can only describe as husky, if I hope to avoid offending fat people, was struggling to maintain position in mid table. Beads of sweat ran down his colossal shaven head, and his body swelled visibly as his lungs grasped for more desperately needed oxygen.

We made our way past huge, ancient looking trees, struggling through dense vegetation. Hopping over great roots and winding our way around the vast wooden columns was easier for some than others, and it wasn't long before John began to succumb to exhaustion.

"Hey..." John spoke wheezing "Hey guys, can we stop for a break?" Lexey and Claire halted at the head of the group and turned.

"Yeah, I don't see why not." Lexey shrugged, the apparent leader of our expedition. I saw no reason to argue, my feet were already becoming sore as a result of my lack of preparation. Not that I owned any hiking boots to bring, had I thought to do so.

"Cool, I'm starving anyway." Elton stated. He perched himself on a rock and dumped his backpack on the ground, digging around for food. Everyone followed suit, John collapsing less gracefully than the rest. I decided to sit against a tree, keeping a little space between myself and the others. Seeing everyone eating made my stomach growl audibly. Along with new abilities seemed to come my inconvenient, insatiable appetite.

"Aren't you eating, Zack?" Elton asked, his face smeared with chocolate.

"Didn't bring anything." I muttered, and no sooner had I finished the thought than I was hit in the chest with a soft thud, and a tinny clang. A foil wrapped sandwich lay in my lap. I looked up to see Lexey, a fair distance away. She had hit her target.

"It's a good thing some of us came prepared." She said, rolling her eyes.

"...Thanks." I mumbled incoherently, vision fixed on the floor.

While I was satisfied with devouring my borrowed lunch in silence, the others seemed intent on conversation.

"Hey kid," the largest in our group spoke, having finally caught a breath that found it all too easy to outrun him "how come you wanted to change to this group anyway? It's gonna be slow as hell getting there with me you know?"

"Oh, I don't care how long it takes," Elton said, gulping a luminous energy drink "they put me in a group with Luke. That guy hates me."

"You really should stand up for yourself." I muttered from my quiet corner.

"What, like you stood up to Charlie?" Lexey broke in with a disgusted expression. Apparently I hadn't muttered quietly enough. I remained silent, admiring the surrounding greenery.

"Yeah, I heard about that. You know, people say you're a psycho but you don't seem so bad to me?" John shrugged casually "A little moody perhaps, but not a psycho." He continued to eat a bread roll. I felt uncomfortable being the subject up for discussion. There was a long pause.

"So why did you do it?" The poster-girl for peroxide decided to chime in. I didn't really feel like responding. What could I say, to stop myself slaughtering everyone in the room? I'm sure that would have gone down well. Their focus remained on me, expectant of an answer.

"Because... he deserved it." That was the response I finally settled on. Lexey gave a derisive snort.

"Violence is never the answer." She helpfully informed me.

"Violence is the only language some people understand." I spoke quietly, but Elton heard. I could almost see the gears in his head turning as he considered the notion.

■■

After an uncomfortable conversation, and a tuna sandwich that was surprisingly tasty, our party ventured forth. Our pace was slow. A team is only as strong as its weakest link after all, so I was thankful when the uneven ground, and the seemingly endless trees made way for more level and open terrain. We had to take another breather on our travels, but the second time I managed to keep from becoming involved in the chatter altogether. Finally, after what already seemed like an age, we reached the halfway point on our map. A gentle stream, which may as well have been the Amazon River considering Claire's reaction.

"I am NOT walking through that!" She bellowed with admirable certainty.

"Calm down," John said panting "no one's walking through, there are stepping stones." He pointed a chubby finger at the wet rocks protruding from the surface.

"Can't we go around or something?" She said, clearly irritable.

"It's not even knee deep? I'll go first, it'll be easy." Elton said, striding to the water's edge. He stretched short legs over the unstoppable torrent, planting a foot firmly on the first rock. Daintily he made his way forward, both slow and methodical. Every step was on the very edge of his stride, but sure enough, he made it to the other side without a single droplet touching him.

"You see? Easy!" Elton beckoned us to follow triumphantly.

Lexey went second. Sure-footed and with the adequate range, she crossed with no trouble, joining Elton on the successful side of the trickling terror. John was up next. He was tall enough for sure, but a little lacking in the balance department. He crossed the first few stones, arms outstretched in an effort to keep himself steady, but as he neared the far side of the raging river, his right foot lost traction. His leg became submerged up to the knee, with a less than dramatic splash.

"Arr, damn it." He sounded more disappointed in himself than annoyed as he stood with one leg in the placid water. "Oh well, no point staying dry now." John hopped in and walked the rest of the way through the shimmering liquid, emerging with soggy boots. With the majority of us having made the perilous crossing, it was the wannabe Barbie doll's time to shine.

"Hey, don't worry. If you fall in, the water's fine!" John assured her smiling. It didn't exactly help.

"I don't wanna do this." She squeaked in my direction. I gave her a quick glance, then ignored her. She let out an indignant grunt and hesitantly stepped forward, breathing deeply in anticipation. She hopped girlishly onto the first stone, and shrieked at a pitch that almost shattered my eardrums. Some people are so inconsiderate. Hands buried in her chest defensively, Claire stood whining and squirming awkwardly in place.

"Come on, it's not a big deal." Lexey said in a tone that suggested she were ashamed to share a gender with her.

Claire took another daring hop forward, making it to the second stone with another shrill cry. From behind I could see her trying to psyche herself up for the next jump. It was crucial that she made it, as evidently she was utterly allergic to moisture. Fearlessly she leapt into the great void between the two stones, her feet landed on the third rock and then immediately slid out from under her. Brand new hiking boots arced skyward, and the rest of her followed. She came crashing down in a bright and beautiful display of aquatic motion. It's a shame she didn't see it that way.

"OH. MY. GOD!" She screeched, sitting up in the shallow stream. She stood and sulked on the spot for an instant before stamping her feet like a petulant toddler. Everyone attempted to stifle laughter as she stomped her way aggressively through what remained of the great lake she had, so far, failed to cross. As she clambered out of the water, the boys burst into great fits of uncontrollable giggles. Lexey smirked, showing a little more self-control. Even I had chuckled to myself a little, despite the fact my ears were still ringing.

"This is not funny!" She clomped the ground again in furious anger, droplets falling from her soaking hair.

"Guess you should have just walked through it, huh?" Elton beamed gleefully. She pushed him, and took him clean off his feet.

"Shut up! Owh, my makeup is ruined!" She whimpered, wiping her face with her hands and seeing the smeared remnants of her former mask plastered on her palms.

"Don't worry. You look better without it anyway." John broke into a charm offensive.

"Shut up!" Claire repeated, arms flailing wildly in his direction in an all out attack.

Whilst they were all too busy laughing at Barbie's first swimming lesson, I was still on the wrong side of the stream. On the stepping-stones, two out of four had managed to get wet, and I personally didn't like those odds. It wasn't far, I was pretty sure with my fresh Lycan powers I could make it. Shit, they might as well be used for something other than giving me a headache right? So whilst all attention was directed elsewhere, I took a couple of steps back, powered forward as hard as I could and pushed away from the ground with all my might. I felt the compact dirt give a little under my feet, then it was all over in an instant. I cleared the water and crashed down to the ground on all fours, almost tumbling forwards with the excess momentum. They all turned at once.

"How did you get over here so fast?" Claire asked, sweeping damp locks of hair out of her eyes.

"Erm... stones?" That was all I could think to say. My mind was running a little empty. Group B looked at me with suspicion, but all words failed. I restlessly shifted my weight from one foot to another, waiting for them to find something better to do.

"Hmm. Anyway, we should get going." Lexey finally broke the silence. "Now, we've got two choices according to the map. You see that rocky verge up ahead?" She asked pointing to the verge in question. She gestured towards the paper in her hands. "This says follow it around, but it's a pretty long way."

"So, what's the other option?" Elton wondered aloud.

"We go over." She shrugged.

∙∙

The craggy slope looked neither too sheer, nor too daunting to me. John and Elton on the other hand, one of whom is rather sizeable, and the other, not so. They didn't look too pleased about being outvoted on the choice of path we take.

"I can't believe you agreed to this Claire?" John said, looking a little betrayed.

"Excuse me, but have you seen the state of me?!" She exclaimed, pointing both hands at her face. "I'd probably look better if I fell off and died, so I might as well climb!" Humble little backpack in tow, she hurried forward to be the first to make the ascent.

"It's official," announced Elton under his breath "that crazy girl has got more balls than us."

Claire clambered upwards like a woman possessed, with a complete disregard for her own personal safety. She slowed for nothing, her rage so prevalent that I momentarily considered the possibility that the rock itself might keel over in an impossible display of surrender. In no time she reached the summit of our miniature mountain and stood defiantly at its peak, teeth still grinding as she swept another sodden lock from her equally sodden face.

"Seriously, how hard can it be you guys?" Lexey spoke to the two reluctant mountaineers.

"Well, in case you haven't noticed blondie, I'm not exactly built like Spiderman over here," John exclaimed, pointing to himself with a single chubby thumb "and I've had taller meals than this guy." He waved a dismissive hand in Elton's direction. Lexey rolled her eyes and exhaled heavily. She marched over to John and tugged the pack from his back.

"Hey what the-?" He murmured.

I was absentmindedly rolling a stone beneath my aching foot, when the rucksack rolled to a halt in my field of vision. My reaction was an incoherent grunt.

"Come on, lead by example. These guys are letting your side down right now." Lexey said, just as a rather substantial rock connected forcefully with John's shin.

"Ahhh, ahhh, ouch, ouch, owie, ouch, shit, shit, shit." He rasped comically, bouncing on his one good leg.

"Hurry the hell up you pussies! I can see the others from here, they're already at the base of that dumbass hill thing!" Claire roared violently. Any femininity she may have normally emitted had completely disappeared, falling prey to her foul mood.

I took that as my cue to begin climbing. I grabbed the backpack and slung it lazily over my shoulder, then placed a tender paw on the jagged rocks. Moving my weight and that of the backpack felt effortless, although I did have an unfair advantage over my fellow travellers. I hadn't been hauling that thing around all day for a start. That, coupled with the fact that I had recently become a creature of legend meant that when I joined the shrieking rock thrower at the top, I couldn't quite understand what all the fuss was about.

"Right, who's next?" Our fearless female leader asked in a tone that suggested her patience was wearing incredibly thin.

"Not me!" They both replied in unison, raising a hand as though they were still in class.

"Ugh, whatever. You two can fight it out amongst yourselves." She told them, drained. She joined myself, and the moistened banshee in no time. We were only two away from completing our set. Unluckily for us, they happened to be our least valuable assets.

"You go first little man, that way if you slip I can... break your fall... or something." The rotund one of the pair argued.

"To hell with that, I don't have the reach to climb this thing. You go first, and I'll just cling to your leg." Another rock came hurtling down, narrowly missing Elton's pea sized head. "Whoa, Jesus!"

"Get your asses up her or so help me God, I will murder you both!" Claire screeched, another stone clutched tightly in her fist.

"Okay, okay! Right kid, if we do this, we do it together." John spoke solemnly, eyes fixed on the fifteen-foot high obstacle he had to overcome. To him it appeared to reach high into the clouds above, an undoable task.

"Pfft, kid? Pretty sure I'm older than you..." He dived out of the path of yet another projectile. Shuddering a little after regaining his composure, Elton finally accepted his mission. "Alright damn it, let's go before she makes good on her promise."

Boldly they marched forth with unflinching stares. Determination personified, they began their heroic ascent. Their bold determination however, swiftly turned into bawling and bad excuses.

"This is actually quite high now!" Elton wailed, having made it past the halfway point. He was tightly hugging the face of the world's smallest cliff.

"Wish I could say the same pal." John panted beneath him, thrusting a hefty arm clumsily to its next handhold. "You're almost there. I'm not gonna make it, just go on without me!"

"Oh for God's sake, quit being so melodramatic." Lexey groaned, face planted firmly in her palm. Elton took another tiny step higher. It was just enough to put him in her reach. She leaned over the edge, grabbing his delicate wrists, and dragged him upwards. His little feet scrambled against the wall, the scuffles voicing his discomfort as he panicked. Finally, he stood on soft grass, eyes closed. Warily he opened them.

"Hey... I did it. I'm up." He smirked.

"Yeah, you're a real hero." Lexey huffed sarcastically.

John continued to climb, in an image not too dissimilar to a Titan scaling Mount Olympus.

"Haul ass, come on!" Claire, who had turned from Barbie doll into drill sergeant in the time it took mascara to run from her eyes to her chin, shouted fiercely.

"Hey, you know what they say," He heaved "slow and steady wins the race."

"Dude, I don't know who *they* are, but from the crowd up ahead I'd say they gave you some bad advice." Elton talked down from the ledge, and I'm sure took much pleasure in the fact that he was, for a moment at least, towering over someone else.

It was painful to watch the hefty boy work his way towards us, at what I couldn't in good conscience call a snail's pace, for fear of insulting the snails. He persevered though, and eventually he was agonisingly close to the top.

"It's no good, my arms are dead. I can't go on..." John breathed.

"You're like two steps away?" Elton replied confused.

"Tell them... I died to save you all." He panted, beads of salty sweat running down his forehead, white hands shaking.

"Oh for the love of God. Zack, help him up." Lexey pleaded, having had more than enough.

I gave her an uncomfortable glace but said no words, obliging in silence. Leaning down over the ledge, I grabbed on to his oily arm.

"Buddy, this is optimistic to say the least." He huffed, realising what I intended to do. Without replying I tugged at his arm and forced my heels into the ground with, I'll be honest, a little more force than I originally intended. I fell back, and landed ever so gracefully on my rump.

"Oh Shit!" John managed to squeak as he was hurled through the air, in the instance before his nose and the dirt became more than just friends. He writhed on the ground, wheezing.

"You're stronger than you look." His words were muffled by the mouthful of grass. He turned his head, revealing a face smeared with mud. "Thanks, I think..."

Elton laughed heartily, right in John's dirty mug. When I lifted myself from the ground Lexey's eyes fell on me. I didn't immediately realise why.

"What happened to your arm?" She asked curiously.

I looked down to see crimson beads trickling from my dark sleeve. It is at this point I should probably just come out and say that, at the time at least, my ability to talk to girls was less than stellar. Can you blame me? With a social group as stimulating to the opposite sex as mine was, I'd have been more comfortable interacting with a unicorn, should I happen upon one. The fact that I knew more werewolves than females was a disheartening realisation indeed.

"Oh, I umm... must have cut it climbing... my arm I mean. On, on the wall... thing." Forget Zack, you can all call me Casanova. She stepped forward and took hold of my wrist, lifting my sleeve to reveal the pre-bandaged wound beneath. I flinched at the unwarranted human contact.

"Well," she said peering at the bandage, turning an ever-deeper shade of red "you've got incredible foresight for someone who didn't even think to bring lunch." I couldn't think of anything witty to say in return.

"Can we get out of here now? This day is *far* from over, and we're just wasting time." Claire said bitterly.

"Is your arm gonna be okay?" Lexey asked, and I nodded in reply. She paused "You're a weird one… What exactly are you hiding?" Whilst I was pleased that my review had been upgraded from 'fucking psycho' to merely 'weird', I was a little taken aback by her statement. I avoided looking into her narrowed eyes.

"I, umm... nothing. I'm not hiding anything." I lied.

■■

So, we finally regrouped with the rest of those unfortunate enough to be on that retarded field trip with us. We were the last to arrive and as such, the heroes of Route B were not entitled to a rest. Thanks to our sluggish pace, the entire journey was now behind schedule. Did Columbus stick to a schedule? I think not, but try telling that to a grade school geography teacher. All that lay between us and the highest point on our side of the horizon was a tedious walk up a gentle incline. The trail we had to take spiralled around in eccentric circles as it made its way towards the heavens.

Claire disappeared into the crowd, no doubt in search of her usual group of friends. After all, she needed to find someone with the relevant skills to reapply the many layers of her face that were now careening somewhere downriver. Lexey had disappeared amongst the others too, seemingly sick of babysitting the rest of us. John was at the back of the babbling conga line, struggling to keep up as seemed to be his way, and Elton matched him stride for stride. I kept my distance as usual, to avoid being dragged into their inane conversation. As I mused at the back of the pack, I came to the realisation that even though our trek was a complete and utter farce from start to finish, it was still preferable to being surrounded by a horde of squawking teenagers.

After a short distance had been covered, Damian spotted me from up ahead and rushed back to speak. It was a talk I was pretty sure I didn't want to have, having played a part in his father's murder and all.

"Hey man." He said as unceremoniously as he could. I responded with a nod of my aching head. "Look, there are a couple of things I need to talk to you about."

"Oh yeah, like what?" I enquired, straining to separate his speech from that of all the rest.

"Erm... okay, let's just get this outta the way. My dad, he's gone right? Like, for good?" I could hear the hope he held.

"Uhuh, believe me. He's not coming back." The fear in Phillip's eyes, that picture of terror on his face, flashed through my mind. I have no problem admitting that it didn't exactly move me to tears.

"Good. Fucking asshole deserved it. I needed to know for sure. Would it be stupid of me to ask about it?" He asked, and I simply nodded. After a thoughtful pause, he spoke again. "Alright I guess... second thing. What the hell is going on with you lately? First Charlie, then that strange old guy you were with, and today down in that poor excuse for a zoo? It doesn't make any sense, dude." I could practically see his mind at work. Damian was trying to put the pieces together, but it was a puzzle far from complete.

"Trust me, you wouldn't believe me if I told you. Hell, even if you saw it, you probably wouldn't believe it."

"Try me. Show me if you have to. I mean come on, how unbelievable can it be?" He shrugged. These were the words I didn't bother to speak. 'You have no idea.'

"Honestly, you're probably better off not knowing." I said as earnestly as possible.

"Ow, what the hell!" Came a breaking voice from behind us, followed by obnoxious guffawing.

"What is wrong with you?!" John sounded outraged as Luke chortled gleefully.

"Goddamn it," I muttered to myself. "you might get to see what I'm talking about after all." I told Damian, as a familiar stirring predictably began. I turned quickly and approached the trio, hoping I could avoid yet another potential massacre. It was becoming almost routine. The rest of the students headed off without us.

"Oh look, it's your knight in shining armour once again." Luke mocked as we arrived.

"What's your problem dumb ass?" A fair question I thought. Elton continued rubbing his head where the bully had struck him yet again.

"No problems here, just putting this little shit in his place. Keep out of it, freak." Now that hurt my little feelings. Luke tried his damnedest to sound threatening.

"In his place, really?" The Lycan begged to be free, as it always did. When would it learn? "Well, I guess you're right Luke. Everybody needs to be in their place." I began walking towards him. Damian looked on, wondering exactly when I had turned from miserable layabout into the Punisher. Little did he know, my intentions were severely more complex than he understood. I wasn't looking out for the underdog, I was trying to stop myself from becoming the orchestrator of the next big high school tragedy.

"Oh, here he comes. What exactly are you gonna do, puke on me? Yeah it's not like everyone's forgotten about that, you fucking weirdo. What, you think 'cause you hit Charlie you're a big man now?" The kid's tone was smug. Truth be told, I was kind of hoping people had forgotten about that whole vomit based escapade. My dark side pleaded with me to hurt him, or set it free. It made clear that it preferred the latter option. Still, I suppose the fact that it was holding back long enough to give me an option at all was an improvement.

"It's fine Zack, just forget it. I'm okay." Elton said meekly, shuffling from one tiny foot to the other. This irritated me, and it.

"Jesus Christ, fucking stand up for yourself!" Lycan and boy spoke in tandem, both my best intentions and my worst had the same message for Elton. It, however, had a personal message for Luke, and I allowed it just a little freedom, the tiniest amount of leeway to say what it had to say. I felt he needed to hear it. I got in close, so no one else could decipher the distant whispers, and I let it speak through me.

"Listen. You can't begin to imagine the things I could do to you." He began to back away but It followed "I could destroy you, do you understand? There would be nothing left. *Nothing*." He took a couple more steps backwards and ended up at the edge of the trail, pebbles and dust rolled down the deep slope at his back. He looked afraid. "Give me one good reason I *shouldn't* tear out your throat."

He trembled visibly, then as is always the way with his kind, his fear turned to fury.

"What is with you? Just stay out of it!" His hands balled up into fists at his sides. "Why do you care about this little pussy anyway?" Luke pointed aggressively at Elton.

"LEAVE ME ALONE!" Elton cried, launching himself headlong and throwing his hands into his tormentor's torso. Luke went hurtling back, arms flailing, careening down the slope and bouncing painfully as he went. He took on the properties of a ragdoll as he tumbled, finally rolling to a halt on a part of the trail we had long since passed that lay beneath us. Suddenly the wolf was gone, and I was back entirely.

Luke didn't move. Elton stood panting, his body trembling as a result of the adrenaline coursing through his veins. Damian and John stood, mouths agape.

"You said to stand up for myself right?" He peered up at me with a stare that told me he was unsure of his actions. The shadow of potential consequence was beginning to pass over him.

"Yeah. Don't worry, he deserved it. Come on, let's get out of here." In silence we marched on to catch up with the rest of the group, leaving Luke to lick his wounds alone - provided he was conscious.

15 Days Until the Next Full Moon

It was after the events of that most undesirable field trip, that I decided school was the lesser evil. I promised myself that never again would I look forward to anything. I would rather do math until my eyes bled numbers than sit in a tin box full of stinking pubescent school kids again. Luke glared the whole way back from behind a slightly bruised face, and a significantly bruised ego. I never managed to shake Elton, who clung to me the whole way home fretting about the possible ramifications. I tried to reassure him that minor assault was probably about the coolest thing he had ever done, but he was having none of it. Needless to say, I was glad when it was over.

The instant the bus arrived back at Shawshank School for the clinically uninteresting, I could not walk away fast enough. I was happy when my sore feet touched down on the chaotic congregation of cloth that was my bedroom floor. My return to gloom was spoiled before my grimacing face could meet the musty pillow though, as is my luck. The phone on my bedside table rattled like an epileptic, not considerate enough to wait until I was safely in the land of dreams before throwing their next fit. Reluctantly I took it in hand. The message was from Locke.

"The usual time tomorrow. Time to meet the family."

I found it impossible to care. The bright light seared the words into my brain, leaving a ghostly impression of them every time I blinked.

"Fucking wolves." I muttered to the walls. Then, though daylight was yet to fade, I fell readily into the world of sleep.

■■■

Clearly I needed the rest. I slept right through 'til early afternoon. Still, if you really boil it down to its component elements, what I had been through was an obstacle course for advanced babysitters, so who wouldn't need some damn rest? It was a course I passed with flying colours, if you ask me. I decided to grab as much sustenance as I could cradle in my arms and retreat back into the darkness for most of the day. Too busy moping to even care about what was coming, I wasted my time watching shows about antiques. The subject matter seemed to include the hosts, who looked old enough to be killed by a stiff breeze. I enjoyed the irony of watching them talk about an ancient and dusty clock, whilst what little of their time remained ticked away audibly behind them.

Soon though, the hour the great phone prophesised approached, and as it neared I craved something warm to prepare myself for the potential horrors that lay ahead. It wasn't walking right back into the wolf den that bothered me. No, the horrors I speak of relate to a much more personal hell of mine. Meeting new people. My skin crawled at the thought. I considered heading for a mirror and attempting to practice my interested face, but ultimately decided against it. After all, Locke had described them as family. If there's one thing I know about family, it's that they have to tolerate you regardless, so bollocks to them.

My quest for something cooked led me to the kitchen. I peered perplexedly at the oven. Then, realising that I'd have a better chance of getting to the moon if you dropped my pale ass in a space shuttle and let me mash at the switches, I called my mom for backup. Luckily for me I am lovable enough (to my mother at least) for her to heed my cries, and it wasn't long before a steaming plate lay before me.

"You sure do have an appetite lately. I don't know where you put it all." She sighed, placing what was left of the raw meat back in the practically empty fridge.

"I'll have you know, I'm going out tonight. That's why I need all this energy." I replied through a mouthful of mashed potatoes.

"And I don't suppose you'll tell me where you're going this time either?"

"Just out with friends again." I said bluntly.

"Okay, I won't pry. I'm just worried. You've been different lately." Mom said with a genuine air of concern.

"Trust me, I'm fine. I promise."

"If you say so. I know how it is with kids your age." She waved nonchalantly. "Your body is going through changes, and all that awkward, hormonal stuff." She chuckled to herself, sweeping sandy hair from her field of view.

"Way to blow the subtext, Mom." I said glancing at my phone, my jaw working overtime.

"Huh?"

"Oh, nothing. I gotta go. I'll see you later." Realising I was late, I shovelled a few more highly attractive mouthfuls into my already bloated cheeks and headed for the door.

"Alright. Don't be too late." I heard her call as I slammed the door behind me.

I could already see the muddy land cruiser sat idled, waiting for its less than precious cargo. A slight sinking feeling began to develop in my gut, which I hoped wasn't down to continued hunger because if it was, I had a real problem. Said feeling was alleviated when I got close enough to see that it was Rita who waited for me, and not the man who saw a belt as a tool for getting his way, rather than keeping his damn slacks up. It was replaced by the speech stopping sensation of a female presence, but honestly I preferred that to the fear of imminent assault. Regardless of our teamwork in taking down father of the decade, I still didn't trust Locke. If anything, he had become even more unpredictable. I got the impression he only helped me the way he did because it suited his own nefarious ends.

■■■

True to form, I said little on route to our destination. I suppose it would have been a shame to ruin any surprises for myself. I was however shocked to learn, through my hard-hitting questioning, that suddenly I was trusted enough to visit the home of our towering pack leader without the aid of a blindfold. I wasn't aware that I had ever had the pleasure of visiting previously, but it turns out that those stairs that so viciously attacked my shins way back at the start of all this madness belonged to the man himself. It all came flooding back when we arrived and I jumped from the vehicle, landing on the gravel drive where my feet had fallen once before. The clattering stones beneath me were oh so familiar.

"Well, here we are." Rita cheerily informed me.

"Damn, this place is huge." I muttered to myself.

There it was, sat beneath a hazy orange sky in the final minutes of a winter's day. The manor house was vast, its tiered roof tapering to a point above the arched oak door. Ivy crawled its way up much of the natural stone walls, and spiralled around the two sturdy looking pillars at the building's entrance. Four golems sat weathered and watchful, high above. Many of the windows were dark and uninviting, only a few giving way to illumination at all. Even seeing the huge residence laid out before me, it was only when I noticed the Bentley parked lazily on the driveway that my hatred truly sunk in. I wondered just how the hell Locke had ended up with such a place.

Rita beckoned for me to follow as she approached the doorway. I trailed behind her, still overcome by a potent mixture of awe and jealousy. I noticed off to my left a considerable distance away, a cellar door jutting out from the ground. I remembered almost fondly being dragged through it whilst doing my best impression of an inmate in Guantanamo Bay. She swung the heavy cast iron knocker. It made a booming noise as it connected with the wooden surface.

"Heh, cute." I remarked dryly as Rita let go, and I realised it was shaped like a huge metal paw. After a short wait the door creaked open, and one weary eye peered through the gap created. Our appearance must have appeased the eye, because it decided to grant us entrance.

As the veil peeled away, the innards of the grand old house were revealed. An ornate ebony staircase spread its steps wide in the centre of the entrance hall, sweeping upwards elegantly to the second storey. A tired looking wooden floor, wearing the scars of a space well trodden ran from wall to wall, and decrepit looking paintings adorned every vertical surface. Interspersed with seemingly reckless abandon was a bunch of antique furniture, or at least I deduced it was antique through my long afternoon of thorough research. Wide, gothic archways framed either side of the stairway, and the rich aroma of food wafted through from beyond.

"Hey Dean." Rita greeted the scrawny stranger kindly.

"Hi." He had the posture of a man broken. "Food will be ready soon, come through." He continued after a pause, then peered at me as though he'd never seen a human being who didn't look as emaciated as him before. My eyes darted from his measly self to the rest of the room, purely for lack of anything better to do, until he finally strolled away. Dean disappeared beneath the arch, and life got a little less awkward.

"Jeez, Locke must be loaded to own a place like this. Why cheap out on the help?" I spoke to myself, forgetting I wasn't alone.

"Oh, he's not the help. Dean's my brother-in-law." Rita stated softly.

"Erm... well... shit." Let no one ever tell you I'm not a master wordsmith, for that would be a lie.

"He's also the one who made you what you are." She turned toward me and gave a weak smile. I cannot describe the face I pulled exactly, having not had the displeasure of seeing it. I can only assume I adopted the appearance of a man who had been forced to swallow a whole bottle of bitter pills. I had nothing to say to that, so consumed was I by disbelief. I was sure there must be some kind of mistake. Rita followed her almost certainly meth addicted brother-in-law and I shuffled behind her, shell-shocked.

We entered a long dining room, complete with a lengthy table fit to seat more bodies than my humble little fingers could account for. Matthew sat in one of the many chairs twiddling his thumbs, engaged in idle conversation with Dean, his brother by blood. His sickly looking sibling leaned against the wall nearby with his pale shaven head in his hands. I recalled that fateful night. Was the terrifying beast, the one with those huge dead eyes, really the pathetic man I now shared common space with?

"Zack!" Matthew called. "It's good to see you again. Come, take a seat." He beckoned. I waved clumsily and did as he said, pulling out the aged chair at his side.

"You finally get to meet the rest of the pack. You excited?" He asked.

"Yeah, I'm thrilled. I'm planning to make a game of guessing which ones voted to off me when I suddenly became your problem." I said, drumming a beat on the titanic table with my fingertips. My eyes scanned the creepy looking framed faces on the walls. Matthew huffed to himself.

"Don't judge them for that. They made that call because they believed it was right. Anyway, it never happened and here you are. Be grateful for that."

Just then, the relative calm was broken by the wolf's paw doorknocker furiously hitting its mark. Muffled bickering came from behind it, inaudible over the deafening metallic clang. Dean hurried away to answer it like a good little boy, as I buried my head in my hands in discomfort.

"Don't worry, your ears are still developing. They'll balance out in time."

"Well when that day comes, I'll be over the moon." I whined. "Hey um, Rita told me that your brother, he's the one who, you know… *made* me." I said to Matthew.

"Yeah, that's true. You two were born on the same night, for lack of a better term. I guess that could almost make you two brothers as well."

"No offence, but he looks kind of sick. Whatever he's got it's not, you know, hereditary or whatever is it?" I asked in a half whisper. Matthew's brow furrowed.

"He is having a little trouble adjusting, that is all." He stated with a hint of controlled anger "And no, that in no way affects you." I was surprised by his unusually harsh tone.

Just then, a bony old crow strode her way into the room. A young girl with deep blue hair trailed in behind her.

"I'm telling you Grandma, you're over reacting." The girl stated in a voice that was close to a groan.

"And I'm telling you, you look bloody ridiculous!" The crow cawed.

"Yeah, that means a lot coming from *you*. I've seen pictures of you when you were younger. You want to talk about ridiculous? You can't say a damn thing, so quit giving me shit you old bat." The youngster retorted.

"How dare you speak to me in that manner, I'd have gotten seven shades beaten out of me if I'd ever spoken to my elders like that!"

"Yeah, well now the only things older than you are fossilised and shit has changed. You don't like it, go play in traffic."

The lack of manners kids have these days is astounding, it really is enough to make you sad. Still, in the war between generations, team wrinkles was losing and she knew it. She hauled out a chair and slammed her bony behind down on it, hissing like a wounded cobra.

"Bloody children." she said wrapping her black cardigan tightly around her (I assume in an attempt at self mummification). "No damn respect."

"It's good to see you, Annie." Matthew tried his hardest to cut through the quarrel and regain some order.

"Have you seen what this pathetic child has done to herself? I mean it's ludicrous!" Annie squawked, neck waddle flapping furiously in the breeze. Dean glided back into the room, silent and near weightless, then took a seat without anyone paying him a second's attention. The girl sat with her arms folded and had murder in her eyes.

"Come on Anne, she's young. If the worst she does is dye her hair, then you should consider yourself lucky."

"Exactly! Just because she doesn't like it, she gets all pissy! She doesn't seem to realise that compared to most people I know, I'm a fucking saint."

"Bethany, you will watch your mouth this instant!" Anne cried.

"Bite me." Beth snapped.

"Don't tempt me you little shit." The old lady snarled.

Well, this was about the moment where I'd had enough. I wasn't going to stand for it any longer. I felt the rage building within me, to a point where I could no longer control it. It became too much, I leapt to my feet and gave a mighty roar! I flipped the table, and they all gasped in horror as I transformed in seconds before their eyes.

"I'm the boss around here now!" I said as a wolf somehow, and then I proceeded to-

Okay so none of that happened. Truth is, I stood and I pleaded. I told them all about how we should just get along. How we're a pack, and a pack is practically family. They began to rally behind me as I gave a rousing speech about honour and loyalty, they all started to chant my name an-

Okay so that didn't happen either. What *really* happened was, I sat leaning my head on my hands for another twenty minutes whilst both cradle and grave screeched like harpies. This went on to such an extent that I considered finding the nearest spoon, sharpening it to a point, and jabbing furiously at my earholes until the whole world was drenched in pure and wonderful silence.

"ENOUGH." Came the booming voice of Locke from outside of the room. Everybody fell silent, and I praised every deity I could think of.

Locke stalked his way into the dining area. His presence held an intensity like no other person I'd ever met. Imagine my surprise when the slight frame of Mr Osborne waddled in behind him.

"Sir?" I said, my mouth charmingly agape.

"Good evening, Zack." He smiled

■■

How could it be? That was all that ran through my mind as I sat gormlessly hovering a spoon inches from my face throughout the whole of dinner. I couldn't take my eyes off of his beardy little mug. The whole ordeal became a considerably quieter affair after

Locke's entrance. People hardly dared to speak, myself included, despite the questions rattling around in my skull. Questions like 'Why is my teacher having dinner with me, also why am I being taught by a potentially homicidal monster?' I mean, isn't it usually the PE teacher who's possibly dangerous and probably hiding something? Not the guy who does Math, surely?

What really struck me though, was his level of calm. I certainly hadn't managed that degree of self-control, and seemingly neither had Locke, or the old bag. Yet Matthew and Mr Osborne, they seemed to show an almost monk worthy amount of restraint. I had to find out how they did it, but not at the world's most uncomfortable dinner party.

Uncharacteristically, I barely ate a thing. I was too trapped in my own mind to realise that my very empty tum was open for business as usual. It considered the meal before I had left the house a mere appetiser, it seemed. Before I even had the chance to notice that I was steadily starving to death though, the festivities took a less than welcome turn.

"Oh my God, I'm sorry." Dean whimpered as half a glass of red wine spilled from the table, seeping into the battered old patterned carpet. Locke glared with inhospitable, merciless eyes and did not breathe a word.

"I'll clean it up!" Dean squeaked, and he dashed off to the kitchen. The dining room was mute as things clattered in the room next-door. He rushed back in, clutching some kind of spray bottle and a cloth in his pasty claws. He dropped to the ground, frantically spraying and scrubbing, spraying and scrubbing. Locke reclined in his large chair at the head of the table and sighed heavily.

"Look at you.'" He boomed lazily. "You're pathetic."

"Locke, please." Matthew interjected.

"It's true. That good for nothing brother of yours is a disgrace to this damn pack. Hell, what kind of Lycan is he when he's so afraid of his own nature? Even the fucking kid here is making progress, and he was a Goddamn mistake." He rumbled, and I shrank into my seat. The room turned cold. Everyone's shoulders were tense and unmoving, apart from the Alpha's. His body looked relaxed, and yet there was a palpable sense that he could explode at any instant. The repetitive sound of scrub and spray began to grate.

"He will get better." Rita spoke softly.

"BULLSHIT." Locke bellowed, and slammed a colossal fist on the table. Mr Osborne opened his mouth to speak, but before he had the chance, the pack leader's head wheeled around. "Keep out of this, Lewis." And he did.

"Your brother is a waste Matthew, see that it-"

"I didn't ask for this!" Dean leapt to his feet, quivering. There was a deafening pause.

"It's what you were meant to be. Something more than human." Locke fired the words with the force of bullets.

"No, no one should be this! It never stops, it never sleeps, the hunger never ends! I DIDN'T ASK FOR THIS!" Dean yelled, voice quaking in a manner so pathetic I actually felt sympathy gnawing at my gut. Then again, perhaps that was just my hunger reminding me I was wasting to nothing.

"Well, this is what you are." The gargantuan man replied frostily. "There's no escaping it now."

"Locke, if you wouldn't mind, I'd like to show the kids around the house a little." Matthew said with his head lowered, submissive.

"Then go."

"Come on, Zack, Bethany…" Matt stood.

"Hell no, I've seen this old place before." Beth stated, seemingly entranced by Dean's gradual mental breakdown happening right before us.

"I'll go." I meant to speak clearly, but it came out more like a whisper. I glanced for a second at old Annie, who was so still that for a moment I was concerned rigor mortis might have kicked in. Then I got up, and as Matthew left the room, I shadowed him closely.

He headed straight for the stairs, I followed silently behind, we reached the top and I tailed him into a room full of prehistoric furniture, covered in dustsheets. He closed the door once we were both inside.

"Thanks for getting me out of there." I breathed for the first time since getting up to leave the dining area.

"I was trying to get you both out of there. Beth doesn't understand who the hell she's dealing with down there, but you, you do. This is why I need your help, I need you to help us kill him!" His whole speech was in furious whispers.

"What, are you fucking crazy?" I returned in my own coarse whisper. "How the hell do you expect me to do that?!"

"You Phase faster than him. We may be different when we walk on two legs, we're stronger and faster, yes, but we are still people. We are still fragile. While you're a wolf and he's a human, you have the advantage. I've never seen anyone change as fast as you do."

"You're out of your damn mind." Suddenly we both turned towards the window, a patchwork of square glass sheets, framed in black. A pitiful squeal could be heard from outside. In tandem we rushed to look. Dean stood hunched in the glow of a security light, weeping on the gravel driveway outside.

Locke stood opposite, the rest of the pack shrinking behind him near the doorway to the house.

"Oh shit." Matthew breathed, it was the first time I'd ever heard him curse. He bolted for the door.

"Phase. Right now." Locke ordered menacingly.

"I can't, I can't do it." Dean pleaded, tears streaking down his gaunt cheeks.

This was the moment, if I could choose only one, when I realised I was in way over my head. I was just like Dean, a member of the pack who shouldn't be, and now Matthew was asking me to help take out their leader. Maybe I should run away, but where would I go? Surely I would need help, but would anyone be willing? I wasn't certain of any of these things, but I knew for damn sure no one would believe me. That was when an idea hit me square in the face, like a psychopath's belt buckle. I took out my phone and tapped the switch to turn the camera on. I stayed as low as I could, mostly hidden by dusty velvet curtains.

"Do it, prove your worth."

"Locke, please don't do this to him. He just needs time." Rita begged on her brother-in-law's behalf.

"QUIET." His voice seemed to make the earth shake. I had it all in frame.

"I'll try harder, honest I will. I'll learn to deal with it, I promise." Dean blubbered. He was truly a shadow of a man.

"No. You'll Phase because you have to Phase." I saw Locke's back hunch up as he let out a deep and terrifying snarl.

"Locke no!" Matthew called rushing forwards "Dean! You have to transform NOW!"

Locke's clothes tore, and the man that once stood in them changed into something else, something altogether far more fearsome.

"I can't!" Dean cried. I watched the human become the Lycan on screen, the sound of bones breaking and reforming, the masses of silvery white fur erupting. It was a truly harrowing thing to see, and I had it all on film. Maybe if push came to shove, the video could be my saving grace. The wolf stood, blocking the security light and bathing Dean in shadow. It snarled ferociously at him.

"Please, I'm begging you. I'll do better from now on, I fucking swear." His voice wavered.

The white Lycan leapt forward and Dean turned to run, but it was too late. He was side swiped by its giant clawed hand. It threw him violently across the ground, gravel clattered as he went tumbling through it. Rita released a horrified gasp.

"Locke, you have to stop this!" Lewis Osborne called, but no one would act. No one would try to stop it. They were too paralyzed by fear, so they all just stood by.

Dean began to crawl, wounded and bleeding, outside of the circle of light on the drive. The wolf pounced and struck him. Then it hit him again, and again, a furious flurry of blows that seemed to be endless. It went on long enough to turn from violent outburst into purest, wilful brutality.

Beth stood, mouth wide open, whether in horror or fascination I wasn't sure. Rita buried herself in Matthew's shoulder. Matthew himself could not look away as he saw his brother savaged right before his eyes. The big bad wolf carried what was left of Dean into the centre of the spotlight, and dumped him there for all to see.

14 Days Until the Next Full Moon

I was fucked. That was my optimistic conclusion as I lay in bed the following morning, repeatedly watching the grisly footage of Dean's demise. The way Locke just dropped him like he was subhuman, even something less than an animal, was enough to bring me out in a cold sweat. It brought home the fact that I could be next, that at any time, it could be me. There was no guarantee I would even see it coming. Maybe one day Locke would just show up at my house, or at school. Maybe he'd treat the whole thing like a mob hit when I became too much of a burden for him to bear. Here today, lunch tomorrow.

I spent an inordinate amount of time weighing up my options. Many of them didn't seem to be options at all. If I hung around, tried to keep my head down, the Alpha could snap at any moment. Then all my walking on eggshells would be for nothing, and I'd be just another corpse on his driveway. If I ran, what would happen to my mom? How far would I get before they tracked me down anyway, and how would I learn to cope with being what I had become? No, that was too risky, I needed another way. I thought about what Matthew had asked me to do, to kill Locke. I wondered if I could really do it. I was pretty sure that guy could break me in half before I even had a chance to snap at his heels. Even if I could, who's to say some of the pack wouldn't be on his side? So yeah, I was fucked, and I needed a second opinion.

"What the hell do you want, it's like 7am?" Damian groaned on the other end of the line.

"I haven't slept. Besides, you wanted to know what happened to Phil right?"

"Okay, okay, I'm listening." He sounded both groggy and intrigued.

"No. No listening. I have to show you this."

■■■

Damian stood in open-mouthed silence as he viewed the video I had taken. The tinny sounds of Dean's pleas brought the whole thing back to me, in the kind of gruesome detail my phone was unable to capture. I heard the fleshy mass that was once a man hit the ground in epic mono sound, and the clip I had captured was over.

"No way, that's gotta be fake." Damian stated with authority.

"I swear it's not. I recorded that myself last night."

"That can't be true, you're bullshitting me." He said smirking.

"I promise you, this is what I was talking about the other day, the thing I said you wouldn't believe even if you saw it. I rest my fucking case." I left no trace of humour in my voice. He stared at me for a long moment.

"Fuck off."

"Oh for God's sake. I'm telling you it's true." I half yelled, frustrated.

"So you expect me to believe you, a miserable, lazy school kid, can turn into a six foot dog?"

"Whoa, bit harsh. But essentially… yes." I nodded rapidly.

"Prove it."

Well, I couldn't exactly change right there in the street. I mean even if I could manage to transform at will, the outcome might not be the most desirable. I'd prove my point, sure. He'd definitely believe me, at least in the moments before I tore his face off. I had to think of a better way. I glanced around, doing a full rotation, trying to come up with a solution. Then I found one.

"Okay, watch this." I stepped over to the wall that ran by Damian's house, separating his front yard from the next. I reached it and swung a clenched fist, it connected with a soft fleshy pat. Bricks shattered, and went flying onto his neighbour's lawn. He sprinted over.

"Holy shit, you're like a super hero!" He said, peering next door at the smashed stonework now lying on the grass. "Didn't that hurt?" He turned to find me cradling my hand, in the phoetal position.

"Ow, ouch, motherfuc-" I mumbled through gritted teeth. My friend, being a friend and all, decided to respond to my pain with raucous laughter.

"Oh, well it was still pretty impressive." He said wheezing. "Hey, damn it. You just broke my mom's wall, she's gonna be pissed."

"Well, tell her I said I'm sorry." I snapped, still more concerned about my potentially broken hand. I breathed deep for a while, and eventually lifted myself gingerly to my feet.

"Well, you're no Wolverine, that's for sure." Damian helpfully informed me, observing my increasingly bruised fist.

"Sucks for you huh? You'd have loved to see me in tights."

185

"Nowadays Wolverine doesn't wear tights." He sighed at me wearily.

"Well excuse me Stan Lee. Look, I need help, are you gonna help me or-"

"WHAT HAVE YOU DONE TO MY WALL YOU LITTLE SHITS?!" Damian's mom hung her head out of her bedroom window and wailed at us.

"Oh crap, lets get out of here." Damian panicked.

"What, to where?"

"To see Venn, now run damn it!" He cried as he leapt into action.

"I'M GONNA MURDER THE PAIR OF YOU, JUST YOU WAIT!" She had already made it to the foot of the stairs.

"I'm really sorry about the wall Miss Wilson!" I yelled, not daring to look back as I ran as fast as I could.

"Oh, you will be when I catch you, mark my words!"

■■

We didn't stop to breathe until we were almost to Venn's house. By then our lungs burned, and our hearts screamed for respite.

"Glad to see... she has... recovered then." I spoke between pants.

"Yeah... no kidding." Damian panted in return. "Why are you... out of breath... anyway. I thought you... were all... superhuman... now."

"I'm good... in short... bursts... asshole." I wheezed defensively.

We stood hunched with hands on knees for a short time, allowing our overworked teenage hearts the chance to recover. Then finally, with a last heavy sigh, we both self-righted.

"Okay, look. Obviously I find it hard to believe that you're some kind of *wolf-man*. The small part of my brain that doesn't think it's still seven years old won't let me believe it. But, I just saw that freaky old guy you were with the other day turn all doggish and tear what looked like a smack-head to pieces. Unless you both know Spielberg, I don't know how that's even possible. I don't get what's happening here, but when we're done with Venn, explain everything to me. I'll help if I can." Damian thought about what he had said for a moment and then nodded, as if to confirm his statement.

"You got it, but be ready for a hell of an explanation. Now, why are we visiting Venn exactly?" I asked. We began walking the final stretch to our near-mute friend's house.

"Because he's gone all AWOL on us, he hasn't been to school at all. I called him yesterday, and he sounded in a bad way."

"So, we're coming to pay our last respects, is that it?"

"I just wanna see what's up with him. That, and I didn't fancy sticking around to see what kind of punishment my mom had in mind. At least now she has some time to cool off before she murders me." The last line carried a sarcastic edge.

"Yeah. That or time to plan." I replied, and he actually looked a little worried.

I had never before been to Venn's house. I mean, he was sort of my friend, but he also barely ever said more than two words. I had a feeling he would be lacking somewhat in the hospitality department. I had no real expectations, and his home met that lack of expectation most admirably. He lived in an attached house on a street full of them. A small park lay opposite, complete with drunken grown men draining beer cans into their open maws on the grass. All that set Venn's house apart from the others was the ear-splitting sound of gunfire emanating from the upstairs window.

Damian rapped on the door, and the most fragile looking elderly man answered it.

"Excuse me, but is Venn in?" He asked in his sweet, talking to a grown up voice (which I made a mental note to imitate later).

"Well it's that, or the Chinese are invading." He smiled softly, revealing a row of purple gums. "Head upstairs boys." There was a sadness in the old timer's eyes that made me a little uncomfortable.

"Whoa, Venn's parents are old, huh?" I said to Damian, as we headed up the stairs and towards to sound of World War Three.

"That's not his Dad, numb-nuts. Venn's a foster kid. You didn't know?" He looked surprised, as I'm sure did I.

"What, no I didn't know, how was I ever supposed to know that?" I lowered my voice as we got closer to the source of the screams and explosions.

"Well, now you do." He mumbled and pushed open the off-white door.

Venn's room was a mess, not too dissimilar to my own. His blinds were down, banishing the sun from his realm. The only light to be seen was flashing intermittently from the flat screen TV that he was hunched in front of. He was far too engrossed in the game to notice us enter. He mashed furiously at triggers and buttons, whilst on screen the enemy team tried in vain to take him down. Their screen names popped up in red every time he landed another kill, and furious trash talk poured from his speakers. It helpfully informed him that he had no life, and was definitely a virgin.

"Hey man. Long time no see." Damian shouted over the incessant cursing of another downed opponent. Venn turned, and on screen his counterpart became riddled with bullets.

"Oh… hi." He said, and turned back to continue his killing spree. He seemed even more distant than usual.

"Where have you been, we haven't seen you at school? You didn't seem to want to talk on the phone." There was a long pause, filled with the screams of fallen enemies." Is something up?" Damian pried.

"No." He responded unblinking, as he threw a grenade that took out four of his terrorist foes. We stood uneasily, hoping for more from him. We should have known better.

"Come on dude, I can tell something's up." Damian pushed, just as both the game and Venn's distraction ended.

He sat quietly for a moment, staring at the statistics screen. His alter ego emblazoned across the top, along with a score and the letters 'MVP'. Suddenly tears started falling, as his self-built barricade began to crumble. Damian walked over to him and I gingerly followed.

"Venn, what's wrong?" Damian asked, his obvious discomfort creating awkward patterns with his features.

"Yeah," I said bemused, looking at the TV "you only died twice and one of those was his fault?" I pointed slowly in Damian's direction. Venn silently wept, ignoring both of us.

"Come on man, just tell us. Maybe we can help?" Damian put what was supposed to be a reassuring hand on his shoulder, then felt weird and promptly removed it.

"You can't help." Venn snivelled.

"We can try?" I added, mostly because I felt left out of the conversation.

"It's… it's Bev." Venn finally announced, fresh tears pouring free from his bloodshot eyes.

■■■

Getting words out of Venn was like drawing blood from a stone, so for your benefit I'll cut a long story short. Beverly as it turned out, was his foster mother, wife to the gentile old man downstairs. Being of a certain age, she had taken a bad turn the week prior and her condition had been steadily worsening as the days went on. The previous Saturday night, the same night I had witnessed the murder of what I was supposed to consider one of my own, she too had sadly met her end. Obviously he was pretty torn up about it, so we weren't expecting to see him at school in the coming days. He needed time to deal with his pain, to grieve. I understood that.

My pain on the other hand was still on its way, thundering towards me unseen, in that terrifying void that is the future. Venn had to be alone, and I had to spill my guts to the only person outside of the Lycan clan who now knew what I was. After we left Venn to his game, the only thing that was keeping him numb, I explained the severity of my situation to Damian. I told him all about Locke, and what he had done in order to force a transformation out of me early. I told him too about Matthew's request, that I help him to destroy their pack leader, to free them from his tyranny. He had no advice, other than to try to keep the wolves onside until one of us thought of something better. I thanked him for nothing, and hoped that should it come to it, the video would be my trump card. I could at least threaten to expose their clan, should it come to that.

As I lay in bed, truly desperate for sleep that evening, I thought about all the things that had led me to that point in time. The deer I had savaged in that cage, and the murder of Phil. I realised then that murder is what it was. As good as my intentions had been when I set out with Locke's assistance to find him, Locke did most of the dirty work. And he didn't do it because the guy had done something to hurt his friend. He did it because he wanted to. Dean had only helped to solidify that idea in my mind. With him gone and Venn's foster mother passing too, it seemed like death had begun to surround me ever since I became the dog that I am today.

REMATCH

"What the hell are you looking at you little shit?" I heard Luke shout from afar. Elton, who had decided to stand uncomfortably nearby whilst myself, Damian and Jackson were engaged in equally awkward conversation, peered up reflexively. He spotted Luke striding purposefully towards him. With an audible squeak, he lowered his head submissively. The bully reached Elton (who shrank is his shadow) and shoved him to the ground.

"When I ask you a question, you answer it." He sneered.

"Nothing! I wasn't even looking at you, I didn't do anything!" The words flew out of him in a hurry, each one clambering over the last.

"Hey, isn't that your friend from the geography trip?" Damian asked, as Elton tried tragically to avoid another conflict. I was kind of hoping he wouldn't notice.

"No," I sighed "it's more like I was his carer for the day."

"Well, it looks like he could use a little caring right now."

I gave him the kind of look I would have given my mom, if she'd asked me to clean my room. The 'do I have to?' look.

"Oh come on Fido, should be a breeze for you right?" he smirked.

"Fido?" Jackson butted in, but we ignored him.

I was a little wary. Walking headlong into a situation that could get heated was exactly what I *wasn't* supposed to be doing.

Still, I had gotten better at controlling myself, at telling the wolf no. It had begun to listen to me, at the time I thought that the two sides of myself were finally beginning to sync up. If only it had been that simple, how different things might be now.

As we approached, Elton began to stand and was pushed back down by an oppressive heel. His phone tumbled from his carefully ironed trousers. It went skittering across the concrete, along with a couple of fancy looking fountain pens. Luke rushed to pick it up.

"Swear you won't tell anyone what happened, or I'll smash this thing to fucking pieces." He snarled under his breath at the whimpering boy on the ground. Hundreds of other students wandered around us, some sat on the nearby grass enjoying their first break of the day. No one paid any attention to the kid close to tears on the pavement. Well, except for Damian who had decided to drag me into it. Luke leered over his prey. When I got close enough, I grabbed the back of his dark black tie and yanked him suddenly backwards. He gave out a strangled wheeze as I snatched the phone from him and then pushed him away. He turned and looked at the three of us, the worst looking team of vigilantes the world has ever known. Jackson was practically baring his teeth.

"What the fuck are you, this kid's babysitter?" The bully rasped as he stroked his tender throat.

"Apparently, I think Damian had an attack of conscience or something. So now, here we are." I muttered reluctantly. I could see the uneducated anger in his eyes, the kind of ill informed fury only someone with a barely functioning brain is capable of. He got defensive, as his kind tends to do.

"What, so you gang up on me, three on one? I can't have people knowing this shrimp shoved me the other day. All I'm doing is telling him how it is." Luke scoffed. It was then that I noticed the fading bruise on his cheek, and other cuts and grazes down the length of his arms. As always, the sensation that I was not alone within my own mind began to creep in, as though the animal inside were stretching off. I ordered it to be calm, and it seemed indifferent to the idea. Perhaps it didn't see what lay before it as a worthy foe. Absentmindedly I rolled Elton's phone over and over in my hand. Suddenly, a determined looking Jackson bound forward.

"Hell no, we aren't ganging up on you. Leave this kid alone or I'll kick your ass myself!" the bespectacled boy wonder announced. I was surprised he didn't put his fists on his hips, as his cape dramatically swayed in the breeze. So naturally, Luke's response was to immediately punch him in the jaw. The fist connected with a dull pat, and all at once my head exploded. The blurred vision and all encompassing heart beat from a few days before returned, and that very same white-hot pain shot through me. The wolf roared a deafening and distorted cry that no one else could hear, as Elton's phone shattered into tiny pieces between my fingers.

I called in my head for it to back down, and as I did so, I caught sight of Luke through the haze and grabbed for him again. I took hold of the tie once more, this time the front of it that dangled from his already tender neck. I pulled it tight, swung him around and pushed my free hand into his back to keep the noose taut. My vision cleared, and I could almost hear the monster in my head chuckling gleefully. I realised it could have taken me then, changed me and took over completely.

"Let… me… go…" Luke croaked, unable to grasp his next breath. He collapsed to his knees.

"Cool it man. Take it easy." Damian said, looking incredibly worried. Jackson staggered to his feet, palm placed on his jaw.

"Screw that, choke this prick." He demanded, and then gave Luke a swift kick in the stomach before shuffling to a safe distance. Luke tried to speak again, but the words couldn't escape. I let him go, he gasped for air and hurriedly removed the tie.

"Jesus, you're fucking psycho." He spluttered uncontrollably. So many people had made the claim by this point, I was beginning to think it could be true.

"You better get out of here, or I'll set him on you again." Jackson called from behind me. Both Damian and I turned to give him an uncomfortable stare. My heartbeat was gradually returning to a resting state, and the incessant hum of surrounding chatter was almost a comfort, a return to normality.

"Off you go, Luke." Damian waved him off. He gave us a wide-eyed stare of confusion, and then stomped away. Damian turned to me then.

"Dude, what the hell was that?" He asked.

"I don't know. It happened on the field trip too. I think I must-" I looked around and realised Elton was still sat on the ground, and Jackson was with us, nursing his wound. "Must have… allergies… or something."

"What the *fuck* are you talking about, Zack?" Jackson mumbled from behind his swelling cheek.

I didn't know what to tell him, but it didn't matter. The situation was about to get a little more complicated.

"YOU FUCKING ASSHOLE!" A familiar voice boomed.

"Oh shit. Just remember, you have to keep your cool." Damian muttered.

I turned to see the hulking figure of Charlie striding towards me. The whole school seemed to be cast in his gargantuan shadow. Everyone turned to look, to find the source of the commotion. He came to a stop opposite me, like a duel in the old west. The earth fell silent. Even the birds in the trees seemed to stop their incessant tweeting. The tension was palpable, at least until I broke it with a snort of stifled laughter.

"What the hell are you laughing at?" Charlie demanded to know. What I was laughing at, ladies and gentlemen, was the mangled remains of his nose packed tightly beneath a big white square of gauze.

"Nothing." I spoke quickly, trying not to let a giggle escape. Despite my best efforts, another small snort managed to wriggle its way free. We became enclosed in a gladiatorial style battle arena, the circular walls made entirely of human bodies. Each pair of eyes was focussed on the two competitors. I tried to breathe slowly, to keep calm and collected. I didn't need to get all bent out of shape, it would only make things worse. I told myself that repeatedly, even as I realised talking my way out of the situation was going to be impossible. My dark side flexed invisible muscles in curious anticipation.

I told myself to think, then realised that in doing so, I was wasting valuable brainpower. So then I smartly decided to focus on the actual act of thinking, which if you think about it, was a step in the right direction. The light bulb went on, illuminating my mind with a bright idea. I would humiliate Charlie into submission, I'd make the entire school laugh at him so he was forced to retreat to the cave he had crawled out of. Then he'd have to live out his days there in agonising solitude.

"Erm… I don't know why you're so angry," I began with impeccable comedic timing "a plastic surgeon would have charged you a fortune to improve your face like that." I delivered my punch line like a well-aimed bullet.

Nothing. No response, no laughter, Charlie didn't rush home to cry to whatever beast had spawned him. For a second I could swear I heard a cricket chirping, in the middle of the day too, the smug green bastard. I thought for a moment my Lycan side might bury its face beneath its paws in shame.

"You suck!" Someone hollered from in the crowd.

"Thanks." I turned in the direction the voice had come from "Thanks a lot." I nodded to the unseen heckler.

"You need to get out of this quickly." Damian muttered, trying to keep his voice low from his place in the human wall. I glanced over my shoulder at him.

"Don't worry, if he hits me first then I can just knock him out. Remember your garden wall?" I smirked with confidence, right up until the unseen fist connected with my temple and I was sent crashing to the coarse concrete ground. There was a unified 'OOOH', and then the crowd erupted into mostly incomprehensible noise. Some chanted the word 'fight', while others seemed to be yelling advice like they were a bunch of boxing coaches, barking orders through the ropes.

"Well, that hurt more than I expected." I said, turning my eyes up at Damian and Jackson from the ground.

"No shit." Jackson spat. Charlie's Heffalump foot connected with my side, and sent me rolling closer to the edge of our ring.

"I thought you said you were good in short bursts?" Damian spoke frantically.

"Fuck you man! He caught me off guard." I groaned, clutching where the kick had landed.

I struggled to my feet as my hidden friend began to let go of his embarrassment, accepting the fact that he had such a worthless host. It gave a silent order - destroy him.

"Shut up, I've got this." I told it under my breath.

I began to circle, sticking near the edge of the makeshift battleground, never taking my eyes off of my opponent. I had never been in a fight before, not as a human at least. I have however, seen a lot of movies. My thorough research led me to the conclusion that circling seemed like the thing to do. Someone at my back shoved me forwards and ordered me to hit him. I didn't turn to see who it was, I had learned from that mistake. For a single instant I caught Lexey's disapproving gaze in the crowd, and felt a pang of irritation.

Charlie hurled himself towards me, throwing his bear-like right hand directly at my fragile little face. I flinched, and instinctively caught it mid-flight. He hurled his left into my stomach, knocking the air right out of me. Then I had somewhat of a eureka moment. I remembered Elton's phone, the fence at the Animalarium, the kitchen table at home. It finally dawned on me that if I had a superpower, a particular skill that I truly excelled at, it seemed to be squeezing things really, really hard. I know, I know, teenager with a strong grip. Insert your own masturbation joke here.

With this revelation ringing out in my mind, I clamped down on Charlie's hand, and he wailed in pain. He lashed out repeatedly, striking my arms, chest and head in quick succession. I weathered the blows as best I could, and squeezed harder. I felt the small bones in the top of his hand give way under my fingertips as he buckled to his knees.

"Let go, let go, let go!" The colossal kid whimpered.

Before I could weigh up the pros and cons of releasing King Kong from my steely grip, Miss Clarke burst through the crowd with the backup of an exhausted looking teacher's assistant I didn't recognise.

"You children will disperse this instant!" She yelled, as she finally freed herself from the tangled mass of limbs that had ensnared her. Kids began running in all directions in a bid to escape. Sure, they'd stand there and watch two people beat the shit out of each other gladly, but as soon as a teacher shows up they all morph back into adorable little cherubs.

"Zachary, let that boy's hand go!"

I released my hold on Charlie's grisly paw, and he collapsed onto his face like a well-felled tree. I was actually pretty glad that someone had turned up to defuse the situation. Though Miss Clarke would not have been my first choice, admittedly. I spun on my heel to face her.

"What seems to be the problem Miss?" I asked nonchalantly, rising up and down on my toes, hands clasped behind my back - The perfect picture of innocence.

As the adrenaline brought on by the encounter began to wear off, I could feel the prickly heat building in my rapidly forming bruises.

"The problem, Archer, is lying on the ground behind you." She glared at me sternly.

"Oh he's fine, he's just relaxing is all. I mean look at him," I turned to glance at Charlie's heaving back on the ground. He let out a pained groan. "I wish I was that relaxed. I mean honestly, you could take a lesson from old Charlie down there. Come on Miss, take a load off." I said cheerfully, beginning to lower myself down to the ground.

"THE DEPUTY HEADMASTERS OFFICE, THIS INSTANT!" She bellowed, and I bolted back upright, startled. Like Charlie's first punch, she had also taken me off guard. I'm not good at being taken off guard. Don't judge me for that.

"Jeez Miss. Okay, I'm sorry." I raised my hands defensively, convinced she might strike me down at any second. She stared at me with her stink eye as I began to shuffle slowly towards the Deputy Head's office. I stopped for a second. "Would it help if I said lying facedown is all the rage these days?"

"NOW!" She screamed, and my sensitive ears exploded. Both of my feet left the ground in shock and I leapt into a speed-walk, fearful of the banshee's cries.

∎∎

This time Deputy Headmaster Granger's tie was a deep purple, and had what I can only describe as badly drawn unicorns running across it. That familiar stench of coffee got right to the back of my throat, giving it an uncomfortable tickle that began to drive me insane. The fake leather belt hung broken and limp from his waist, like an apathetic snake that had long since given up. The sweat patch on his back seemed to be ever growing. Of course, I couldn't really blame him because the heat in his dank little room was stifling. My stomach growled loudly, giving me a hit of much needed focus.

"Are you even listening to a word I'm saying boy?" He turned to glare at me. Then returned to peering through the blinds at the other kids making their way to class.

"No. I mean yes! Yes sir, I am listening. I am indeed."

"Then what did I just say?" The Deputy stared at me for a long moment, one eye bulging.

"You said erm… that the end of year exams are coming up… and that I should keep my nose out of trouble…" My confidence noticeably waned as the fabrication went on. His one giant eye remained creepily focussed, as he seemed to analyse me. I considered the notion that he might be a robot in disguise, and that all he could really see were numbers and algorithms.

"Lucky guess." The android finally murmured.

"Sir, would you mind opening the window?" I requested, as a desk fan set in a sweeping motion turbo charged the old fart's body odour right into my nostrils. He said nothing, just clumsily fumbled beneath the blades of the steel blind and mercifully pushed the window open with a creak. The sound of babbling students joined us in the stuffy room.

"Now Zack, you seem to be becoming more of a problem than usual lately. You may not see me often, but word does get back to me. I trust you understand that?" I nodded. "Good. Now don't take this the wrong way, it's simply my duty as an educational professional to ask, and I would ask anyone in your position right now. Are you having any problems at home, or at school? Has anything changed? What, in your opinion, could be causing us to have these issues?"

I remembered the ridiculous conversation with my mom a few days before.

"… hormones?" I said, squinting. This didn't seem to impress him. "Anyway sir I-"

There was a gentle knock at the door. Granger motioned with his hand for me to be quiet for a second, and told whoever was interrupting to come in. The door opened with a squeak and in strolled Miss Clarke, probably to sell me down the river.

"Sorry to interrupt, but there's someone here who wishes to speak with you regarding this matter, Mr Granger." She announced. Elton's tiny little legs carried him silently into the room, like a mote of dust caught in the breeze. He stood in gormless stillness as Granger looked on.

"Well come on, out with it boy!" Elton's body stiffened at the Head's sudden outburst.

"Oh, well I just wanted to say Sir, you know if it wasn't too much trouble and stuff, I thought you should know that erm…" He received a grave look from the increasingly impatient almost-leader of our school. "Zack didn't start the fight Sir, that's what I was trying to say. You've got the wrong person in your office right now."

The Dep-Head mulled it over for a second, analysing what he had heard.

"Well be that as it may, the *right* person, *if* what you say is *true*, is on his way to the emergency room. Whether this young man started the fight or not, I'm afraid this cannot go unchecked."

"I understand that Sir, but Zack, he didn't want to fight. He tried to avoid it. He wanted to do the right thing." Elton interjected, feet shifting uneasily beneath him.

I was taken aback. The irritating speck from the bus had stuck his neck out to defend me. No matter which way I tried to spin it, I definitely owed him. Just for the effort alone.

"As much as it pains me to say it Sir, this student has never been in trouble, he's never caused a fuss. I have no reason to doubt what he says, and I am personally willing to vouch for him." Miss Clarke spoke, then her eyes connected with mine. "At least in this instance."

Granger ran his tie between his fingers, deep in thought. I decided that with two people jumping to my defence, I was better off keeping my mouth shut.

"Okay, I think I'm willing to believe that he was not the instigator here. Charles Brooker doesn't exactly keep a low profile at this school either. Honestly though, that boy is a lost cause."

"Deputy Headmaster, should you really be talking about a student in that manner?" Miss Clarke asked with an intentional air of professionalism.

"Perhaps not Sharon, but I trust that it will never leave this room." Granger turned towards me. "You Zack, are just a pile of lost potential thus far, which is why it troubles me that you seem unable to avoid this kind of drama. For today, you go home. Consider yourself on short-term suspension. Tomorrow I want you in school, on time, with no incidents. I'll be arranging a meeting with your parents."

"*Parent.*" I corrected him.

"Excuse me, parent. I look forward to seeing you there. I think we're done here."

He waved his hand, indicating it was time for us to leave, then took one gangly-legged stride towards his beloved coffee maker. We walked single file out of the room, and the instant we were over the threshold, the door slammed shut. Miss Clarke spun to face us, and a lengthy silence followed.

"What you did today young man, was very admirable." She finally said to Elton, her chin raised high. He mumbled some kind of appreciation.

"I trust you will heed the Deputy Headmaster's warning, Zack?"

"Sure will Sharon." I felt a pang of glee at using her first name.

"Do not call me Sharon. I am a member of the faculty, and I will be treated with the proper respect." She demanded.

"Okay, sorry *Miss.*"

She let out a small grunt, told Elton to be sure he wasn't late for his next lesson and then strode away down the empty hall, leaving him and I alone. I stood motionless, not knowing what to say, and I could tell he was having exactly the same issue.

"Thanks for helping me out with Luke again." He murmured to his shoes.

"Yeah, no problem. Thanks for having my back through this whole thing." I replied, waving my hands at the situation.

"Sure thing."

Another all too long pause. Suddenly it was broken as a rusty old school bell mounted high upon the wall, erupted into deafening life. The sound sent an almost blinding pain shooting through my skull, and I clamped my hands down on my ears in a vain attempt to drown out the sound. I gritted my teeth against the onslaught. When the bell finally halted its furious attack, I breathed a huge sigh of relief. Steadily, I removed my palms from my ringing ears.

"Well," Elton spoke and I winced at the sound "guess I better get to class. I'll see you around."

"Yeah… See ya." I whispered gingerly. And with the tap of well-shined shoes fading into the distance, all I could think about was how I seriously needed a solution to my perpetual earache. I refused to be caught off-guard like that again.

BLOODLUST

I didn't hear what Matthew said when he pulled up to whisk me away again into the land of lunacy, reason being that I had finally found a use for my phone that didn't involve it being the bearer of bad news. The erratic sounds of every day life were gone, replaced by the glorious predictability of electronic music. Everything was in order, and every beat knew its place.

"Why the headphones?" Matthew asked as I lifted one oversized earmuff.

"I finally found a solution to my hearing problems." I told him with an obvious sense of pride, and climbed into the same old 4x4.

On the journey to Locke's secluded abode, we talked little. My stomach felt uneasy, and that sensation only increased the closer we got to the grand old house. It was my first time going back there since witnessing Dean's demise.

"So… what's happened since… you know?" I couldn't bring myself to speak Dean's name. Not to Matthew, not yet.

"Nothing. Locke… disposed of him. It's like he never existed." He replied, a glimmer of sadness in his voice. Images from the video I took flashed through my mind. Dean may have been gone, but he left one big, bloody footprint on my memory card. "If any modicum of good has come from that day, it's that *now you know,* Zack. You understand the importance of what I've asked you to do." He said grimly. I replaced my headphones, and all was lost to the bass.

■■■

When we arrived, I tailed my courier around the outer walls of the building. As we crossed the driveway my eyes fell upon the spot where Dean had met his end. It had been bleached clean. We ended up at the rear of the house, where the welcoming committee was already waiting. Beth sat on a fancy looking garden chair, her feet thrown lazily on top of a rusting old table, seemingly made up of interlocking metallic vines. She swept deep blue hair from her eyes to get a better view of whatever game she was playing on her phone.

"Motherfucker!" She groaned through gritted teeth. I assumed she was losing.

Anne, the bony old crow, was inside the house, casting a hateful gaze across the grass through the lattice window. I took a shot in the dark and made the assumption that if the sunlight touched her skin, she'd crumble into dust. I considered inviting her outside to join the rest of us. Rita sat solemnly on the step by the back door of the house. She kept her hands in her lap, and her face seemed devoid of all emotion. I couldn't really blame her.

Locke, man-mountain and bringer of misery, stood as though frozen, staring at the treeline. I knew from our brief foray into first-degree murder that just standing as he was, he could be picking up the scent of prey on the winds. At a safe distance from him was Mr Osborne, hands clasped behind his back - the very picture of tranquillity.

"Today, we hunt." Locke stated as myself and Matthew got a little closer to the rest of the group. See? Sniffing for prey, I totally called it. I stopped and he took a giant stride towards me, then suddenly grabbed my arm and lifted my sleeve. He saw the healing knife wound on my shoulder.

"Well, at least it's not infected. Today, you lead us kid." He stated, and I swear, I pooped a little.

"Wait, what?" I said, hurriedly tugging my sleeve back down, skin cold in the brisk evening air. "I can't do that, I still suck at this stuff."

"You'll do as I say." He spoke in equally icy tones.

How dare he, who was he to order me around? I began to get worked up, if he wanted to throw hands, I'd throw hands, make no mistake. I thought about how I was going to call him out 'Man versus man or dog versus dog, how do you want it bitch?'

That was what I thought, but when I tried to collect all those thoughts and spit them in his face like a dragon's jet of flame, all that came out was a barely human whine. He was exactly right. I would do as he said. You know why? Because he's bigger than me, and on at least one occasion, probably two, I've known him to actually eat people. If that's not a good enough reason for you, then I'd like to hear a better one.

"Don't worry Zack, you can do this." Mr Osborne assured me.

"Yeah, that's easy for you to say." I spoke in a low, harsh whisper. "You see me as a student. If I fail this, then that guy see's me as lunch, wrapped in a t-shirt."

Locke turned one dark and piercing eye in my direction. It was more than enough to cause another sudden bowel movement.

I hadn't even gotten the Phasing thing down yet, and I still had next to no agency when in wolf form. It felt like Locke was dooming me to fail, just waiting for the first opportunity to show that I was a burden not worth carrying, so he could dispose of me swiftly.

"Trust me, Locke tells me you've already developed some self-awareness. That's great progress, especially considering the age at which you became Lycan. It's not easy for anyone, let alone youngsters. The fact that when you change isn't a total blackout is astounding."

"Yeah, and it's bullshit." I heard Beth call. "How come this kid gets to join the pack already? I'm destined for a spot, and you make *me* wait."

"Because Bethany, Zack is the result of unforeseen circumstances. We would never have made one so young out of choice." Matthew interjected.

"Unforeseen circumstances, you mean like the ones that led to Dean being spread all over the driveway? The same ones that led to you pushing back your little hunt here?"

"Watch your tongue, child." Locke snarled.

"Fuck you." She shot back, and my level of respect for her went through the roof. "Why are you so against making teens into Lycans anyway?" Beth asked, waving her hand erratically.

"Because, it causes complications. A human being is already in a state of rapid development. The mind and body is changing, and without a stable base to work from, becoming one of us can have undesired side effects." Matthew explained, trying to keep the situation from escalating any further.

"What kind of side effects?" I asked, suddenly feeling like I should be kept in the loop. There was a long and empty silence.

"Honestly, we've never had to deal with it before. From what we know of the past though, and from other packs, the results vary. Sometimes it just means they take a little longer to adapt, even some adults can struggle with the change. Dean for example. Sometimes however, it can be… catastrophic." Matthew explained, and I appreciated his none answer more than the blank stares I got from most of the others.

"Give me an example." I said monotone. I listened to the wind, and felt invisible for a while.

"Well, there was a story of a seventeen year old wolf out in Romania." Lewis Osborne began.

"No, maybe we shouldn't? We can't be sure about any of this stuff." Rita spoke for the first time, still perched on the step.

"True, but if anyone deserves to hear this, it's him Rita." Osborne gave her a gentle look. She cast her eyes back towards the ground. "On one occasion she is said to have Phased. It was far from her first time, but for some reason, she became trapped in her wolf form. After a day or so… she completely lost her mind. This all happened seemingly out of the blue, or so the story goes. Her pack had no choice but to hunt her down. It's no easy task in any case, but some amongst them were her own flesh and blood."

"Well shit… anything else you want to tell me about?" I muttered.

"There was one other that we heard tell of in recent years. It supposedly happened to a fifteen-year-old boy in France. He got… stuck, for lack of a better term, mid transformation."

"Oh, yeah I heard about this." Beth butted in. "They say he became a gross, twisted thing. Couldn't speak, could barely move at all. Then they had to put him out of his misery. Don't believe in these fucking ghost stories."

"Call them what you want, Bethany. All I know is there's a reason our rule goes so far back that none among us can recall its origins. I for one don't want to keep him in the dark. We do know for certain that terrible things *can* happen. He has every right to be aware of this."

"It's a horror story you tell to kids to keep them down, and that's all it is." Beth stated with finality.

"I feel it's important to note, "Osborne turned to address me, "that just because there can be complications, it doesn't mean there will be. I relayed those stories to you, Zack, purely for the sake of transparency. We've never had that kind of complication arise amongst our ranks. Regardless of the hearsay, you seem to be doing better than we ever dared hope for, take comfort in that."

I remained silent, mulling over what I had heard. It sounded like a folk tale. The kind of hearsay that, if you trace it back far enough, always leads to nothing. Still, I couldn't help but find it unnerving. I decided to push it back, far into the recesses of my mind. After all, I had more immediate concerns.

"No more stories. Kid," Locke said, his stony eyes meeting mine. "Phase and lead the way."

"Okay…" I muttered with a total lack of confidence.

"Zack, believe me, when you change you'll want to hunt. Just allow instinct to take hold." Mr Osborne patted me on the back. I breathed a heavy sigh, and then finally nodded.

I began to undress, placing my bulky headphones onto my pile of clothes. Locke, Rita, Matthew and Osborne all disrobed along with me. Feeling a little flushed, I made certain to avert my gaze from Rita entirely.

"Dear God, Sir this is just bizarre, could you not?" I pleaded as my teacher's hairy chest became exposed.

"Man the fuck up. He's not rocking anything you aren't." Beth hollered. She had already returned to her game.

I stood on the cold grass in naught but my underwear and closed my eyes, hoping that by some miracle, it would help my concentration. I tried to rouse the wolf within from its slumber, and I felt its phantom form move reluctantly. I peeked as the four humans around me contorted into strange, inhuman shapes. I shut them out again, and heard bones break, flesh tear, their cries of agony. All except for Locke, who barely made a sound.

"Get the hell in here." I heard Anne caw, followed by a blue haired girl's weary sigh. The door slammed.

I told my dark side it was free, that it could smell the scent of prey and had permission to hunt it down. Then it took notice. In just a momentary flash of white, an instant of molten misery, I was something new, more than human. Suddenly, I was no longer gazing at the soft and pasty hands I was expecting to see. I was looking at ferocious claws, and jet-black fur. It whispered silent words to me. It wanted to feed.

The scent of living flesh overwhelmed my senses, and my body burst forth at unstoppable speed. The sheer power was awe-inspiring, but it was not my own. Limbs moved, dictated by the beast in my head. I struggled to gain some semblance of control as it sprinted towards the treeline, but it was as though I was tugging uselessly at the reigns of a stampeding stallion. I seemed to drop in and out of consciousness rapidly, like a movie skipping frames.

It glanced behind, and I was swept along with it. Tailing us were the others, the great silvery wolf that was Locke, galloping head and shoulders above the rest. The sandy dog that was Rita darted nimbly between towering oak pillars. At her side was Matthew, whose fur was a patchwork of darker tones. The wolf that I knew was Osborne was smallest, and coloured an earthy brown.

We charged through a shallow stream, sending cooling spray up into the evening air. We leapt and weaved seamlessly through the trees, sending decaying leaves spiralling upward as we passed. Flashes of blackness continued to disorientate me, but the wolf in charge stayed on task. We were on something's tail, the scent was becoming all the more potent the closer we got. I wrestled internally for control of what I still considered to be my body. I fixated on each limb as the beast's anticipation of warm blood grew. I demanded that it listen to me, and fought to overthrow its command. We would get to feed, I promised it that.

Suddenly my shape felt alien. I momentarily gained control of my body, and then instantly realised I had no fucking clue how to use it. The smooth, flowing motions stopped dead, then both paws and furry hands disappeared from beneath me. I tumbled into an uncontrollable roll and collided heavily with a tree, which tilted dangerously. Spinning out, I managed to get a brief grasp on the ground only to stagger gracelessly forward, losing all the rhythm and pace that that Lycan had built up. I cursed in my mind.

Then my head was filled with upbeat emotion, the congratulations of some of the pack. Apparently my bail was something to be proud of. I slid to an unsteady halt, tearing the earth as I tried to cling to the dirt. I sat inelegantly on my furry butt, like a baby who'd only recently discovered the skill. The chocolate brown wolf that was Osborne bounded up to me, and batted playfully at my giant, cumbersome head. As though we were linked, I felt his positive reinforcement leak into my consciousness. He could tell that I had turned some kind of corner. All at once, the feelings of the others also joined mine. Matthew seemed relieved, and Locke gave off a vibe of peaked interest. Rita however seemed enveloped by sorrow, giving the ethereal equivalent of a weak smile.

I shuffled back onto my paws, and gingerly tried to test them out. The earth felt a little steadier beneath my feet. All the while the silent voice of the Lycan in my head was trying to make its hunger known. I pushed it down, and buried it beneath intense concentration. Synapses began to fire, and quickly made the connections to the part of my brain that already knew what it was doing. I hit a kind of trot experimentally, and managed not to break any bones.

Locke's essence overwhelmed all others as he strode through the group, a low rumbling growl emanating from within his broad, white chest. He glanced over his shoulder at us and jerked his head forward. The swirling notions I felt were all overwritten with his. Follow. Keep up.

He exploded into a powerful run, and the pack fell into step behind him. I hung at the back, keeping up with the pace as best I could on wavering legs. I breathed in deep, and the smell reminded me of why we were out there. There was a break in the tree line, and beyond it was a small clearing. Within the clearing a family of deer grazed peacefully. That is until our thunderous approach caused them to sprint for their lives. Rita darted ahead and dived upon the slowest one, sinking razor sharp fangs into its flank. It kicked its spindly legs in the air momentarily; another crushing bite to its throat was the killing blow.

The stench of blood ignited our senses, the Lycan fought for control once more. Its hunger was far stronger than my ability to keep it under my orders. All too suddenly, it took the reigns again. Locke swiped the second deer, which seemed to crumble beneath his vicious blow. We sprinted past him, heading for the final target. It dashed out of the clearing and into dense woodland. We felt the sensation of an order to stop, but a terrible pain seemed to split our head in two.

■■

The next thing I remember was the end of the chase. The deer ran out onto a secluded back road. Not secluded enough however. We were within range to pounce and so we did, spearing through the air, fangs bared. We sunk dagger like claws and equally sharp teeth into the exhausted animal. Just as we hit the ground, a beat up old pickup truck came careening around the trees, and slammed right into the side of us. We were crushed painfully beneath the wheels, the truck bounced and twisted, then rolled rapidly down the winding lane. Glass and warped metal flew in all directions, until finally it came to a stop. We were devouring rapidly, wound from the collision already healing, when Locke descended and swept us from the road back into the cover of the forest.

His rage filled my mind, and cleared my head. The wolf within had gotten its fill and settled down, leaving me to take the fall. I jumped up, and once more felt the uncomfortable sensation of regaining control of a body I wasn't all that familiar with. Locke peered at the wreckage through the trees. I didn't dare look in that direction. I had no idea what kind of damage I'd caused, or who I might have hurt. A pang of guilt struck a very human part of me.

Locke glared at me with those cold grey eyes. His stare told me he was far from impressed with my takedown. He jerked his head again to indicate that I should follow. The storm within his mind was also raging inside mine as we turned tail and headed for home.

■■

"What the hell were you thinking kid?!" Locke bellowed. It was a far cry from his usual intimidating calm.

I didn't reply, just threw my shirt back on and wondered what became of the people I had left behind in the truck.

"Zack, what happened out there?" Osborne asked, thankfully already clothed.

"It just took over. I fought it for control, but I lost. I don't know what else to tell you." I said meekly.

"Fought it for control, what do you mean by that?" He looked at me quizzically.

"You know, *it*. The Lycan."

"I don't understand. You are the Lycan, Zack. You realise that right?" Matthew joined the discussion. Locke paced like an animal caged.

"Yeah, I get it's me and I have to learn to control it. I don't understand how you guys stop it from taking over though?" I stared at my bare feet on the grass, so pale and delicate.

"Control it? There is no *it*, there's just you." Locke snapped.

"But, but what about all that shit you said before? 'He was in there'. You know, when we fought?"

"He was talking about being able to sense you as a part of the pack. You must have felt it? It's as though we share a consciousness. That doesn't occur until you stop blacking out, and start to become self-aware as a Lycan." Matthew explained.

"Yeah I felt that today, with all of you. So... I don't understand. How do you guys stop the wolf from having its way?" I asked.

"It doesn't have its way." Rita said, looking at me concerned. "Early on, it's hard to manage your phasing, especially when you're angry. Having this kind of power is dangerous when you're mad, especially when you still black out."

"Yes, I thought that with you being created so young, you might have more trouble with it than most. Which is why I warned you about it." Matthew added.

There was a soundless dark chuckle within my head. It was enjoying watching me squirm, as I came to the realisation that I was the only one. None of the others had that presence in their minds.

"You're lucky you show such potential kid. I promise you though, the moment you become a liability to this pack, I will remove you as an issue personally. You came close to that tonight." Locke grumbled sternly.

"Other than this sense of… separation you seem to have, is there anything else unusual you think we should know about? Any strange effects beyond what we've already explained to you?" Matthew spoke softly.

I thought about the intrusive, overly sensitive hearing. That, and the increased sense of smell that seemed to come and go as it pleased was all a part of the process. Elements of development they had explained to me beforehand. Then something else crossed my mind. The situation in the Animalarium, then again when Luke hit Jackson. The intense pain, the blurred vision, and that deafening roar that drowned out everything else. I glanced at Locke, who stirred impatiently as he awaited my answer.

"No… no there's nothing else."

10 Days Until the Next Full Moon

It was a frosty day, and we all stood shivering in a line. Our matching blue shorts, quivering in unison at the slightest shudder-inducing breeze.

"So, there I was feeling all guilty thinking I might have killed some random strangers. I'm up all night, beating myself up. Then first thing in the morning, I crawl downstairs half dead and see the people I took out on the news." I muttered to Damian, sure my words were being lost to the others around us, dissipating on the cruel winds.

"Damn, what did they say happened?" Damian asked, teeth chattering.

"Get this, the woman was claiming whiplash. The guy was claiming all sorts of shit; he even had a neck brace on. He told the reporter that a weird looking bear dashed out in front of his truck, and he intended to sue the people who owned the land." I kind of resented the 'weird looking bear' part. I liked to assume I was quite a handsome pup.

"So, his plan was to take legal action against a forest?" Damian said, peering through one sceptical, narrowed eye.

A gust of epic proportions hit the whole sorry squad of us. The entire line grimaced in tandem, and from the far end I heard an angry soul shout 'Fuck this shit!' I took a moment to ponder which of my limbs might succumb to frostbite and drop off first.

"Seems so." I replied, peering at my trembling hands. It would be the fingers first, I was pretty sure. "The best part is though, when the reporter explained there was no land owner, the guy threw a hissy fit. Tore off his neck brace and slammed it on the ground, overturned a table and started wailing about who was going to pay for his pickup."

"Jesus. Some people are truly clueless." Damian, teeth chattering, let out a disbelieving laugh.

"I know right. I just pray they were that stupid before the crash, otherwise I really do have something to feel guilty about." I snickered.

"Hey. Would you guys mind, you know, involving me in this conversation?" Jackson yelled over what had become a roaring wind.

"Sure, we were just talking about how rude it is when people butt in." Damian yelled back, self-satisfied.

"God, I hate you both *so* much." Jackson seethed overdramatically. Damian replied by sticking out his tongue and blowing an admirable raspberry. Much to my dismay, the winds changed and carried the resulting spray in my direction.

"Ahh, splash-back!" I cried, shielding my face with a short sleeve that wasn't up to the task. "Watch where you aim that shit." I complained. The two of them giggled themselves silly in the midst of my unplanned shower.

"Alright, listen up!" Mr Goth, the schools senior PE teacher finally returned after heading to the stock room to get the equipment for our lesson. "Today, we'll be playing softball." A groan ran through the entire group.

"But sir, softball's gay." A stocky ginger kid, Carl Wilson piped up. There was some guffawing from the other students.

Goth (or the Dark Lord as we liked to call him, for no reason other than his name) dropped the bag of equipment to the floor. He reached one hairy knuckle up towards the sky, and used it to scratch the bald spot at his crown. Breathing deep, his already bloated stomach inflated further. He let out a heavy sigh. The laughter gradually died out as he stood defiantly in the face of it all. Silence fell, and he reached down and took one of the balls from the bag, spun it on his palm, and then suddenly let fly.

The ball hit Carl in the gut, and took all the wind out of his sails. He keeled over, leaning into the wall for support. Even the gale seemed to hold off as the entire class inhaled in shock. The Dark Lord surveyed his subjects for a moment. He strode over to Carl, and bent his head low. They were face-to-face, and close enough to taste each other's breath.

"Gay it may be Wilson, but apparently it's not as soft as you." Goth said, completely deadpan. Then a smirk played across his lips, and he straightened up. "Anyone else have a similar, riveting opinion they feel they need to share?" He glanced around. "No? Then let's begin."

That day, the balding old geezer went some way to earning his title. After seeing Goth put the Wilson kid in his place, Damian, Jackson and I all exchanged a knowing glance, and then nodded in appreciation.

■■■

After an hour and a half of standing still on a field, and watching Elton dart back and forth, awaiting a ball that would never come, the truly difficult part of PE was upon me again. I thanked all concerned for the fact that physical education seemed to be so low on our schools list of priorities. The lessons were few and far between, but when they did come, I had to do my utmost to hide the far from subtle scars that ran down the length of my body. The mark from the blade on my arm hadn't left a trace, it disappeared completely the last time I Phased. However, the ones caused by the Lycan were permanent, and more than a little noticeable. Up to that point I had managed to keep them concealed by facing the wall, and quickly switching out my blue shirt for my white one. On this day though, things were a little different.

Damian and Jackson flanked me on either side. Damian wasn't an issue, since he already knew the details. As bizarre as those details were, he had seen more than enough proof to convince him that they were legit and as such, a strange kind of acceptance had washed over him about the whole werewolf thing. Jackson however, seemed to be becoming increasingly suspicious of our hushed conversations that were forced to stop dead as he approached. I changed out of my shorts, and waited for Jackson's attention to be elsewhere. Quickly, I threw my shirt off. Whilst I was in a state of undress though, I heard someone call my name.

"Zack... Hey, asshole." I recognised the voice of Luke immediately. I glanced over my shoulder. Twisting my torso revealed just enough for Jackson to catch a glimpse of the scars. Luke held up my phone and waved it around, smug as can be. He then scurried from the changing rooms, slinging his bag over his shoulder as he went. I let out a mournful huff, and resigned myself to having no phone. I also used that time to vow mute revenge.

"What the *hell* happened to you Zack?" Jackson asked, mouth agape. In a flash, I knew he had seen.

"Oh… I got attacked by a dog." I told him somewhat truthfully.

"No fucking way."

"It was a really big dog." I added.

"Why are you lying, no dog could do that, how did you even survive *that*?" His eyes scanned me through his thick specs, analysing as best they could.

"Erm… dude?" Damian spoke over the hum of those still getting changed. "Luke took your phone."

"I know." I spoke back, glad for the change of subject. I picked up my big dumb headphones mournfully. "What am I gonna use to drown out all your bullshit now?"

"No, I don't think you get it. *Luke took your phone.*" He stressed, squinting at me strangely.

After a few seconds of ignorant silence, the stuttering cogs in my head finally began to turn. Luke had the phone, and the phone had the footage. If Luke saw it, he was sure to have several difficult to answer questions. Questions such as 'why do you have a murder video on here?' and 'who is that oversized canine?' I felt my eyes widen with panic, as the potential severity of the situation finally began to sink in.

"Fuck, we have to get it back." I proclaimed. I scratched at my head, perhaps hoping the friction might create the spark of an idea. I needed a plan.

"So, go take it from him? Can't just let people get away with stealing your stuff." Jackson spoke unconcernedly. He had no idea about the possible ramifications of me becoming involved in yet another heated confrontation. The voice in my head whispered agreement with my bespectacled friend. I felt a deep unease in the pit of my stomach, and tried to convince myself I didn't hear it.

"No. I've gotten in too much trouble lately as it is." I told Jackson. I left out the part about needing to keep Locke onside, and making sure the presence in my mind stayed a secret. "Sir, Luke just stole my phone." I told Mr Goth.

"I'm not your mother, Archer." He groaned as he gathered up the loose equipment in the changing rooms. "Deal with your own problems."

"But Sir, I'll get myself expelled at this rate." I protested, as dismay descended upon me. If I ended up fighting over the stupid thing, I was guaranteed to cause no end of drama for myself. That was if I managed to keep control at all. On the other hand, if I did nothing and the video ever got out, Locke would see to it that I never had the chance to tell anyone what I know.

"Well then, be creative. You're supposed to be smart right? God I hope you are 'cause lord knows you can't throw for shit." The cholesterol-ridden old man pulled tight the cords on the equipment bag, then strode out of the room without another word.

"Fine. We'll have to think of another way." I said, turning back to my pair of friends.

"Whatever. I'm in if it means getting under Luke's skin. I'm gonna find out the story behind those scars though, don't for a second think I've forgotten. I've got a detective's eye, me. You can't keep anything secret forever." Jackson beamed confidently, relishing the idea of having something to investigate. 'You can't keep anything secret forever.' The words stuck with me, and I worried that he might be right.

■■■

"Alright, now's our chance Elton." I said in a rushed whisper.

"Guys, I'm really not sure about this. You didn't even speak to me for the whole of PE, why am I suddenly involved?" He mumbled.

"Come on, it's now or never! I've got your back." Jackson tugged Elton along with him, and with that, the plan was in action.

Jackson and Elton strode forwards, marching in step down the crowded hallway. Jackson split off, removing his blazer as he walked and slinging it confidently over his shoulder.

"This is like an incredibly low budget version of Ocean's Eleven." Damian muttered as Jackson continued to strut, seemingly in slow motion. I let out a single bark of laughter from our position at the mouth of a mostly empty storage room.

It was the transitional period between our fourth and fifth classes. Everyone was heading to their final lesson of the day. Our mark, Luke, came out of a Gen Ed room with our target, his backpack, slung lazily over his shoulder. Elton headed straight towards the goal, seemingly shrinking as he approached. Luke's eyes caught sight of him, and his features became etched with something close to utter bewilderment. The tiny little victim stepped right to his long time bully. Elton took off his bag and dropped it to the ground.

"I wanna fight you." He squeaked, almost inaudibly.

"What the fuck did you just say?" Luke glared, a disbelieving expression on his trailer park face.

"I said… I wanna fight you." Elton spoke up, but barely. Luke erupted into a fit of laughter, clutching at his sides melodramatically. Damian set off down the hall towards them.

"Really, you're actually saying this *to me?* You wanna go?" The bully's tone was one of arrogance. He threw his backpack at the wall, it hit a display case and fell to the ground. He didn't notice Jackson, leaning unceremoniously against that same wall, waiting for his moment.

"Yeah, bring it on… pussy." Elton said, and raised his fists weakly. It was a truly cringe worthy moment.

"You got it pipsqueak." The bleach-blonde bastard cracked his knuckles menacingly.

Quick as a flash, Jackson sprang into action. He leapt unseen behind the mark, and in one smooth motion, swung his blazer by one sleeve around Luke's ankles. He caught the other sleeve as it whipped around, and tugged with all his might. I'm sure in his head the crowd was going wild. He was having visions of people talking about our heist for years to come, of it going down in history as one of the greatest manoeuvres ever pulled off by confidence thieves such as ourselves. All of that was shattered though, as the shoddily stitched blazer let him down. With a loud rip, one sleeve came free in his hand.

Luke turned to see Jackson crouched on the ground, ruined blazer in his grasp.

"What the *fuck* are you doing?" He asked the hunched boy aggressively. Jackson didn't look up.

"PLAN B!" He hollered at the top of his lungs.

"Oh god, oh god, oh god." Elton muttered. He was really hoping it wouldn't come down to plan B.

Elton reached forward reluctantly and grabbed Luke's waistband. With a sharp tug downwards, he exposed him to the world. Everyone turned, pointed and laughed as Luke panicked. He tried foolishly to run, but tripped and fell. The volume of their incessant giggling only increased as he struggled to redress himself on the floor. Damian strode behind the chortling mob and, completely unnoticed, he kicked the bag with the back of his heel. It slid smoothly across the polished surface. As it reached the storage closet I was hiding in, I snatched it inside.

"I'm gonna kill you, both of you!" I heard Luke w\ail. Usually the roar of laughter would be enough to plunge me into madness, but that time despite the volume, it was music to my ears. I closed the door, and began to search.

I rummaged through Luke's stuff, finding a bunch of old papers. Battered books never read, homework assignments uncompleted, an old magazine about cars for some reason. There were pencil shavings but no pencils, an ancient and dusty yo-yo, and a handful of long forgotten jellybeans. I tipped the bag out, hoping for more, but there was nothing more to be found. I cursed under my breath, then left the storage room to look for Damian and the others.

"You will all get to your classrooms right now!" Mrs Stonehall bellowed as loudly as her lungs would allow. She waddled towards the congregation of kids, bingo wings flapping frantically. As they dispersed I saw Luke, thankfully clothed and fighting back tears. His bloodshot eyes blew his cover. Elton was sat on the ground, covering one side of his face with an open palm.

"How dare you hit this boy. You should be ashamed of yourself!" Stonehall screamed, her spit splattering Luke's shirt.

"But, but, but!"

"To the deputy head, NOW!" The teacher screeched. To be honest, I was just glad it wasn't me for once.

∎∎

Through the window in our following class, we saw Luke wandering through the school grounds, escorted by the Deputy Head. He had been ordered to vacate the premises for the rest of the day. Perhaps in the hope that the memory of his bone white buttocks swaying in the breeze would die with the daylight. I spent the remainder of my lesson worrying myself half to death about the prospect of the footage being found. I tried my hardest to theorise about where a criminal mastermind, such as Luke Boon, might hide his ill-gotten gains. Alas, no instant of inspiration gifted me with the answer. All I was certain of from Elton's close inspection was that it wasn't in his pockets.

It was only later that evening when Damian knocked at my front door and made the confident proclamation, 'We are retards' that the phone's probable location became apparent. His locker. It was so obvious. We were indeed retards, and I was proud of my friend for using all of the evidence at hand to come up with that most conclusive conclusion. Pretty soon though, he was wishing he had never had the brainwave that brought that realisation to mind. He was less than happy with the situation when the two of us were crouched low in the school grounds, hoods up, shrouded in darkness.

"This is nuts, what the fuck are we doing here? We can't even get in." His voice was raspy. Anger threatened to betray his attempts to remain quiet. The light of a semi-present moon made the bare skin on my hands tingle.

"We can't with that attitude, Negative Nancy. Quit complaining, and help me find a way." I whispered back, and with that we began to stealthily approach the school's lower building. I pulled the handle on the building's main door. It was locked tight.

"Good effort genius." Damian murmured sarcastically.

"Well, you don't know unless you try. Jeez you're like a spoiled kid, can't take you anywhere."

"This isn't exactly a day at the fair, we could get expelled for this! Why don't we ever go to the fair, like normal people?" He continued to whine.

"Because you're too tall for human rides, Lurch." I rasped back at him, as I tried to open several of the classroom windows. They were all locked. Even if one of them happened to be open though, the classroom doors would still have blocked our advance. I spotted a window that lead directly into the hallway.

"Maybe we can use the fire escape, see if there's a way in from th-" Damian began. The sound of shattering glass cut him off.

"WHAT THE-" He began, and then realised he had forgotten his whisper. "What the hell are you doing?"

"I'm getting us inside. You do realise if anyone finds that video I'm dead right? Now get in here." I said, clambering through the broken pane.

"Jesus Christ, you owe me big for this." He told me. Pulling his hood lower, he followed me inside.

The hefty rock I had used to so subtly gain us entry lay amongst the shards on the ground. I am nothing if not a master of stealth. Seriously though, I knew we didn't have long to work with. There were plenty of houses nearby, one of which was my own. Someone would have heard, and soon an apathetic cop on a nightshift would be sent to investigate yet another minor disturbance.

The school was an eerie place at night. The usually bustling halls were barren, and all too silent. Impenetrable darkness lay ahead of us. The lockers in that particular building were on the second floor, which was where we needed to head. Damian rummaged around in his pocket, and pulled out his cell phone. He hit the camera button, and turned on the tiny flashlight. It illuminated the darkened hallway just enough for us to proceed.

"This is creepy as shit, let's make this fast." He mumbled. I nodded, and as we began to move forward, I struck a sneaking pose. Then I began my rendition of the Mission Impossible theme, making a terrifying gun with my out stretched hands. "Could you not?" He asked in a grim, grown up tone.

"Oh, lighten up." I replied, gun fingers still ready to fire. He slapped me on the back of the head, and the clap echoed in emptiness. I was motionless for a moment. "Okay, I deserved that."

We crept down the sterile hallway, what little light we had refracting in the glass panels of the display cases. Badly written work stapled to the walls drifted in and out of focus as we made for the stairs. Our steps echoed, and seemed to be amplified by the empty space. Damian pointed his makeshift torch upwards, revealing the mountain we had to ascend. We shared a fleeting nervous glance, and then made our way up the steps.

Thankfully, nothing waited there in the dark to molest us. We reached the top of the flight without being sodomised, which if you think about it should be a bonus in anybody's book.

"Alright, so the lockers are down past the library and on the left." Damian said.

"We have a library?" I asked, genuinely surprised. He just shook his head, an expression of shame in the shadows.

We picked up our pace, powerwalking our way down the hall, following our guiding light. When we rounded the corner, a seemingly endless bank of blue boxes awaited us.

"How the hell are we supposed to find out which is his?" Damian asked, defeatist. I had the same concern. That is, until I remembered one of the distinct advantages my furry little friend gave me. It knew the thought as soon as I did, and it swelled with pride. Then I thought about how it was still a massive pain in the ass, it picked up on that too.

"Well, he's a bully right?" I turned my attention back to Damian, abandoning the stirring presence.

"Yeah, he's an asshole. What's your point?"

"I'll just look for the locker that smells of TV dinners and parental neglect." I slowly stalked my way down the hall and inhaled deeply. I muttered to the wolf in my mind, asking it to make itself useful for once. It had as much to lose as I did, and I think it must have realised that because to my amazement, it fulfilled my request. It had become more than familiar with Luke's stench due to our previous encounters with him, and as the smells I began to recognise flooded my nostrils the wolf growled so that only I could hear. As I got closer to my goal, the volume of its rumble steadily increased until finally it stopped, all of a sudden. My eyes fell on a single navy square that reeked of my schoolyard nemesis.

"It's this one." I stated, certain that I was right.

"You're sure?" Damian asked, and I gave a single nod. "Whoa, that's some super hero business… well if you're right anyway. Now how do we get it open?"

I grabbed the locker's protruding handle and gave it a sharp yank, the door tore off with ease. The whole Lycan deal was definitely beginning to have its uses. Within the locker lay the prize that we were searching for. My phone sat, screen dark, at the centre of the metal space. I grabbed it and slipped it into my pocket.

"Well, that works I guess." My friend mumbled.

A gentle wave of light passed through the window, and over our hooded figures. Damian hurried over to see whose headlights had just spoiled our fun and deprived us of much deserved celebration. I heard a pair of car doors open.

"Shit, it's the cops!" He panicked, rushing away from the window and crouching low. I dropped too, and headed to get a look for myself. Two uniforms clicked their torches on, and instantly spotted the broken glass.

"Fuck. We have to move." I said, and began furiously tearing locker doors open.

"What the hell are you doing? We've gotta get out of here!" He yelled. All attempts at remaining quiet had been abandoned.

"Making it less obvious what we came for, head for the stairs!" I shouted back, still frantically removing the wretched blue doors. As he ran towards the staircase I pulled the whole row of lockers down, sending possessions in all directions. Then I took off after him.

We reached the bottom of the flight and heard the cops call out to us.

"We know you're still in there, give yourselves up or you'll only make things worse." The beams of their torches flashed across the wall at the far end of the hall.

"Damn it, now what?" Damian asked, eyes darting, searching for options. A cop's boot appeared on the windowsill opposite our hidden position.

I glanced around, and could just about make out the murky silhouette of a classroom door in the gloom. I leapt forward and kicked it open, the lock tearing free as it gave way. We ran inside, and Damian pushed what was left of the door closed. I toppled a shelf to block their advance. Within me the wolf was stirring, whispering sweet words about how it would be *so* simple to destroy them and walk away. I told it 'not now.'

"Great, now we're trapped. Any more bright ideas snoopy?" Damian bawled at me. I could make out his frustrated expression in the pale moonlight. The Lycan inside made its opinion clear. It would not allow us to be caught.

"Relax, I'll handle this." I said to the wolf, not meaning to speak out loud. I looked at Damian, who thankfully assumed I was talking to him. "Just let me think."

Boots began to hit our makeshift barricade. Every foot that connected with the already damaged door brought us one step closer to capture. I stepped away from the sound, mind filled with panic and uncertainty. The wolf began to become impatient. I raised a hand, trembling with adrenaline, to clutch my head nervously.

The moonlight touched my skin, which burned as though it were suddenly aflame. My skull seemed to tear in two, and the Lycan let out a demanding roar. Vision blurred, and I collapsed on to all fours as the volume of the whole world seemed to drop to zero once again. I clutched at my head, begging it to stop, waiting for the now familiar sensation to pass, grimacing in pain. As sound began to return, I heard Damian again.

"Not this, not now!" He yelled, and dragged me to my feet. "Come on man, we've gotta go!"

The door began to tumble, barely kept upright by the flimsy shelf I had dropped in its way. I shook in an attempt to clear my mind, and regained a little of my visual clarity. I pulled my hood as low as possible and tugged my sleeves down, trying as best I could to keep the fiery moonlight from finding my flesh. My eyes fell upon the fuzzy outline of a teacher's heavy wooden chair, sat behind a wide oak desk. I dashed over, grabbed the back of it and swung it at the window, allowing the acidic beams of the moon to hit my face in the process. The window gave in, and shards went flying out into the night sky.

"That's your answer for fucking everything." Damian groaned, and leapt his way through the hole I had made.

I tried to follow just as the door fell down. As I clambered onto the window's frame, another pain shot through me. My consciousness was filled with deafening, monstrous cries, causing me to tumble out, and fall with a thud on to my back. Damian, who was already fleeing, turned and spotted me lying on the ground. He sprinted back and grabbed me by the arm.

"Come on you dumb ass, no time to be lying down." He said, tugging me to my feet as the torchlight swept in our direction.

"Stop right there!" The two out of shape cops shouted in unison from behind us. I held onto Damian as he steered me, in my less than stellar state, to freedom.

9 Days Until the Next Full Moon

The next morning, first period wasn't exactly what we were expecting.

"We will not tolerate vandalism at this school." Headmaster Starkey stated to the room. Every student had been called to an emergency assembly; apparently there had been some kind of break in the night before. Who knew?

"We suspect that it might have been some of our very own students that perpetrated this crime." He said, shaking his head in disappointment. Damian and I exchanged uneasy looks, and then pretended not to know each other.

"The officers on duty last night informed us that there were at least two criminals involved. I've called this assembly together to let all of you know that once we discover who is responsible, they will be prosecuted. Those accountable, should they turn out to be students at our fine establishment, will also be expelled with immediate effect." The room was deathly silent as he surveyed his subjects, jagged beak pointing towards the sky.

"Great. We are so fucked." Damian muttered through gritted teeth.

"Young man." Damian flinched in his seat as the Headmaster snapped. The tiny dictator then reverted to a calm tone, although he seemed fit to explode at any moment. "Do you have something to say regarding this matter?"

Damian froze like a rabbit in the headlights. He couldn't seem to formulate a response. Starkey motioned for him to rise. He shot to his feet like a bullet, tangling his fingers in nervous anguish as he stood.

"Erm… I was just saying to my friend here," He pointed at me, and I dropped my head into my hands. Damian suddenly leapt into fake aggression. "that it sickens me! It… it sickens me, that someone in *our own school* might be responsible… and if I knew who it was, I would kill them dead Sir!"

I don't know if that last part was supposed to be a joke, but if it was, it hadn't hit the mark. All was silent for a moment, then someone who I'm pretty sure must have had cholera, broke into an extended coughing fit. That only served to make the moment seem all the longer. Damian shrivelled, becoming a ghost of a boy. Despite towering over the Headmaster, he seemed to shrink to microscopic size.

"What I meant to say is… I would definitely report them." Each word seemed to rush over the last in quick succession, then Damian immediately dropped like a stone back into his seat. His body was as tense as a coiled spring. The headmaster eyed him for several seconds, a bewildered expression colouring his features.

"Well…" He finally began, looking concerned and unsure of what to make of the freak occurrence. "It's good to see that you're passionate about your school, boy…" I'm sure at this point he was making a mental note. Order the staff to keep an eye on the creepy kid, the one who expressed a desire to murder in front of his peers.

"Smooth move. You ever thought of public speaking as a career?" I mumbled, barely moving my lips. He managed to punch me in the leg whilst scarcely moving at all.

■■

Damian spent the entire school day expecting men in suits to come and drag him away, to lock him up and throw away the key. I tried to explain to him that they could prove nothing. We were the only ones who knew what we had done; the cops weren't about to get a forensics team involved for the sake of minor damages. All we had to do was remain calm and go on living, like it never happened. That didn't stop him jumping out of his skin every time a classroom door opened, but hey, at least I tried to calm him down.

Elton, sporting an impressive shiner after playing his part in our exquisite plan, was on a high like I'd never seen before. He hung around with us all day when he wasn't in a different class, and beamed to himself periodically as he recalled the events of the previous day. The break-in meant nothing to him. He didn't even consider that a major event, not when compared to Luke's public undressing. Elton grinned every time he caught another glance of his former tormentor shuffling around the school, an introverted shadow of his former self. The guy was getting abuse from all sides, and Elton enjoyed nothing more than a bully being brought down to the level of a victim. He also came up with the nickname 'Full Moon Boon', which spread like wildfire. It could be heard resonating through every classroom, and every hallway that Luke had the unfortunate honour of being in.

When the lessons were over, Damian's shattered nerves could take a well-earned rest, and Elton's joy sadly had to come to an end. I wasn't done with school. Tragedy though it was, the night of my parental meeting was upon me.

"Mrs Archer, it-"

"It's Miss." My mom corrected.

"Apologies, Miss Archer. It has come to our attention that Zack here has been… struggling shall we say. He fails to pay several teachers the respect they deserve, and on top of that, he has been involved in an incident of a more serious nature." The Deputy Head explained.

"Oh, and what serious incident is this?" She asked, twisting in my direction, the hint of a scowl appearing.

"A kid started a fight, and I finished it. What was I supposed to do, let him beat the crap out of me?" I said, getting a tad defensive.

"You mean, he didn't tell you about this?" Granger raised an eyebrow.

"I didn't think it was important Sir. It's not like she wasn't gonna find out from you anyway." I spat.

"And how does that make you feel, Miss Archer?" He asked from behind his ridiculous salmon pink tie, plastered with cartoon cats. Honestly, it's like he thought it was a fucking therapy session.

"He should have told me. If the other kid started it though, I see no issue." She replied, soft but firm, hands placed neatly in her lap.

"Miss Archer, I'm sure you understand, we can't have our students involved in violence here." The Deputy Head added with a humourless chuckle.

"Then perhaps you should be more proactive in dealing with the students that instigate violence." Her lips curled into a small, false smile.

The Dep mulled this over for a second, chewing on the inside of his cheek. He then decided to pursue a different point. He took a large slurp from his seemingly bottomless cup of coffee, and swallowed it with an irksome gulp.

"Maybe so. However that doesn't even relate to the real issue here." He stated.

"Then why did you bring it up?" Mom asked, without missing a beat.

I felt like high fiving her there and then. I was pretty sure she would have more than a few words for me when we got home, I did neglect to tell her about the Charlie incident after all. Despite that though, there and then, she was willing to defend my actions. And rightly so, if I do say so myself. Granger let out a huff, glancing from me to her. I wondered if the resemblance had suddenly become more apparent to him.

"Miss Archer, your son in recent weeks has gone from doing next to nothing, to doing nothing at all. I hope you understand that this cannot be allowed to continue." The Deputy drawled.

"Don't you worry, I'll make sure he gets his act together." The woman opposite him stated, and her conviction worried me slightly. Granger's eyes looked me over. I sat motionless and quiet. No comment. The Deputy Head breathed another weary sigh.

"Look, can I speak to you alone for a moment." He asked her.

"Sure. Zack, step outside for a second." She motioned with her hand for me to go, never taking her suspicious gaze away from Granger's own fixed stare.

I drummed on the seat's uncomfortable wooden arm rests for a moment, then used them for support as I undertook the arduous task of getting to my feet. Glancing over my shoulder on the way out, I saw the two of them sat silently, waiting for me to leave. I stepped outside into the empty hallway, as the door drifted to a soft close behind me. With little else to do, I leaned against the wall and continued my drum solo, anticipating the call back for the final verdict.

Well into a wall-based rendition of 'Eye of the Tiger', my teacher and fellow Fido, Lewis Osborne, happened to stroll around the corner. I gave him a cheery wave between beats. He strode up to me, his expression stern.

"Why did you break into the school?" He asked in a whisper that held some tension. His question took me off guard.

"Wait, what?" I replied blankly.

"Your scent was all over those damaged rooms, why?" The tiny teacher asked, his face still set in serious lines.

I guess at times, I forgot I wasn't the only one who had the abilities tied to being Lycan. It never even occurred to me that Osborne could figure out in an instant that it was me who broke in, just by sniffing at the air. Fortunately, I hadn't yet been dragged away by angry men in uniform, which meant he had so far kept that knowledge to himself.

"Well, this kid stole my phone." I began.

"And you saw this as a reason for breaking and entering?" He eyed me doubtfully.

"Well no… kind of… shit. If I explain, you can't tell Locke about this, or he will kill me, and I mean literally." My shoulders drooped; I resigned myself to coming clean.

"Zack, Locke is our pack leader. Having said that, whose side do you think I'm on?" He asked, his eyes locked on to mine. I wasn't sure I understood. After my brief and ignorant silence, he decided to elaborate. "It is in the best interests of the pack, for you to remain a part of it."

He was in on Matthew's plan. I couldn't believe a seemingly intelligent man such as him would give any credence to the idea, that *I* of all people, could take out the pack's fearsome leader. Regardless, I would take any ally I could get.

"Okay, well you're not gonna like this." I warned him.

Lowering the sound on my phone, I showed him the footage I had taken of Dean and Locke's terrifying encounter. As it went on I explained how Luke had taken the phone, stashed it in his locker, and how I desperately had to get it back. Osborne watched stoically, his lips pursed together in a hard line. The clip came to an end. He seemed to process it for a few moments.

"What made you take this?" He asked, without looking in my direction.

"Validation, I guess. And I thought that it might be of use somehow, to prove what he's doing you know?" I lied.

"Has anybody else seen this?" Osborne scratched at his beard thoughtfully, and proceeded to twist facial hairs between his fingertips.

"No. No one has seen it. I didn't know if I should show it to Matthew or…"

"Showing it to Matthew will achieve nothing, and we can't get rid of Locke through any conventional means. You could never show that video to anyone without outing us all." He emphasized the word 'anyone'. I thought of Damian. He wouldn't reveal what he knew, I was certain. "Might I make a suggestion, for future reference?" He asked.

"Sure. Go for it Lew." I responded.

"Next time you find yourself in need of something that's locked up in the school, something of the utmost importance such as this. Remember that I'm a teacher." He groaned wearily, shaking his head slowly from side to side.

Just then, the door to the office flew open and slammed against the wall. My dear mother marched out, the very essence of rage.

"How dare you!" She spat, indignant.

"Delete the video." Osborne muttered before turning on his heel, and disappearing down the hallway. I hurriedly shoved my phone into my pocket.

"I meant no offence, Miss Archer. It's just that we have to keep our students best interests in mind. It is our duty to protect them." Granger stammered apologetically.

"To suggest that I would *ever* hurt my own son! Come on, we're leaving." The woman scorned grabbed me by my sleeve before I could even think, and began to drag me down the hall.

"Miss Archer, I meant nothing by it. It's school policy to consider every possibility." Granger pleaded.

"I have never been so embarrassed in my life." Mom snorted as she tugged me along.

"Jeez, don't take it out on me." I moaned, as she forced me out through the school's main doors. "It's not my fault you beat me." I grinned.

She gave me a terrifying look. The sort of stare that would make the most battle hardened soldier fall to his knees, and beg for forgiveness and mercy.

"What, too soon?" My face contorted as I struggled to deal with the distressing scowl.

7 Days Until the Next Full Moon

"Honestly, she went mental." I explained over the sound of clinking bottles, as Damian grabbed another beer from a plastic bag.

A couple of days had passed since the parent teacher conference that almost branded my mother as a child abuser. The five of us sat on a field that seemed to have given up on life. Patches of pathetic yellow grass withered all around us, and the stench of the nearby sewage outlet was enough to make my toes curl. Despite this, it was often a place where students such as us would congregate. I'm sure the fact that it was a secluded location in which to partake in underage drinking had nothing at all to do with it.

"Well, I guess it could have been worse." Elton spoke up, twisting his bottle absentmindedly in the dirt. His black eye was still yet to completely fade.

"Yeah, she could have killed Granger." Jackson said, seeming to find that hypothetical outcome amusing.

"I don't get it." Damian took a swig from his fresh bottle. "Your mom usually seems so mellow?"

"You've never accused her of beating minors." I gave him a crazed look, and took giant gulp from the gargantuan carton of fruit smoothie I had brought in place of alcohol.

A large huff burst forth from Venn, our long absent and still grieving pal. He rested his head on his hands, eyes low, toying with a bent bottle cap. Poor kid, he didn't seem at all the same since he lost his foster mother. We had barely seen him, but Venn is very similar to a movie's ambient sound. You don't even notice it's there, but once it's disappeared you can tell something is missing.

"Hey, it's good to have you back man." I tapped him on the shoulder, hoping to get some response out of him. I got nothing. He had gone from being quiet and distant, to practically none existent.

"How's your old man holding up?" Jackson asked, his brow furrowed. Elton took on the visage of someone crashing a funeral. He was new to the party after all, and actually hadn't even met Venn until that day.

"He's still in denial, walking around smiling like she's not even gone." Venn mumbled. "When it hits him, it's gonna be bad."

"Well, maybe he's just coping with it in his own way." Damian suggested. Venn cast the bottle cap into the vile smelling sludge of the sewer outlet, and as its surface broke, my nose wrinkled. I focussed on the scent of dead grass, and the smell of human faeces faded to a tolerable level.

"So, has Zack told *you* about his secret scars, Venn?" Jackson changed the subject to the only thing I wanted to speak about less than dead relatives. Venn shook his head morosely.

"Secret scars?" Elton seemed thankful to have a reason to get a word in.

"Oh yeah, huge scars all over. My theory is he's some kind of demon hunter, that's why he does so badly in school. Too tired from twilight battles with the devil to concentrate." Jackson smirked. Even though he joked about it, a burning curiosity was evident in his eyes. I wished he would just let it slide.

"I heard he got attacked by a pack of raging Chihuahuas." Damian's mouth twisted into a wry smile.

"Yeah, I'm not buying the whole dog thing." Jackson waved it off dismissively.

"Oh… you really should." My friend in the know shot me an informed look.

It was then that our relative harmony was shattered by the obnoxious ramblings of a group of miscreants. They strode across the bridge spanning the shit river, shoving each other and yapping at a higher volume than I (in my infinite wisdom) deem necessary. I recognised the dog first, the canine companion of the assholes who harassed us on the day this recount began. It barked indiscriminately, seemingly having the same amount of social restraint as the people on the other end of the leash.

"Goddamn it. Those guys are trouble." Damian muttered.

"Yeah, maybe we should go." I added. I had become so uncertain of myself. The strange outbursts that began when I stood before the tiger's cage had only increased in frequency and intensity over time. I feared what might happen if the wolf should push just that little bit harder. I worried it was a case of when, and not if.

"Screw that!" Jackson broke in. "I'm not moving because of those pricks. We were here first."

"What, are violent scumbags the only thing you *don't* have some kind of allergic reaction to? Isn't the pollen too much for you around here anyway?" Damian said sardonically.

"Jesus Damian, don't be such a bitch." Jackson spluttered.

Elton and Venn exchanged a glance. Elton again seeming as out of place as possible, and Venn, the very picture of indifference about the whole situation. They looked away from each other, finding no common ground. Then my sights fell on a familiar face, framed by a blonde pixie cut.

"What the hell is she doing with them?" I asked the group at large. The squabble came to a halt as they looked at the approaching gang.

Lexey, who had in her time at our school gone from being 'the new girl' to just being a girl, marched in step with the group. She seemed completely at ease amongst the mob, despite appearing to belong to a different species.

"Guess she fell in with the wrong sort. I always knew she was a bad egg." Jackson announced, sounding ashamed of her.

"That must be why you asked her out." Damian laughed. "Were you hoping to fall in with the Lost Boys over there too?"

"Hell no. Do you really think I'd ever wanna be like those dumb asses? I actually *have* a future."

"Yeah in politics right? Up until you carpet bomb Turkmenistan for calling your mom fat." I jabbed. His response kind of took me off guard.

"My mom is fat, the stupid bitch!"

There was a drawn out and awkward silence between us. All that could be heard was the steadily approaching squad of wasters.

"Well that escalated quickly…" Elton broke the rising tension. "Hey, that girl you were talking about is coming over."

The group had taken their own place in the foul smelling field, and were proceeding to crack open cans of cheap alcohol.

Sure enough, Elton was right. Lexey had split off from the crowd, and was heading in our direction. She glided towards us, hair whipping violently in the breeze, and came to a standstill before our sorry looking troop.

"Hey Venn." She spoke in a higher register than any of us were accustomed to hearing. "How're you doing? I'm sorry for your loss, you know." Venn looked up at her. The pain was clear to see, held within his tightened jaw.

"And how did you know about that?" Damian asked, sounding a tad suspicious.

"Overheard you guys talking about it in class." She replied matter-of-factly, gesturing towards Damian and I.

"That's a little rude don't you think? Sorry dude, we weren't trying to tell the world. Didn't expect anyone to listen in on our conversation." Damian cast a dark look in Lexey's direction.

"I don't care." Venn groaned, eyes back on the yellowing ground.

"Look, I just wanted you to know, you're not alone." The blonde eavesdropper raised her voice against the blustery winds. Venn cast another momentary glance at her. She gave one short nod, and his eyes fell back to the dirt.

"So... I trust your arm's healing up?" She said.

"Huh? Oh yeah, can't even tell anymore." I waved off her question, but detective Jackson latched on to it.

"What was wrong with his arm?" He cut in. His eyes shot from her, to me, back to her.

"When we were on the field trip, he had this big gash on it that opened up." Lexey told him, unaware she was fanning the flames of suspicion.

"Which arm?" Sherlock demanded, and she pointed to where the now none existent wound had been.

Jackson leaned forwards, and tugged up the sleeve of my cosy hoodie. It became considerably less cosy as the cold air began to bite at my bare skin.

"Get off me, you freak." I groaned drearily.

"No, I wanna see."

"But it healed already." I told him.

"Then there's no problem with me seeing where it was right?" He snapped, and I sighed.

"Nope. Guess not."

He rolled up the sleeve the rest of the way, until it was a tight, uncomfortable bundle above my shoulder. I felt like a cadaver as Jackson asked Lexey where the injury was, how deep it looked, and how much it had been bleeding. They poked, pointed and prodded at me.

"Look, I told you. It healed." I was losing my patience.

"That quickly, without a trace?" He said sceptically.

"What are you, a fucking doctor now?" I barked.

"Whoa, take it easy. You're doing yourself no favours acting so defensive. What exactly are you hiding?" He peered through narrowed eyes, made large through thick lenses.

"I'm not hiding anything." I stated.

It was then that the malcontents took notice of their missing member. The dog yapped on as they realised where Lexey had gotten to.

"What're you talking to those bitches for?" One of them yelled. He wore a striped blue sweatshirt and was missing some teeth, but I'm sure his lost fangs were not important to him.

"Yeah, get back over here!" A gum-chewing girl with black hair, pulled back in a dangerously tight ponytail. Her lip curled in distaste as she eyed us.

"I'll be over in a second." Lexey yelled back, and then huffed in exasperation.

"Fuck that, don't waste any time with those faggots." The one holding the leash called. His grey hood and sweatpants matched perfectly, I'm sure he thought he was the very definition of high fashion.

Venn's body tightened noticeably. His mouth turned from a weary gape into an expression of contempt. The gang laughed heartily at what, let's be honest, was a sub par and overused insult at best. Venn stood, clutching an empty beer bottle in his hand.

"You alright there, V?" Damian asked, eyebrows raised.

Before we could do anything to stop him, Venn cast his arm back, winding up for a powerful throw. He slung the bottle straight at the chuckling retards; it narrowly missed the one with the dog and hit the ground. Broken glass showered the others. Various curse words filled the chill air, and their whole group stood. Venn was motionless, chin raised, taller than I'd ever seen him before. The dog snarled viciously.

"Holy shit!" Jackson proclaimed. It was indeed the holiest of shits. We'd never seen the like. Venn – poster child for silent apathy, had taken action.

"Do you know who the fuck you're messing with?!" The one in grey bellowed to a chorus of demands to kill us and kick our asses. I'd have preferred if his pals were at the very least, consistent on the severity of punishment they desired.

"Aaron, let it go." Lexey pleaded. Her voice made it clear, she'd seen this sort of thing enough already.

I had never before witnessed someone care less about a threat. Venn, seemingly returning to form, didn't speak a word. Unlike his usual self though, he was not backing down. Determination seemed to emanate from his very being.

"Guys, let's just get out of here." I suggested, feeling the likelihood of another unwanted conflict growing. The wolf had other ideas. It savoured the thought of taking on the group of thugs. That was what worried me.

"Yeah come on, let's move." Jackson agreed.

"Oh, not so brave now I see." Damian glared at him accusingly.

The one with the dog handed the leash to the girl with the Croydon facelift. He began to stride over, his arms wide, as though he had decided to be a fridge for Halloween but forgotten his costume. Venn held his ground, completely calm and completely still. Aaron reached Venn, who stood head and shoulders above him. He spread his arms even wider, as if he were considering hugging a barrel, but couldn't quite work up the courage to make the first move. He got uncomfortably close.

"What now huh? I'm right here." Aaron bared his teeth.

"Hit him, rip his fucking head off." Some girl in the crowd shrieked. I felt bad for the litter of kids she almost certainly had at home.

Venn stared at him, dead eyed. Inside, the mutt was asking why, why wasn't I putting this pathetic creature in its place? I breathed slowly, keeping myself composed. I needed to be very careful about what I chose to do next.

"Who the fuck do you think you are, you have no idea who you're messing with do you?" Aaron snickered.

Venn still refused to back away, or lower himself to the thug's level. Said thug responded by spitting right in Venn's face, much to the amusement of those behind him. Disgusting tar ridden saliva streaked down our friend's cheek. The mouths of us all fell open. It was such an insult, an incredibly vile and disrespectful action to take. Still he never wavered, hell he never even blinked. The voice in my head grew louder, instructing me to murder and maim. To give these grotesque human beings the fate they deserved.

"Leave him alone, Aaron!" Lexey demanded, shoving him. It had little effect.

"The big man over here can't defend himself? You're fucking pathetic." He cocked his left hand and swung fast for Venn. He saw it coming, but did nothing to stop it. The fist connected flush with Venn's eye socket, to the underwhelming soft pat of real violence. His head turned with the strike, but his feet remained rooted to the ground in defiance.

My brain erupted again into animalistic fury. The desire to kill overwhelmed me, and for a second it was all there was. The same white flash, the deafening roar, the same dizzying pain, and blurred vision. Only this time, I fell flat to the ground. I felt myself slipping away.

"Zack! Zack are you alright?!" Damian's muffled voice, as though I were hearing him underwater. The dog's incessant bark turned to a fearful cry, before a single high-pitched tone replaced everything else.

I told myself not to pass out, to hold on, but I felt weary. I was slipping into darkness. The wolf was winning. I knew it held a grin full of razor sharp teeth in that moment, the wicked smile of victory. I pushed back, but it seemed hopeless, I was leaving the world behind, and leaving my body to the whims of the werewolf within.

Suddenly a cold liquid hurled me back into the real world. I shook my head, and wet hair sent droplets of beer flying in every direction. I gasped for air - it was borderline hyperventilation.

"Thank Christ!" Damian was never usually the religious sort, so this just went to show how thankful he really was. The panic he felt was easy to see, he was breathing almost as erratically as I was.

"This one fainted!" Aaron announced, and his group of greasy friends laughed enthusiastically. Only a few seconds had passed since the scumbag had spat at Venn.

"Come on dude, let's get out of here." Damian hauled me to my feet, and I stood on shaky legs. The Lycan growled in frustration. 'Not this time' I told it.

"Let's go." Lexey demanded, grabbing Venn (who still hadn't budged) by the wrist. Damian supported me as we staggered towards the bridge, and our escape. Lexey dragged Venn, and the other two trailed behind us.

"Where do you think you're going?" Aaron yelled at his little blonde pet.

"Go fuck yourself." She shouted in return, which I thought was a fair response.

The gang began yelling, and hurling cans of beer at us as we made our way over the shit river. They disturbed the stagnant water, unleashing disgusting odours that even my more human companions found intolerable. When we reached the other side, we were out of range. We crossed the grass to find our feet back on familiar stonework.

"Jeez, why were you even hanging around with them?" Jackson asked Lexey, in their first exchange of words since he so heroically got shot down.

"Well, me and Briana had kind of a falling out." She said, finally letting go of Venn's arm. "Don't worry, I won't be making that mistake again."

"Yeah, make sure you don't. I can't believe you were ever that stupid in the first place." Jackson replied.

"I guess I'll take that as a compliment." She rolled her eyes.

"So, where to now?" Jackson posed the question to our ragtag band of losers.

"I've gotta get home before dark." I mumbled gravely.

I recalled the moonlight on my skin, how it burned, and seemed to play a part in triggering my volatile responses. Damian glanced at me, understanding my thought process. I released myself from his well-meaning grasp, as I felt far steadier on my feet than I had a minute prior.

"What are you, twelve?" Jackson demanded.

"Dude, I smell like a damn brewery. I'm gonna head off, you kids have fun without me." I waved a weak goodbye, and separated myself from the group.

The moment I rounded the nearest corner, I pulled my phone from my pocket and scrolled through the numbers until I found Matthew's. He answered, emotionless, and I asked him if he was free to talk. Thankfully he was, because I had a lot I needed to lay bare. I told him about the pains in my head, and all that came with them. That they were seemingly becoming more common as time went on. I also told him about the acidic moonlight, and how it seemed to have a very strong effect on me, helping to trigger my weird episodes. I explained to him what had just happened in the field, how I felt myself slipping away. I left out the part about the voice in my head, and the fact I had his brother's murder on film.

He explained to me that this was strange. The burning moonlight was not unheard of, but only usually occurs on a first transformation. He didn't know what to make of the episodes I was having. I was his little project though, his one hope for a pack without Locke, apparently. So he had some advice for me.

"Don't go out at night. Stay out of the moonlight altogether. On the eve of the full moon, make sure you're here with us."

I agreed to his terms. I didn't usually need an excuse to hide away. Truth be told though, I was terrified. The risks were all too real, that fact had finally hit home. I had this horrible feeling that if I did the wrong thing, shit would get very fucked up, very quickly. It was time to play it safe.

4 DAYS UNTIL THE NEXT FULL MOON

So I had been laying low, as Matthew had suggested. I went to school and I kept my head down, for the most part. Then I went home, closed the damned curtains, and suffocated the remaining hours of the day one by one. It was tedious as all hell, but I felt safer. I felt at peace. There was barely a stirring from the Lycan, it had no enemies to face and no moonlight to try to spark its next frenzy. I kept cool and collected as it lolled around, probably as bored as I was. I was in relatively high spirits when I went into class on that Wednesday morning.

The class in question was Geography. I strolled in, and even stopped at the desk to greet Miss Clarke.

"Good morning, Sharon." I jerked my head and gave her a wink.

■■

You know, being outside wasn't so bad. Standing beside the mobile classroom, and watching all the round faced little cherubs waddling towards their next lesson was kind of relaxing. Their backpacks were so high up they were practically wearing them as hats. Momentarily, I yearned for the days where I too was a new student. Then I remembered all the teasing, and not knowing where any of my classes were. Then the crappy food that seemed to aim to make us all obese, and the weird social cliques that I could never understand. I came to the conclusion that school was stupid and always will be, when the classroom door shot open.

"Hey, dumb ass." Lexey called spiritedly. "She says you can come back in now."

I nodded to her in thanks, for keeping me well informed. This time when I entered the classroom, everyone was seated and ready to go, textbooks open. Miss Clarke still sat at the head of the class. I wouldn't make the same mistake twice though. Using her first name, bad move, I made a mental note. I leaned on her desk with one arm.

"Good morning, Miss Clarke." I said, and pulled out the same head jerk-wink manoeuvre.

■■

You know, being outside was even better without all the smelly little kids around. I got to stand contemplatively in the early morning sun, letting the cool breeze waft up the sleeves of my sharp looking blazer. It was considerably sharper than Jackson's, which had had the previously removed sleeve stitched back on haphazardly. I looked out across the field, the same one we had crossed when our journey to the woods began. It was the journey that changed everything for me, the one that made me a Lycan. I had all of about five seconds to reflect, then the door burst open again. The same blonde bob poked out.

"She said, 'you can come in again if you promise to shut up'." Lexey mimicked Clarke's well-mannered speech.

"Well, isn't she a ray of sunshine." I followed her back into the class.

Lexey took up her seat next to Venn again, who was sporting a black eye of his own since his run in with Aaron. He remained sullen, still woefully down about his loss. I felt for the kid, but to be honest, I couldn't relate. The only parent I had ever lost, got lost of his own accord. He upped and left in a time before I can even remember. As such, I didn't really know how to console Venn. Still, Elton was over the moon that he and Venn had briefly had something in common with their matching shiners.

Lexey herself had still not reconciled her differences with Briana, who gave her spiteful looks from across the room at every given opportunity. She instead had taken to hanging around with Venn all the time, to the surprise of us all. Because of this, there was nowhere left to sit amongst my friends. Damian and Jackson were nestled together, Lexey and Venn too. Elton, the little speck, wasn't even in our class.

"Sorry dude. Looks like you're flying solo this lesson." Damian pointed to an empty table.

"Yep, Zack 'Third Wheel' Archer. That's what they call me."

"Don't you mean *Zachary?*" Jackson peered at me smugly.

"So help me, I will cut you." I shot him a dirty look, as I sat in my uncomfortable plastic chair.

Finally the lesson had begun. I drifted in and out as Miss Clarke babbled on about something called 'the water table'. It couldn't have been important. I mean if you ask me, there's nothing worse you could possibly make a table out of. Due to my incomparable logic, I chose to disregard pretty much everything she said. Instead, I focussed my efforts on drawing a kick ass picture of a dinosaur on a scrap of paper. But not just any dinosaur, a dinosaur with *guns* on it. I was just adding the rocket launcher, when Lexey turned over her shoulder.

"What the hell is that thing?"

"For your information, it is a T-Rex." I educated her.

"What kind of T-Rex has rockets coming out of its back?"

"The best kind, obviously." Honestly, some people don't have a clue.

"Zachary, that better be work you're doing." Miss Clarke stood, and barged her way over.

"Of course it is Sharon," I covered my picture defensively. "I'm drawing *all* of the water tables."

She loomed over me. I, and my two dimensional T-Rex, were nothing in her shadow. She snatched the picture from under my hands. The teacher examined it for a second, and puffed out a despondent breath.

"Not only are you wasting your time, but this picture is factually inaccurate." To my horror, she screwed up the paper in her hand.

"What, did I make the tail too long?"

"It has machine guns on its arms!" She snarled, throwing my compacted dino into the wastebasket. The room chuckled at me in harmony.

"What's your point?" I gave her a squint eyed look. Clarke glowered at me, lips pursed, and then returned to reading a stack of papers whilst everyone else worked. The room settled down into a silence only broken by rattling stationery. I took another piece of scrap, and began work on T-Rex 2.0.

I had gotten as far as sketching the creature's tiny claws when I heard laboured breathing from the table in front. Lexey had a reassuring hand placed on Venn's back.

"It's okay, just keep it together." She whispered gently. He struggled to fight the emotions that were rapidly getting the better of him.

"What's the matter man, girlfriend picking on you?" A nobody called Chris said jokingly, trying to brighten the mood. Venn remained mute.

"Nah, everyone knows Venn here is gay." The longhaired boy next to him announced, in an equally light-hearted way.

Venn stood, eyes bloodshot and on the verge of leaking, towering over the seated students. He shoved his way past those around him, grabbed the boys' table, and flipped it. Their books and belonging went sailing across the room, the table tumbled and slammed down right next to a freckled ginger girl, who shrieked bloody murder. I had never seen him so filled with rage. Even the incident at the field wasn't like this. There, he had seemed cold. In that classroom though, he seemed furious, his body was tense and shaking as he stood over them.

"Whoa, sorry man!" Chris said.

"Yeah, we didn't mean anything by it, chill!" the other one added, hands raised defensively.

"Venn Armitage, control yourself!" Miss Clarke leapt to her feet, slamming her hands on the desk. Silence fell. It was as though we existed, for a time, in a vacuum.

All eyes were on our enraged friend, but even we couldn't think of a word to say. After a time, he strode back to his seat, but only to grab his backpack. He then stormed from the classroom without another word.

"Class, excuse me for a moment." Miss Clarke said graciously, and chased after him. As always when a teacher left, the room descended into mindless chatter.

"Hey, Lex." Jackson called. She sat with her head on her hand. "What's gotten into him?"

"Sorry. I promised that whatever he told me, I'd keep to myself." She spoke without turning to face him.

"What? That's bullshit, you've known him for like five minutes." He snarled, indignant.

"Sorry." Lexey shrugged.

Jackson muttered something I couldn't hear, so I'm going to assume it was a series of curse words. I didn't pry about Venn, she seemed miserable enough without me poking my nose in where it most certainly wasn't wanted. I was worried about my near-mute pal though, he seemed to be deep in the grasp of serious depression. What concerned me the most, is the thought that his mental state might get worse before it got better. Boy, was I right about that one.

2 Days Until the Next Full Moon

I have been called many things in my day, most of them highly unpleasant. One such moniker I have never been granted however is 'psychic'. Yet that, I felt was undoubtedly what I must be when I got the call a couple of days later.

"Dude, dude! You've gotta come to the industrial estate!" Damian hollered at me over the phone the instant I answered. I winced, and moved it away to a safer distance.

"Jesus, relax a second would you, what the hell's going on?"

"It's Venn, he's on the roof of that old warehouse where they used to make car parts." Damian said, gasping for air.

"What the fuck, what's he doing there?" I asked, confused.

"He wants to jump man! I'm just around the corner now." He heaved, and in the background I heard Lexey's feminine tones.

"Please, just come down Venn!" The familiar voice pleaded.

"Shit." I had just been settling down for another night of safe, warm shelter. An evening of no worries or cares before I had to head back to Locke's huge abode the following day, to ride out my first full moon with the rest of the pack. Every instinct I had told me to avoid the moonlight at all costs, to stay home and stay safe. I couldn't just leave him though; the poor kid was in such a sorry state. "Alright... I'm on my way. Just try to talk him down."

I killed the call, and headed for the door. I got as far as the stairway before I noticed the dying light through the window. I considered my options, then went back to my room and grabbed a hoodie, gloves, and I tucked my trousers into my socks. After tugging the hood as low as possible, I was as prepared as I was going to get. I rushed down the stairs, and my mom yelled something I didn't quite catch as I bolted out of the front door and took off down the street.

■■■

I arrived in record time, thanks in no small part to my ungodly speed advantage. Thankfully, by the time I got there Venn was still sat high upon the roof, rather than being smeared across the pavement. I panted, clutching my chest like a dusty old heart attack victim. Acid ran through my veins, and I couldn't catch enough air to speak a single word.

"Come on dude, we don't want you to do this!' Damian called to Venn, who sat on the edge of the high rooftop, feet dangling. His eyes were bloodshot, and tears streaked his cheeks.

"Please, come down Venn." Lexey begged, welling up. Her hands shook with a mixture of adrenaline and anxiety.

"I got here… as quick… as I could…" I struggled.

"We don't know what to do man. He's not listening to us." Damian kept his voice low.

"No matter what you're feeling right now, we'll help you through it I promise!" Lexey called up to the broken boy.

"No, you can't help, my dad has lost his mind. I'm too weak to cope with this. I'm fucking done!" Venn sobbed, and my heart broke a little. Seriously, I must have come down with a swollen empathy gland or something. "I'm done with all of it."

"You aren't weak. Now you listen to me, you can fucking do this!" Lexey said demandingly.

"We have to do something." Damian mumbled in my direction.

"Lexey, you keep him busy. We'll try to find a way up, fast." I gulped in air and set off.

"Just stay there Venn!" Damian called, as we dashed around to the side of the building.

There was no way up, just a sheer steel wall. Our heads darted, searching for a path. We ran to the rear of the warehouse. There was a shorter, concrete building attached to the steel structure, but it was still far out of our reach. A water pipe jutted out of the shorter building, leading the rest of the way to the roof.

"Fuck." Damian breathed. "If we can just get on to this part, we can use the pipe to go the rest of the way."

I spun around, hoping for some kind of miracle. All I found was a long shot. Over a chicken wire fence behind us was a manufacturing plant. It had a ladder leading all the way up to the roof. An image of my jump across the river on route B flashed through my mind. It sent a tingle up my spine. I couldn't even believe what I was considering.

"I have a really, really stupid idea." I stated.

"What is it?" Damian, still frantically looking around.

"Just wait here." I ordered.

I ran to the fence and clambered over it, using the holes in the chicken wire for grip. I dropped from the top, and landed in an ungraceful heap on the gravel parking area. Dashing across it, I reached the ladder and began my ascent.

"What good are you gonna do over there?" Damian shouted, a panicked hand running through his short, dark hair.

"Just trust me." I called back, still climbing.

Honestly, I didn't even trust myself. What little bravery I possessed evaporated as I reached the top, and turned to see the distance I had to face, and the drop that awaited if I failed.

"I'm gonna fucking die. That's it, this is where I die." I muttered to myself.

"Zack, you can't be serious?" Damian hollered.

"Trust me, I've got this." I tried to sound confident, even as my voice cracked.

"You're gonna kill yourself!"

"Yep." I replied.

Taking one last look at the fall, I began back stepping. I needed a monstrous run up, of that I was sure. My mouth became dry, and my breathing, shallow. I started to shake as my system flooded itself with adrenaline. I held a trembling hand up to the setting sun. 'No going back' I told myself. I repeated it like a mantra, silhouetted fingers still shivering in the wintery breeze. I clenched my fist, ordering it to stop. The wolf began to awaken, its sense of self-preservation rising to the surface. It told me I could destroy us, and I told it that we look out for our own. It shifted uneasily, as without a second thought, my feet sprang into motion.

I sprinted across the roof, my footsteps clanged on the corrugated surface. Before I knew it, I had taken off. My feet left solid ground, and I was hurtling uncontrollably through the brisk air. My arms swung frantically, and in that airborne instant the concrete rooftop looked impossibly far away. Wind whipped my face as I tore my way through the orange sky. For a second, I was sure I wasn't going to make it. My body twisted, bracing itself for the impact to come.

Unexpectedly my ankle clipped the edge of the building. I had made it, just barely. I crashed down, and an ear splitting crack reverberated off of every surface, a fraction later I howled in agony. The wolf inside roared, feeling my pain. My arm was broken, I had felt the bone give way. I whimpered and winced, and felt all around sorry for myself as I clutched the damaged limb. For a long moment I just lay there in the phoetal position.

"Zack, are you okay?" Damian isn't always the brightest penny.

"Do I sound okay?" I spoke through gritted teeth.

I dragged myself up on to my feet, using the good arm for support. My ankle was shot too, and this only became more apparent as the discomfort built with each step closer to the pipe. I could just barely hear Lexey and Venn continuing to speak, him still weeping and her still pleading. By this point I was already promising myself that if, after all I had been through, Venn jumped and somehow survived, I'd kill him myself.

I grabbed as high as I could on the cold pipe with my working hand, and hauled myself toward the clouds. The only way to progress was to use the small bolts that protruded from the steel wall as footholds, but I was barely able to find any traction. I wrapped my broken arm around the water pipe and hugged it tightly, as I placed the good hand higher once more. As it bore my weight, the pain rocked me. I felt dizzy, like I could pass out at any instant. Painstakingly, I inched my way up the warehouse until finally, my fingertips fell upon the roof's edge. I pulled myself up, kicking away from the wall to gain much needed momentum, before I sprawled onto my back atop the vast building. The distant conversation had become more heated.

"You guys don't understand, you don't really know what I am." Venn sniffed and struggled to breathe. "I can't do this." He climbed to his feet.

"VENN, NO!" Damian and Lexey cried in unison. I staggered to my feet, and ran towards him with an embarrassing limp.

"I'm sorry." He blubbered. Then my friend stepped out into the abyss.

I forgot the pain in my foot, and the broken arm. I pushed forth with everything I could muster. The two below yelped as Venn's feet left the rooftop behind. I leapt forward towards the edge just as Venn disappeared from view, reaching my good hand over the ledge in the hope that I might be able to grasp something. To my surprise, I actually did.

I caught a hold of the fabric at Venn's collar, there was the terrifying sound of tearing as the material took his weight, and I was pulled off balance. I thought for sure I was going over with him, that we'd get a seat in the carpool lane on our premature journey to the great world beyond. I tumbled out into open air, and barely managed to get the crook of my battered arm over the metallic lip of the roof. As gravity tried to tug us downward, my fractured appendage took the brunt of it, and I screamed for the second time that day. My teeth ground, as a solitary tear rolled down my cheek. I held back the rest, I suppose fearing that should I show further weakness, God might see fit to revoke my testicles.

The seconds of blinding agony felt like centuries as we hung there, far above the ground. I told my body I only needed one more thing from it on that cursed evening. My final request was for it to sling Venn back on top of the building. I swung him to the left and then with all my strength, up to the right, and heaved him onto the rooftop. I felt the satisfying clunk of his body reaching safety, and in that moment I could have died happy. In hindsight, it would have been better if I had.

In my instant of inner peace, I barely felt the hands on me as the friend I had just saved, saved me in turn. Too busy was I celebrating my success with a party, held exclusively within my head. When I lay panting on the cold steel again myself, a dreamlike sensation overtook my senses.

"Zack, what are you doing?" I snapped back to reality, Venn's flustered face hovering over me.

"Stopping you from becoming a human milkshake, you retard." I groaned, gingerly sitting up. "Never mind me, what were you playing at?" Sorrow filled his eyes as he considered his answer.

"I just... I can't take it anymore." He mumbled sulkily.

"Bullshit you can't. You said your old man's losing his mind or whatever, how was this ever gonna help? You'll send him over the edge."

"But I... I didn't know what to do. This felt like the only way out, you know?" Venn stared down at his feet, he wiped at his face with an already damp sleeve.

"Well, this isn't the answer. You can't just give up. You've gotta look out for him, and we'll be the ones to keep an eye on you." I said, cradling my ruined limb and nodding my head at Damian and Lexey. They were yelling for us to come down. "How the hell did you get up here anyway?" I asked him, with an eyebrow raised high.

"There's a fire escape on that side of the building. Why, didn't you use that?" He jerked his thumb in the one direction Damian and I *didn't* check.

"You've gotta be shitting me? You don't even wanna know how I got up." I mumbled, face dropping.

Venn smirked for a moment, then his expression returned to a stony personification of despair. He chewed nervously on his cheek. I became a tad more impatient when I noticed that the day was breathing its last. I was about to talk when he beat me to the punch.

"Look, it's not just my dad… and losing my mom. There's something else as well." He said in such a way that I feared his guts might literally spill out across the roof, and stain my shoes.

"Well… what is it?" I looked at him quizzically. Venn took a deep breath, as though he were about to plunge himself into icy water, and wasn't sure he'd ever be coming out again. There was naught but the rustling of the wind for a few incredibly drawn out moments.

"I'm gay." The words finally left his lips, words that he had kept inside for far too long. He locked eyes with me, awaiting judgement.

"Jesus, is that all?" I sighed overdramatically. "And here was me thinking it was gonna be something important."

"You mean you don't care?"

"Of course not, who would?" I glared at him moodily.

"I thought you guys might not, you know… be able to accept me or whatever. My mom… well my foster mom, she was the only one who knew and when she…" Venn mumbled, his face turning red. "I just felt alone and I...I guess it doesn't matter anymore." He smiled weakly.

"Venn, you were almost spread thin across the parking lot. I can't believe you didn't just say before, did this really seem like a better option to you?"

"I don't know." He sounded confused. "What with everything that's happened lately... I just felt... lost."

"Well consider yourself fucking found. Can we go now?" I pulled my hood as low as possible as the final rays of sun started to disappear, and the night began to take a stronger hold.

"Yeah, I guess... I'm kinda embarrassed though." Venn's lips twisted in distaste.

"Look, they aren't gonna care either, and we'll all forgive you for scaring the crap out of us. We just want you to come down off this roof." I pointed down at the other two, who were beckoning us with their hands. "I'm in a bad way, and I really have to get home before dark. But I'm not getting off of this thing until you do, so are you coming or not?" I asked him bluntly.

I felt the frosty wind on my face, as I awaited his answer. The temperature seemed to drop all at once, and the damp line on my cheek began to tingle. Then it dawned on me, that *this* was the longest conversation I had ever had with Venn. It took his near death experience to make it happen. I hoped that with his secret out in the open, he would in future, feel that he could leave his reclusive persona behind. We could help him through his grief after all. Finally, he gave a small smile and nodded. We got up, and slowly descended via the fire escape. Every metallic step on that thing sounded like mocking laughter to me.

From Shit to Worse

As I stalked my way home, keeping my ruined arm supported beneath the not so ruined one, I began to shiver. My breath hung in the air before me. I reminded myself that I would only have to deal with the pain for a single night. Then I could go to the Lycans, and they could make sure that I Phased somewhere else, and my shattered bone and bruised ankle would be right as rain. This was little comfort to me. I could almost feel the light of the low moon weighing down upon my shoulders. Thankfully I was covered from top to toes. I kept my head low down, so the burning beams couldn't reach my bare skin.

The wolf was restless. So close to the next full moon, the one-month anniversary of its inception, how could it not be? It too could feel the weight of the moon, lazily drifting in the early night sky. Feeling its hunger, I muttered to it to hang in there. One more day, and it could feed within the ranks of the pack. That was all I asked. My life is nothing, if not a series of unanswered requests.

I marched as fast as my battered foot would carry me. I hadn't yet even left the industrial estate where Venn had almost checked out of the life hotel early, when I heard a distant dispute. It was muffled and far off, so I told myself it wasn't my problem. My good deed for the day was done and frankly, it should have covered me for the whole year. Still, I couldn't shake the feeling that something about the voices was familiar. I stopped for just a second, ensuring that I didn't raise my head and allow the treacherous moonlight beneath my hood.

I tried to focus on the sound, but my developing ears were still uncooperative. They'd amplify any noise to jet engine levels when I wasn't expecting them to, but when I needed it, nothing. I did the unthinkable and roused the dog; its interest was peaked by the sounds too. Somehow it helped me to focus, our strange symbiotic relationship at work. Just for an instant, the stifled sound became clear.

"Get the hell away fr-" Lexey's voice. It came from somewhere to the east.

Then it returned to its inaudible state for a few seconds, and suddenly sparked back into life.

"-ust wanna talk." Aaron, I had heard him only a few times before, but I couldn't have mistaken him for anyone else.

Dread filled me completely, and consumed all emotion that was there before it. The Lycan bared teeth, growling in anticipation. I had a terrible decision to make. Do I leave Lexey to her fate, whatever that may be? Head home and go into hiding again, away from the moonlight. Or do I go to her aid and risk it all? If it came to blows, I'd be at a disadvantage. I mean, I had a broken arm for Christ's sake. With the Lycan's hunger already becoming an issue, I'd be taking a huge chance. 'Better to walk on and forget it' I told myself, which is why I was surprised when my feet began taking me straight in her direction.

■■

I managed to run, out of necessity, on my injured foot. I grimaced the whole way, and when I reached the source of the sounds, the two respective scents were strong. Dim light came from inside one of the warehouses, thrown from the high windows. I tried the door first, a huge metal thing that was locked tight. Even in good condition, I couldn't have got it open. Clattering metallic objects could be heard inside; Lexey was throwing stuff at him.

"I'm not letting you out until you fucking listen to me!" He yelled aggressively.

"Just stop, I want nothing to do with you. I should never have listened to you. Open the door and let me go!"

As quickly as I could, I scouted around the edge of the building. There was a rear shutter, equally as fortified as the front door. That was no good. My other option was a fire escape; thanks to Venn I was now aware of their existence. I began to clamber up it, hoping for an easy way in. The wolf was practically salivating, awaiting the conflict to come. I warned it that we were getting in there and getting her out, nothing more.

The windows I had seen from the ground were indeed small, too tiny for me to fit through. Even if I could have gotten in that way, there was a sheer drop to the ground below. I carried on up until I found myself on the rooftop. The same dull light poured from a skylight, spilling out into the black air. I shuffled my way over to it, trying to be as stealthy as I could manage. Reaching the edge, I looked down into what turned out to be a factory.

Beneath me lay several huge machines, with walkways between each of them. Through the central walkway, Lexey was backing up as Aaron relentlessly approached.

"Don't touch me!" She sneered.

"Just stop and talk to me you bitch." He demanded. She kept backpedalling, grabbing what she could and hurling it at him. "Fuck this!" He cried, and ran for her.

I didn't know what he was going to do when he caught up, and in all honesty, I didn't want to know. I couldn't stand by and watch. That ridiculous urge to do right was strong in me. So, I did the only thing I felt I could do in order to keep my conscience clear. I told myself I was sure to regret my actions, the being in my head concurred, and then I went ahead and acted anyway.

I drove my foot through the skylight, sending glass petals down into the factory. Then, against my better judgement, leapt through the gap. I was aiming for the top of a titanic machine, and landed gracefully upon it, like a cat made of cotton wool. Of course, I'm kidding. I did at least manage to get my feet onto the machine I was shooting for, only to glance off of the side of it and fall painfully for what felt like the thousandth time that day. I ended up in a bundle between a couple of work benches.

"Zack?!" Lexey yelled in surprise. Even Aaron had stopped and turned to see what the cause of all the commotion was.

"Yep." I groaned from the floor, doing a pretty good impression of a beanbag. "I'm everybody's hero today." I used one of the benches for support as I climbed to my feet, feeling utterly destroyed.

"What the fuck are you doing here?" Aaron snapped. I asked myself the very same question.

"Look, just let her go, and we'll forget this ever happened." I said reasonably, clutching my useless arm again.

"How did you even find me?" Lexey asked, but I just waved the question off.

"This has got nothing to do with you. I just want to talk to her." He grabbed a hammer from a tool bench next to him and pointed it at me threateningly. "So you better get out of here. Don't make me force you."

The wolf found his threats laughable. I could tell it was just hoping he would come for us, hoping that it would get its chance to unleash all hell on him.

"No, I've got this covered. Back down." I mumbled to it. Aaron gave me a confused look.

"Final warning." He stated. The wolf growled menacingly.

"She's coming with me." I told him. He gritted his teeth, furious.

"Okay, well you asked for it." Aaron said, spinning the hammer in his hand.

He took a single step forward before Lexey sprang from behind him, and smashed him over the back of the head with a rusty looking wrench. He tumbled to the floor, momentarily clutching the point of impact, and then spun unsteadily to face her.

"What are you doing you crazy bitch?!" Aaron boomed, as ruby droplets pooled, and began to form tiny rivers on his grasping fingers.

The wolf exploded. The scent of blood was overwhelming, and it cried out in my mind, craving flesh, chaos and brutality. I tried to control myself, but it was a part of me. I craved the blood too. 'No, we have to keep control!' I demanded, but the monster desired violence. It was ready to feed.

"NO!" I yelled, my protest leaking out into the real world.

"Zack, are you okay?" Lexey asked, fear in her eyes. She took a careful step backwards.

"No, we can't." I growled, grinding my human fangs together.

I had to stop it, however I could. I was fading to blackness again, and I knew if I let it win it would take complete control. Its thirst was too strong. It was driven mad by the moon, and as a result, so was I. I had to do something fast.

I leapt at Aaron, and drove him into the ground with inhuman strength. I felt no pain anymore, just the all-encompassing need to feast. I had to unleash the beast's fury without letting it take me. I swung a hammer like fist at Aaron's jaw, a nauseating crunch followed. The need only got worse, and rage grew within me. The tell-tale burning in my chest intensified. I rained down blows upon him, each one opening up a fresh wound on a visage that looked increasingly less human. In the distance I heard pleas to stop, shrieks of terror. The Lycan began at a snarl, and as I pummelled the unrecognisable mass beneath me, it built up to a terrifying roar. It, and I, cried out in unison.

Suddenly, the world became silent. As my clothes tore, making way for a body they could not contain, I felt the fiery moon upon my skin.

THE FINAL DAY

In the moment between sleeping and waking, there was the purest of peace. It was quickly shattered. When my eyes flew open, another pair stared lifelessly back at me. Lexey, or what was left of her. Her mouth was frozen, agape in horror. She lay with me in the shimmering pool of gore. Fragments of memories flashed into my consciousness, a flicker of claws, a mouth filled with flesh and blood. My mouth… their blood. Where the blonde girl's legs should have been, there lay a trailing mass of internal organs.

I began to wretch uncontrollably. Hurriedly, I hauled my weary body up off the ground. As I squatted on all fours, feeling the bile and body parts within me rising up, claret raindrops fell from my stained skin. The vomit came quickly. I felt like I was drowning, as I projected the foulest of substances into the space between my slickened hands. Pieces of what I saw were unmistakably human. I breathed heavily, taking in as much air as I could before the second onslaught came. My eyes watered as I was suffocated by the savage slime.

When it stopped once more, I waited, anticipating the next round, but it never happened. My naked body was two-tone, half an earthly pink, and half a darker shade of red. Face split down the middle in a startling divide. I gradually elevated myself to my feet, which slid uneasily beneath me. When I could finally survey the room, what I saw was a disturbing tableau.

The girl lay on one side, the half of her that still existed. What was left of Aaron, which is to say not much at all, was spread around the room. The destroyed machines had scattered their parts far and wide, seeming just as much the victims as the humans did. Nothing had avoided the carnage unleashed. In the middle of it all was I, stood at the centre of a crimson spotlight, the star of my own personal horror show.

My next breath caught in my throat, when the severity of what I had done suddenly hit me. She was dead. Lexey was dead. Panic struck. I bit down hard on my lip. The guilt was overwhelming, what was I supposed to do? I squeezed my hands into tight fists, trying to regain some sense of control. This just forced the congealing liquid to seep between my fingers, the silken sensation made my empty stomach turn. I looked down at the disgusting state of myself and realised that I was filthy.

I shuffled towards a water-cooler, trying to forget the terrible sight behind me. An unsettling patter accompanied every sodden step. Pulling the switch, a thin stream began to fall from the spout. I splashed myself with it, but it barely did a thing to remove the grotesque viscera. My efforts became more frantic, so desiring to be pure again. I doused myself more and more, and tried to wipe the stuff away, but it only served to smear it further. The sense of dread was escalating. I tore the canister from the dispenser and dumped its entire contents over myself. It drained all too quickly, and though much of what marked me was gone, I still felt death clinging to my skin.

"FUCK!" I cried out, hurling the empty plastic husk across the room. It made a loud boom as it struck the steel wall. My entire body shuddered, and I clung to the cooler as my legs buckled beneath me. My thoughts fluttered in every direction, but each path they took lead to another locked door, another dead end. I cried out, my wail echoing, reflected right back at me by the steel box I was trapped in. My outburst did nothing to alleviate. I squeezed my eyes tightly shut, still holding on for dear life. Breaths came quickly, and my eyes began to sting as uncertainty's cruel hands closed around my throat. I collapsed to my knees on the dusty ground.

For a minute, I didn't move. I became numb. Ragged breathing slowing to a steadier pace. I kept my eyes tightly closed, and focussed on the safe, predictable darkness. When I regained some semblance of control, legs still wavering, I stood once more. Looking up, past the grimy glow of the filthy old bulb that still buzzed and flickered high above, I could see the dim light of a new day. It finally dawned on me, I had to get out as quickly as possible. I became terrified of what might happen to me if I were to be caught. I'd be taken away, branded a psychotic killer. In prison it would be impossible to hide what I was for long, there would be nowhere to run, and no one to help a young werewolf like me.

Taking a deep breath, I plucked up the courage to take another glance around the putrid space. Seeing her twisted form again hit me hard, my throat seemed to close and my cheeks ached, as I fought the desire to break down there and then. I whimpered, and then finally remembered how to exhale.

Across the warehouse were a bunch of storage lockers. I had to find something to wear. I walked speedily across, trying to maintain some degree of composure, as the world seemed to crumble around me. Reaching the lockers, I tore the first one open.

Empty, aside from a few random bolts and a battered tin lunchbox. I broke into the second and third, neither one held anything of use. When I opened the fourth, a grubby blue boiler suit lay inside, carelessly balled up. I uncurled the musty material. It smelled strongly of oil and sweat, but it was the best I could hope for. I unzipped the front and climbed in, the coarse fabric rubbed uncomfortably against my bare flesh, but I was thankful to be covered at all.

I could hear the engines of passing vehicles. I had to move. The businesses on the estate would soon begin their operations. The gargantuan machines would awaken once again. I couldn't be there when the sorry bastard who had the job of opening up that morning came to work, and stumbled upon the mess I had made of it all. I strode for the shutter, it was held down by huge and heavy chains. I removed the thick steel pins holding them in place, and began to pull the shutter upwards. Then, I realised I was leaving something behind.

I dashed back over to the brutal display at the centre of the room, and scanned it rapidly. I tried not to take in any of the details, I was looking for only one. The black box that was my phone lay face up in the slurry. I took one step into the ooze, and pulled it out. Matter stuck fast, and tore away with a sickly sound. I wiped it on the sleeve of the boiler suit, then made back for the shutter. Tugging hard on the chains, the door began to rise. I pulled hand over hand, until enough of the piercing light of day broke through the space I had created. I fixed the chain in its new position, crouched low, and was bathed in the sun's warming glow.

On bare feet, in my ill-fitting outfit, I headed for home, soles increasingly sore with each rough stride. I closed off, mentally distancing myself from what had happened, and from the world around me. It was as though the few people I saw as I made my way home somehow knew. They knew that I had done some terrible wrong, and stared at me judgementally as I passed them by. Their accusatory glances stung almost as much as the light of that terrible moon.

Finally, I looked upon my familiar front door. I shifted the potted plant that so cleverly concealed the emergency key. Letting myself inside, I took ghostly, silent steps up the staircase. Nothing in the house stirred. I reached the doorway to my bedroom, my ever-present sanctuary. Still drifting like a phantom, I made my way to the bed. Then, I dropped like a stone. Grabbing the pillow and pressing it close to my face, I howled in exquisite anguish. Images flashed rapidly through my mind, the only memories that remained of my terrible deed. When they stopped, I convulsed violently as my body was overcome with the deepest of sorrow, and the most potent sensation of dread. The moisture of the tears against my cheeks was far too reminiscent of blood.

■■■

The phone vibrated against my chest, where it was uncomfortably lodged in the pocket of the boiler suit. I hadn't moved, I knew not for how long. I took it out and the name on the screen said 'Damian'. I wasn't much in the mood for talking, so I let it ring out. It stopped suddenly, only to burst immediately back into life. I was too busy sulking. I just wanted to lay in the dark, and wait to starve to death. Don't feel too sorry for me just yet though, boys and girls. The day was still young, the world had not yet begun to truly fuck me over.

When the phone rattled frantically for the third time, I decided to get the unwanted conversation over with, rather than delay the seemingly inevitable.

"What?" I said sullenly, after I hit the answer call button.

"Have you seen the news, what the fuck happened?"

"The news?" I murmured, a fresh sense of unease piling on top of the trepidation that was already there.

"Channel three. Look. Like, now." He ordered. I shuffled around through fallen clothes to retrieve the buried TV remote. I turned the box on and switched to the channel, only to be greeted with a blurry CCTV image of my own weary face.

"-for questioning about this horrific incident. He was spotted on the security camera at the rear-loading bay of the warehouse. The building's skylight was shattered but, due to its height, this is not thought to be the way those involved gained entry. It is suspected that the second victim, who is as of now unidentified, worked in the unit that was the backdrop for this vicious slaughter."

"Oh shit. God, I'm fucked. I never meant for it to happen!" I babbled near incomprehensibly.

"What, what happened?" Damian's voice filled with concern, his tone expectant of bad news.

"I heard them arguing, and I went to help her, and now they're both dead." I rambled, words flying into the receiver in quick succession.

"Jeez, calm down, and just try to speak clearly. Who's dead?" He asked uneasily.

"Aaron and Lexey." The other end of the line remained silent for a while, as I tried to keep my breathing controlled.

"You killed Lexey?" The voice finally returned.

"I didn't mean to! I went to help her because Aaron was there, but it all went fucking wrong. She hit him, and the blood set it off! It set the wolf off... you've gotta believe me, I didn't mean to." I poured my tiny heart out, as I sank deeper into anxiety. The line fell silent again.

"I do believe you." Damian finally spoke. "Look, I don't know how long this story has been running, but your damn face is on the TV. Someone's head's gonna roll because that shit's on air before they even had the chance to send the police to your door, but that might just be your saving grace. You can't let the cops come to get you. If that happens, then you'll really be fucked."

"So what do I do?" I was on the verge of a panic attack.

"You have to go to them, go to the Lycans. They're the only ones who can help you now."

"Shit. Goddamn it, you're right." I wheezed. "Thanks Damian, seriously thanks for not just... just leaving me alone on this, you know?"

"You know I'd never do that to you, asshole." He gave a short, humourless laugh, like he wasn't sure he was making a play for the right side. Suddenly there was a loud knock at the front door.

"Oh God, that could be them." I panicked.

"Alright, you've gotta go. Head straight for your wolf friends, and make sure you ditch the phone." He instructed hurriedly.

"Okay." I squeaked. It occurred to me then, that I might never see or speak to Damian again. Not after what I had done. Things would never be the same. "Thanks for everything man." I said, and hung up.

I listened hard as I stripped the blue boiler suit off, and began throwing on whatever I could find on the ground. My mom answered, and seeing who it was, she sounded concerned.

"What's all this about?" She asked. Obviously she hadn't seen the news yet.

"Miss Archer, we're here to speak with your son Zachary regarding a crime that took place sometime last night." The formal voice explained.

So that was it. They were there to take me away from everything, and everyone I ever knew. I tugged a stale smelling shirt down over my head, and grabbed another hooded sweater. I knew I would need it if I had to be outside after dark. A memory of the aftermath I awoke in sprang to mind, and I prayed that it wouldn't come to that.

"Zack, could you come down here for a second?" Mom yelled up the stairs, the worry sent a quiver though her.

"Yeah, I'll be down in a sec." I called back, trying to sound as innocent as possible.

I squeezed my grubby feet into an old pair of training shoes that were a little too small for me. They turned my toes into uncomfortable bundles, but I had no other options to choose from. I slid open my bedroom window, planning to jump. Then, I hesitated. Realising what I thought about Damian also applied to my mother, the woman who brought me life, I couldn't just disappear without a word. I snatched a scrap of paper from a pile of other useless shit, and grabbed an almost entirely blunt pencil from my bedside table.

"Mind if we just head straight up there?" I heard a cop ask, but his feet were already hitting the steps.

Rapidly I scrawled a message. 'I'm sorry Mom, I never meant for this. Please forgive me. I love you.' I dropped the pencil on the table, and gracelessly climbed on to the windowsill. Leaping out, I met the ground with a thud, and sprang immediately into a run. Clambering over the garden fence, I sped up even further as I hit open terrain. I pulled the phone from my pocket and hit call.

"Matthew," I talked when he answered. "I fucked up. I fucked up bad. I'm coming to you guys now, please, I need you to hide me." I panted.

Ending the call, I snapped the phone in half and cast the broken pieces aside. I set my sights on the treeline, as the home I once knew grew distant and small behind me.

LAST RESORT

I arrived at Locke's enormous house panting
uncontrollably, and hoping that the grand old place would be my
safe haven. My reprieve from the chaotic maelstrom my world
had become. I strode quickly across the gravel drive towards the
huge wooden door, and slammed the wolf's paw knocker
repeatedly. My heart pounded in my chest, I could hear nothing
but the colossal roar of the swirling winds. Dark clouds diffused
the daylight, muting all colours to a uniform shade of grey. The
door opened.

"Get inside." Matthew snapped, and pulled me over the
threshold. "Did anybody see you?" He asked glaring.

"No, I stayed within the treeline." I wheezed.

"What the hell happened last night?" He barked. It was the
most animated I had ever seen him.

"I got caught out after dark, and I tried to help someone.
Then the blood… and I just couldn't stop it." I rambled. Matthew
looked me up and down with a furious scowl. "I killed two
people…" I finally stated.

"I told you not to be out after dark." He snapped.

"I couldn't help it! My friend was in a bad way, I had to go
to him, then this girl got attacked and I couldn't just leave her!"

"And exactly how much good did you do by rushing to their
aid?" Matthew glared at me.

No good. No good at all. I had taken two lives, one of which I felt was actually a loss. However, it was still too high a cost for my actions. I gritted my teeth, and tried not to sulk.

"Look, I made a mistake. Now I need your help. I'm sorry alright?" I yammered, choking up. "I can't change what I did now, but I'm screwed without you guys. I've got nowhere else to turn."

Matthew sighed, and scratched uneasily at his shirt-covered shoulder. He beckoned for me to follow. We paced beneath the archway under the stairs, straight into the dining room. Locke awaited, sat at the head of the table with a dark look in his eyes. He placed his hand on the sturdy surface. It creaked loudly beneath his weight as he raised himself to his feet. He began striding menacingly towards me.

"Locke. I'm sorry I've caused so-" He grabbed me by the front of my clothes, opened the door on my left side, and threw me down a set of winding stairs.

I tumbled dangerously, bouncing off of each stone step. I curled into a pathetic ball as I fell, then came to a sudden stop on the dusty floor of the wine cellar. Breathing in the soot, I choked and spluttered as the ashen substance irritated my throat. Plodding steps grew louder behind me. Before I could stand, he was on me again. Locke grabbed me by the hood, closing off my airway in the process. The huge silver haired monster then towed me across the room, and slung my tiny frame haphazardly into a space that was very familiar. I remembered the bars well.

"You stay here, until we figure out what our best course of action is." Matthew said, arms folded, stood at the mouth of the staircase.

Locke proceeded to snap the giant padlock into place, sealing me once again inside the cellar cage. A sense of déjà vu swept over me.

"But wait, why are you putting me in here, it's not like I've got anywhere else to go? I came to you for help, why are you locking me up?" I babbled in confusion.

"The full moon is almost upon us, you're unpredictable right now. This is the safest place for you, Zack." Matthew told me.

He and Locke made their way back up the staircase, and I heard the door slam shut. The sickly yellow light from my first day as a Lycan embraced me like an old friend. I shuffled my way to the corner and sat with my back against the cold bars, staring at the ceiling in the spaces between them. I was trapped, with or without the cage. What was I to do? Would I be kept in hiding forever, would I head to somewhere new where no one would know of what I had done, or would my story end in that very basement? Body softening into a defeatist mass, I lay unmoving, and feeling incredibly sorry for myself.

In the deepest recesses of my mind, the wolf began to wake again. It had tasted the blood it so desired, and satiated its hunger for a single night. How could that ever be enough for a growing pup? To the Lycan, that was a mere appetizer, a small bonus before the real feast began. I guess I can't blame it, it's just in the dog's nature. It was the night of the full moon, after all.

■■■

I focussed on the sound of heavy raindrops coming from outside. Water found its way in through odd little nooks, and had started to pool in random spots around the cellar. Timid, shuffling steps came from the stairway I had so gracefully descended before. I knew not how long I'd been moping in the low light, when Bethany peeked her blue head around the stone archway.

"Beth, what are yo-" She shushed me aggressively, and tiptoed her way over to the cage.

"Don't talk you dumb ass, do you think I'm *supposed* to be down here?" She rasped. I closed my noise hole. "They announced who you killed a little while ago. A young girl, you realise people are gonna call for your head now right?" the fourteen year old spoke in the manner of a grownup.

"Yeah I know. They're right to..." I muttered, gazing at the floor, fresh guilt rising in my throat.

"Well I'm glad you think so, because they're talking about offing you up there right now." Beth whispered harshly, flicking her eyes up to the ceiling.

"What, who is?"

"All of them. Lewis, the teacher guy, is the only one fighting your case." She placed a hand on the lock, and tugged on it as quietly as possible.

"What about Matthew?" I asked. Surely he would be on my side. I was his great hope for taking out Locke, or so I thought.

"He says you're too much of a risk to keep around now," She shrugged. "thinks you'll bring trouble. Says he can't think of a way we can get you out of this."

I felt betrayed. The one person in the group I had thought I could rely on, and he was just as willing as the rest to throw my lifeless body in a ditch somewhere, or worse. To him it was all for the good of the pack, I wondered how much good would be done if Locke knew what Matthew had been plotting. Still, I recognised he kind of had a point. The cops would be after me. Anyone who knew what I had done would be baying for blood. I couldn't even go willingly and face the consequences for murder, eventually what I was would be revealed, and that was not an option. I had never felt so alone, and so hopeless.

"Bullshit. The reason I risked my ass coming down here is because you don't deserve this. You didn't ask to be what you are, and they just sent you out into the world and told you to keep it a secret. I mean, what the fuck did they expect to happen? Locke goes all rogue, and starts messing with you. *Experimenting*, that's what it was."

"Experimenting?"

"Yeah, because you became Lycan young, just like him." She explained, moving closer to the bars.

'Just like him'. Locke and I had more in common than I first realised. I was an accident, and I had become nothing more than his plaything. I began to wonder if I was ever considered a part of their so-called pack. Was I just a freak to them, kept alive first by Matthew's guilt, and then by Locke's fascination? I stood and crossed the cage, coming face to face with Beth.

"How do you know he's the same?" I asked her thoughtfully.

"The old bitch let slip once, she's the only one who's been around long enough to know that. The others don't have a clue." She smirked, a little smug that she was privy to this information. "Don't get me wrong though, he's not the same. Apparently young wolves are always unpredictable. You'll be weird in your own special way."

"Okay, great." I mumbled miserably. "So, what do I do now?"

"Hell if I know, I just think it sucks ass that they're talking behind your back about taking you out. After they caught me listening in, they won't even let me back up on the second floor."

"So I'm fucked anyway, now I just know it's coming?"

"Yeah I guess. If I could get the key, I would. But Locke has it, and they wont let me get anywhere near them." She breathed heavily in disappointment.

"And if he caught you, he'd take your head off." I reminded her.

"Pfft, nah. Locke won't hurt me." Her lips curled into a devilish smile. I looked at her, perplexed. "He has to keep a promise he made a long time ago." Beth explained with a flash of white teeth.

"There's really no way you can help me get out of here?" I asked, resigning myself to a grisly fate.

"Nope, sorry. If you do get out though, it's raining right now. Just saying." She gave a quick wink. "Good luck to you, Zack. If it's any consolation, I feel a little better about them not letting me become a werewolf now. So, you know, there's that."

"Yeah… glad I could be of service." I collapsed to the ground, morose. Bethany ran fingers through her deep blue hair, gave a feminine wave, and quietly disappeared up the stairs.

I knew I was going to die, and I was almost convinced that it was right to be that way. I teetered between selfish self-preservation, and facing the fate a part of me felt I deserved. The wolf had different ideas. It silently demanded that I search for a way out. There was no way for it, or I, to defend ourselves within the confines of the cage. Locke could shoot me through the bars. There was no one around for miles, so who would ever hear? If the wolf took over, it could only thrash uselessly against the formidable cage, one that was built for the very purpose of keeping a ravenous Lycan contained. Even it understood that to try to snatch control would be fruitless.

I lay on my back and spread out, as though I were creating an apathy-ridden snow angel. It was hopeless. I would disappear from the face of the earth. Never to be seen again. Forevermore I'd be branded as a crazed teen killer. The media would talk at length about how I once saw a movie with a gun in it, or how I was obsessed with violent video games. They'd ask what mistakes the parents made, if my absent father was the final nail in the coffin and how, just how could this continue to happen? They'd chat about how the world is going to the dogs and something *must* be done. All of it covered in a ten-minute segment before breakfast.

Of course you'll all be thinking now, cut to the chase. We know you made it out of there, you're telling this story. You aren't buried in some ditch, so how did you get out? Well you're right. At least I think you're right. Who knows, maybe by now I am in a ditch. However on this occasion, I was struck with a bolt of inspiration. Staring at the gross yellow light, and those bars all stood in sequence, I was reminded of a detail I had noticed the first time I was locked in that place and looking for an escape. The bars at the top were big enough for me to fit through. Sure, they were pressed against the ceiling, but if there just so happened to be a hole in said ceiling, there's no reason my slight human body shouldn't be able to pass through. They designed the cage to keep a Lycan contained, not a boy. This flaw, this overlooked detail, would be my salvation.

I jumped up high, and pressed against the wood experimentally. It was very sturdy, sure, but so was Damian's garden wall. For a moment I considered the possibilities, whether I could actually escape, and if I even deserved to. The thing that swayed me was Matthew, and his treachery. He would drag me into his world through his own negligence, and then push the idea that I should be disposed of, all whilst trying to betray the Alpha. No, if the Lycans were against me, I wouldn't give them the satisfaction. Maybe I didn't deserve to live, but if so, neither did they. Matthew and Locke had created the monster, I just had to share a mind with it. Why should I be held responsible when I was just trying to do the right thing?

I resolved to try to stay alive, for at least long enough to deny them the gratification of cleaning up the mess they saw me as. That was if I even had the strength to escape. I'd have to be fast, after the first hit to the heavy boards separating me from freedom, they would hear it. I had to be out and running before they reached me. I took a deep breath, and grabbed two of the bars above. Turning myself upside down I braced one foot against the ceiling, and prepared the other to strike. If I tried it, there would be no going back. Either I made it through, or they'd catch me in the act and kill me on the spot. My resolve outweighed my fear.

I stomped down as hard as I could. There was a loud crack as the wood gave a little. I had passed the point of no return. I kicked it again, this time it flexed and began to splinter. They would be getting up from their little round table by now, wondering what all the fuss was about. I hit it a third time, and a fourth. They'd be realising something was wrong, speeding up their approach. The Lycan demanded freedom. With a final powerful kick, the wood gave way, and a dining chair above was sent soaring. I dropped to the ground briefly, only to leap back up and grab the splintered ledge I had created. As efficiently as I could, I swept myself up through the hole and sprinted for the back door, barging my way straight through it.

I bolted out through the harsh rain, grass slick beneath my feet, and dove into the woodland as quickly as I could. Weaving between trees, I turned my sights back towards the town. Knowing the rain would wash away my scent, they could try to give chase but all I had to do was be faster. I dropped my head, and ran harder than I had ever run before. In the distance, a furious cry rang out. I bid the big white wolf a silent farewell.

MOONRISE

The moon hung high in the air, its oppressive weight bearing down on me. I kept my hood low, and my hands tucked into my sleeves. This time however, it wasn't just the moonlight I was hiding from. A security camera swayed robotically back and forth. As it turned in my direction, I shied away from its mechanical stare.

Rain beat down heavily on the roof of the train station's platform. I had no money, nowhere to go, and no choice but to leave. It was the very same spot Locke and I had lured Damian's father from. We brought him out of the shelter, and into our realm of beasts. The one seemingly selfless act I have ever known him to commit, rushing to help someone in need, just so happened to be what got him killed. I think that really says something about the world we live in.

I sniffed and snivelled, holding back the tears that threatened to burst forth. I would have felt incredibly isolated, if it weren't for the monster in my head that stirred impatiently. The magnetic force of moonbeams made it all too active in my mind.

"We need to escape." I muttered to it. I buried its urges in the darkest corners of my subconscious.

The closest thing I had to a plan was to get on the train and get as far away as I could from town before getting kicked off. That, and hope not to be recognised. Sure, it's not exactly a flawless strategy, but I had to put as much distance as I could between myself, and those who searched for me. Once I was somewhere else, somewhere far enough away, I could find a place to hide. It was my only option.

My empty stomach growled, and I grew impatient. I was starving, but the very thought of eating made me want to puke again. I tightened the grip my arms had around me, doing my best to fight off the bitter cold. For a second, I feared the heavy raindrops might become crystalline in the icy air, forming deadly, piercing shards. All I wanted more than anything else was to be enclosed. To escape the spiteful weather, and to be far away where I could do no more harm.

There was a trundling in the distance, and bright lights approached. The train was slowing, preparing to come to a halt, to carry me off into an uncertain future. A future where I knew nothing would ever be the same again. It was a rickety old two-carriage thing, nothing sleek or impressive. I just hoped it was warm. The doors slid open, and my heart began to race. Could it really be as simple as all that, just boarding and leaving without any resistance? I wished for the best as I clambered on-board.

Sadly there was no heater, but it was a relief to be out of those biting winds. Each seat was worn; exposed foam and unrecognisable stains marred every single one. I grabbed one that was rear-facing, dropping like a rock into its uncomfortable grasp. The whole carriage stunk of smoke and stagnant urine. I peeked up, surveying the people around me, praying to God none of them had been paying attention to the news.

There was a group of six noisy teens, speaking in an accent I didn't recognise. They must have been from the city. Then, there was a gentle looking couple. The man slept heavily on the lady's shoulder. She was awake, but distant, possessing a look of contentment that I envied greatly. The woman toyed with the gold pendant around her neck. Finally, there was a homeless man, he was the closest to me. He wore a battered old jacket and had a few plastic bags, full of who knows what. He was dozing, I'm sure thankful to be sheltered from the elements.

The train pulled away. Through the window, I watched the platform disappear. I glanced again at the couple and the homeless guy, and one of those two pictures seemed far more likely to be in my future. The noise of the youths, loudly engaged in conversation seemed to meld together with the rumble of the train. It all became one indistinct hum, as the countryside flew by.

I tried not to think back, keeping my mind on what lay ahead. I wracked my brain, attempting to come up with some long-term course of action. I got nothing. Right then, the trundling locomotive was my refuge. That was all I needed in the moment. I made a conscious effort to keep my head down, I couldn't afford to be seen, or caught in the light. I stared at my ill-fitting shoes as I bounced along the tracks.

A grunt sprang from the homeless man. I was so strung out it made me flinch. Glancing up, I saw that the old timer was just stirring in his sleep. My galloping heart eased momentarily, and then leapt back to racing speed as I caught the eye of one of the teenage group. We looked right at each other, a fraction of a second that seemed to stretch. My eyes shot back to the ground, and I began mumbling to myself.

"He didn't recognise me. No one has noticed. No one even knows. He didn't recognise me. He can't have." I babbled. I thought I could feel eyes upon me.

Cautiously, I peered up. This time they were all staring. I ducked once more, hoping they were just trying to be intimidating. I would gladly let them believe it had worked, shrink back into my shell like a startled tortoise, and remain there until they decided to move on to prey more willing than I. Their obnoxious conversation had turned into a hushed and private affair. Nerves took a hold, and I began to shudder. I folded my arms in my lap, and buried my head, praying that the darkness would swallow me whole.

The next time I peeked, they were filing their way between the seats towards me. My head spun toward the window, watching skeletal trees flash by from beneath my hood. I didn't dare look in their direction again. I tried to act relaxed, bored even, but I'm sure the tension in my body was obvious. Suddenly, we shot into a tunnel. The train's low rumble became a deafening roar. Each of their gawking faces were reflected in the blackness, and my own features were just as plain to them in the filthy glass.

"I'm telling you, that's him." One of them said in that unfamiliar way. I was caught. One of them grabbed me by the shoulder, and twisted me around with a heavy hand.

"Holy shit." Another spoke, the glare of his phone's screen lighting up his face. "It is. The internet's been blowing up about this kid all day. He's linked to those murders last night!"

A third, wearing a flat peak under his hood, eyed the phone sceptically. He examined the image that the news sites and TV stations had been spreading since morning. Glancing up at me, he analysed my features, comparing it to the picture.

"It really is him." He muttered. "You killed that girl."

"No. I have no idea what you're talking about." I squeaked nervously. He stared again, his eyes hidden in the shadow beneath the peak of his hat.

"You did, you murdered her in cold blood. Messed her up so bad they wont even say what you did." He snarled, grabbing the front of my clothes and pulling me to the edge of my seat.

"I didn't!" I blurted. "It wasn't me, I swear!"

"Then why're you running, Zack?" A heavyset member of their group asked, his eyes bulging.

"You don't seem like such a badass now. Guess you're only a big man around girls?" The one in the cap seemed to be their leader. "You know, people fucking hate us, but we just do what we've gotta do. You… you're something else." He pulled a shining object from his pocket. With a sudden click, a blade shot into view.

"Mess him up, Loz. We'll be goddamn heroes." The fat one spoke to his superior, but never broke eye contact with me.

"Jesus, what are you guys doing, I didn't do anything?!" I protested.

Loz raised the knife, pointing its tip at my throat. I gazed open-mouthed, not daring to move. He raised his chin to the sky, and for the first time I saw his eyes. They radiated uncertainty. I felt then that I had a chance. I could talk my way out of it. He wasn't a violent thug, he was putting on a front, just like all the rest. The blade in his hand made him anxious.

"Admit it. Admit what you did." Loz demanded, his grip tightening.

The Lycan gave a ghostly smirk. I looked at the knife, and the dog's influence told me that I should snatch it away. Then, bury it in the kid's throat. I refused, there had to be a better way. I'd keep them talking until the train's next stop, shove them all of out of the way, and make a run for it. I could be on a different train headed somewhere else before they had a chance to report me. Even as the plan formed, the temptation to turn the blade on its owner was strong.

"Okay." I sniffled, gulping. "I did it, but I didn't mean to. Let me explain." I would spin some bullshit. Keep them occupied until I had a chance to make a break for it.

"Explain what?" The scrawniest among them yelled, he stood next to the homeless man, who stirred at the sound. "There aint no reason for that, killing a young girl. We should fuckin' waste you right here."

The others jeered, and told the one with the weapon he ought to use it. My eyes focussed on the knife in his hand as they all barked orders at him. 'Fuckin kill him man he deserves it' and 'Bitch doesn't deserve to live' pretty much sums up the message they were trying to get across.

"Hey, leave him alone!" The woman with her partner saw what was going on, and yelled at the gang.

"Shut the fuck up, lady." Loz stated coldly. His hands were shaking.

"Come on Loz. Don't be a pussy, fuckin' stick him." The round one ordered, shoving Loz with a doughy hand. The knife swayed dangerously close. The others all continued to goad him.

"Look, I know I fucked up." I raised my hands in submission "I'll hand myself in. When we get to the next stop, I'll get off and give myself up." I lied. Loz's eyes darted uncertainly, as he was jostled and harassed by his peers.

"Do it, stab him!" the skinny one bawled. We left the tunnel and its seemingly endless darkness. A flash of moonlight caught the back of my hand, and the wolf gave me a sharp reminder of its hunger. I winced in pain but maintained control, dropping my arms into my lap, shielding the bare skin. The train was back out in the wilderness, carving its way through the landscape.

"Come on, you don't want to do this and you kno-" Cold steel pierced my chest.

The woman shrieked. The gang erupted into an animalistic frenzy. That same shaking hand pulled the knife free, and plunged it into my flesh a second time. I croaked as fluid began to fill my pierced lung. The Lycan roared within me, and demanded freedom. A third knife strike opened up a fresh wound. Warm liquid ran down my chest, and over my ever-present scars. My attacker sidestepped as I collapsed forward, and fell gracelessly between the seats.

A furious battle began in my mind. The wolf wanted revenge. It wanted to save its host, to save me. As I lay dying, I began to think that perhaps it was for the best. To bleed out right there, to have my life cut short by someone else's hand. It would be a very similar fate to the one I had forced upon Lexey. I could pass on into the great beyond, be tarnished forever, and considered a murderer. That is what I am after all. It's an ending befitting a monster like me. As feet began to stomp down on my wounded body from all angles though, a very human weakness took hold.

The stench of blood, my own blood, filled my nostrils. Then the desire to feed returned in full force. I tried to fight it. I knew I was about to die, to breathe my last at any second. Real fear washed over me, and the instinct to stay alive began to grip more tightly. 'I can save us' the wolf spoke in mute whispers. It was attempting to snatch my body away, to change me into a beast, so that we would live to see another day. A powerful terror began to bury me, the horror of the unknown, the mystery of death.

"Okay…" I blurted, speaking out loud to the voice in my head. Guilt clung like tar, as I reluctantly accepted the monster's offer.

The feet gradually stopped, as the woman's incessant pleas finally hit their mark. The teens strode away, heading back to their seats like nothing had even happened. The lady dashed to my aid, her man sitting uselessly, unsure of what to do.

"Oh my God, you're bleeding. We need to get you help." She spoke in high and beautiful tones. We wouldn't be bleeding for long.

We hauled ourselves to our feet, pain rocked us but we didn't care. The wolf and I shared a gleaming smile. His was pearly white, mine was stained with blood. The youths turned to face us, we were sure they weren't expecting a second act in their little show. We took a staggering step forward, and our leaking body was pure agony. We caught onto a seat to stop ourselves from falling. The demon within desired nothing more than to bathe in the moonlight, for us to finally, truly embrace what we are.

"What the fuck…" Loz whispered, horrified. We turned to the lady as we gasped for air, drowning from the inside. I snatched back control for long enough to speak a single word.

"Run." I said weakly, eyes beginning to water.

Then, in a truly selfish act, we tugged the hoodie from over our head, and felt the searing heat of the moonlight on our flesh. The wolf erupted in delight, and snarled in fury. Of course, they didn't hear that. All they saw was little old me, as we cocked our head in canine fascination. We were deciding which one we were going to disembowel first. There was a poignant sense of déjà vu. The dog had me, and with a devilish smirk, that was it. I descended into darkness, but in that final moment before I was gone, I remember its piercing howl as it tore through the night.

Rebirth

Awaking amongst broken body parts should never become a familiarity. That was my reality though, as I regained my faculties once the slaughter was done. I lay upon shattered glass, and when I opened my eyes, there was destruction in every direction. It seemed as though nothing had escaped my self-centred wrath. I began to wretch – I still hadn't gotten a taste for raw flesh. Immediately I spewed a vile sludge that pooled amongst the human remains. I had to go, I couldn't look upon what I had done for any longer. I took all those lives just to save myself. To see the remnants of the massacre laid out before me was too much. What had I done? Flashes of the spree came back, a truly disturbing display.

I raised my naked body from the slime, and felt like I would never be clean again. I whimpered, knowing full well the severity of my actions. Even Lexey paled in comparison to this. Hurriedly, I searched amongst the carnage. It was a bizarre sight. Seats jutted out from the walls, and I walked on broken windows. The row of ceiling lights to my left were mostly shattered, but a couple still clung to life, flickering feebly. The frosty breeze chilled me to the bone, and I resorted to the unthinkable. I began to strip clothes from some of what remained of the teens. I grimaced as I peeled the cloth free from their sticky corpses, cobbling together anything that would fit me.

Finally, I threw on my own hoodie. It was slick and sticky. As it fell down, lying heavily on my body, I felt disgust with myself the likes of which I had never before experienced. The desire to survive pushed me onward. I walked in shoes that were not mine to the rear of the train, keeping my eyes up high to avoid looking upon the bodies at my feet. My stomach burbled, and I felt yet more vomit on its way. Quickly, I busted open the emergency door, and clambered my way out into the early morning air.

Then I collapsed to my knees on the tracks, and heaved up more of the disgusting slurry. This time though, a glimmer of gold caught my eye. The woman's pendant lay amongst it all, a shining symbol of my self-serving act. I had to go, to run and never look back. My airways seemed to close, as I was overcome with grief and regret. I stood wearily, aching from my transformation, and began to run. Feeling light headed I collapsed, but quickly got back to my feet.

Turning, I saw the train. Its front-end lay off of the tracks, its wheels buried in the dirt. The rear was on its side, a ruined mess. Small pieces of organic matter had been thrown from the wreckage and were scattered in the earth. I promised myself that that would be the last time I would look upon the mess I had created. I would do all I could to bury the memories of that night deep within the recesses of my mind. I was too afraid to die, to do the right thing and destroy myself, but I knew I could no longer be amongst other human beings. I was too dangerous for that. My gaze turned towards the treeline.

I burst into a sprint, unsteadily at first, but I gained my footing. I dashed into the forest, a vast wilderness in which I could hide forever. Weaving through the trees, I made my way ever deeper into the dense vegetation, with the desire to be as far from other people as I could possibly get. The intention was to exile myself, so that I could no longer be an unpredictable and devastating force. I ran until my lungs burned, and then continued on. My eyes stung as the freezing air rushed past me. I'm uncertain of how long I had been running, but eventually, I could go no further. I staggered, considering every footstep another small progression towards my goal of separating myself from the rest of humanity, until finally I fell face down in the dirt.

Tears surged free. I wept as I allowed all my emotions to spill out. The shame and the regret washed all else that was me away, leaving nothing but a husk of a human being. Even subhuman was too kind a label for me. I fought for air as I sobbed, and wept loudly, knowing full well that no one could hear me. There would be no one to judge, and by extension, no one to hurt, no one else to kill. The first flakes of snow began to fall as I lay with my head on the jagged and frosty soil. My eyes were squeezed shut. I didn't have it in me to move.

Something cold and wet nudged at my cheek. I peered up blearily. A wolf, speckled grey and white, loomed over me. Startled, I shot up on to my hands and knees. It stepped back, keeping one paw raised. Its intelligence was evident from its curious stare. Looking around me I realised, I was surrounded by an entire pack. My eyes widened with fear as the wolf approached again. Before I could move, it licked at my cheek. Blood, the blood of too many people, stained its tongue. It nudged me with its wet nose again, turning the white fur on its face, crimson.

I couldn't comprehend in the beginning. Why hadn't the feral creatures torn me limb from limb? As the snow began to settle around me, it all became clearer. The lead wolf turned its head towards the sky, and let out a colossal howl. I felt the creature's call resonate within me, and understood the connection I had with it. The others that encircled me, all joined the call in turn, and finally I understood.

So, how do you think this ends, do you think I get torn apart by wolves in a show of karmic justice? That I live out my days amongst the animals in peace, leaving my humanity behind? No, my dearest companions, the story just told is one of my origins. How I became something more than a mere human being. How I tried to cope with what I was turned into, and how ultimately, I failed. It is the tale of a sixteen-year-old boy, thrown into a world he didn't understand, the tale of a kid who lost everything. This story is far from over though. You've heard about my transformation, and my fall from mundane teenage grace.

Settle in though my friends, because now, I'll tell you how I changed the fucking world.

A Note from the Author

Congratulations dear reader, on making it to the end of my first novel, Stray. Writing this thing was a lengthy and taxing process, and I'm happy to finally share it with the world. Feedback from readers, and building a close community is very important to me as an independent writer. As such, here are a few ways to contact me, and a link to a page where you can become more involved in all the things I do. I hope to see you there.

luxnoctistales.com
facebook.com/NoctisNeverSleeps
noctisneversleeps.tumblr.com
Twitter : @TheLuxNoctis

As a small bonus for anyone interested in Horror, the following is one of my original short horror stories. Part of an on-going series, these tales are available on my website, and on my Tumblr blog. They will always be available for free, to anyone who wishes to read them.

Kindest regards,

Lux Noctis

WITHIN THE WALLS

Alastair stared intently at the oil painted crow. It hung from the wall in its dusty, olive frame. The bird's likeness had been rendered so perfectly, its feathers seemed to capture light from an unseen source beyond the scope of the image. Its beady eye stared back at him. So lifelike was its approximation that, for a second, he could have sworn he saw it move. A sudden loud ring broke the bird's hold over him. It was the bell on the counter. The two guests stood in front of it came into focus.

"Aren't you forgetting something?" A portly woman asked him. Her dangerously slender husband with a grey, pencil moustache stood meekly at her side. Alistair gaped blankly, seemingly unable to grasp the meaning of the words.

"Our room key." The lady smiled in a good-natured manner. Her American accent softened each element in her sentence, every syllable flowing smoothly into the next.

"Oh, of course!" Alistair replied, the gears in his mind finally beginning to turn. His Scottish twang contrasted starkly with his customers sweeping sounds.

He tugged open a dark oak drawer, and began rummaging through sets of keys. A hand fell upon the key to room seven.

"I've decided to upgrade you to our finest room Mr and Mrs Cooke. At no extra charge, of course." Alistair's soft, weather-beaten face stretched into a smile. Mr Cooke flinched as his wife squeaked gleefully.

"Well that's just wonderful, I can't wait to go check it out." Mrs Cooke snatched the keys from the Scotsman's doughy palm.

"Come on George." She said, jabbing her husband in the ribs with her elbow. He immediately grabbed their suitcases.

"Would you two like a hand with those?" Alistair asked, looking a little concerned for George's safety.

"No, we're fine." Sylvia Cooke stated, waving her flabby arm dismissively. She headed up the stairs.

Her skeletal husband trembled beneath the weight of his cargo. He shot Alistair a look that told him poor old George might just consider death a merciful alternative. The ancient staircase creaked uneasily, as the frail old man struggled his way up the mountainous flight. After an uncomfortably long time, he finally disappeared from view.

Alistair smirked to himself; manners had kept his face stern, right up until the guests had left his presence. The smirk swiftly turned to a frown when he considered the fact that the Cooke's were his only guests. Business had been incredibly slow, and it was gradually bleeding him dry. He sighed wearily to himself, glancing around at the entrance to his guesthouse. It was his pride and joy, but it had fallen into a somewhat sorry state.

As Alistair mused, his ear picked up a faint melody coming from the room behind him. He stepped through into his shambles of an office. It looked as though it had been frozen in time many years ago. The whole building was seemingly stuck in the past. Battered old guest books, full of the signatures of previous customers were spread haphazardly on shelving, tables and floors alike. Gas lighting cast elongated shadows that danced across the walls.

As he strode across the ancient floorboards, they strained beneath his weight. The haunting melody grew louder as he approached the sturdy door to the storage closet. He turned the black, iron key that was always left in the lock. He inched the door open and the music became as clear as day. Sat atop the pile of long forgotten coats, left by guests who had never returned for them, the music box stood. The headless dancer twirled infinitely, bathed in shadow, moving to her never-ending melody.

He ducked low and reached inside, removing the old box as a pang of sorrow struck his heart. The music box had belonged to his wife; he hadn't seen the thing for well over a year. Hadn't heard that music since before the illness took her from him. The box's incessant chime only brought him pain. He snapped it shut, and ran a worn out hand across the gold vines embedded in its ebony surface.

A sudden thump startled him, coming from the closet. He poked his head back inside curiously. Nothing. Then, the sound of movement to his left, and the soft crackle of falling debris. It seemed to be coming from inside the wall. Alistair placed his palm on the cold stone and traced his touch along where the noise seemed to originate. Whatever it was seemed to notice his presence, then darted furiously away. The room was finally silent once more.

The gentile Scotsman wondered what it could have been. He considered a terrifying notion – rats. That was the last thing he needed with things going the way they were. He groaned to himself, and hoped it would be nothing quite so sinister. His thoughts returned to the box. How had it gotten to be where it was, and stranger yet, how had it been opened? Even this thought was quickly replaced by a deep emptiness. He slumped in a rickety chair, dropped his head into his hands and allowed himself to wallow in misery. She was never coming back.

■■■

Alistair's sleep was restless. He was plagued by memories that made drifting deeper into dreams impossible. Every blink seemed to throw him forward in time, yet he felt like he hadn't switched off for a single moment. His eyes flew open as dust caught in his throat, causing him to cough and splutter uncontrollably. Moonlight, just enough to see by, filtered through a grimy windowpane. Its beams highlighted the falling matter. The ceiling above him seemed to groan.

A tiny crack formed in the paintwork above his head. As the low creak moved, the crack spread along with it. The gaslight hanging above shuddered, causing the glass to clang noisily. Alistair leapt from his bed, his pale and sagging body jerking into motion. He followed the sounds above, keeping his eyes fixed high. It passed out into the hallway.

Momentarily he considered returning to his room, shutting his eyes and leaving the mysterious happening unsolved. He could not though. Before he could willingly make a decision, his hand was on the doors cold, brass handle. Something was pulling him forward, an invisible and immeasurable force. He pushed the door open, it whined in protest. His feet touched down on the musty carpet of the second floor hallway. With each muted step down the darkened corridor, a familiar melody seemed to rise.

He passed closed off and empty rooms, and felt remarkably alone. A dim light flickered ahead of him, creeping through the tiny gap between the door and its frame at the end of the hall. He

313

longed to stop, to turn around and retreat to the safety of his bed. However with each timid stride, the melody grew louder still, and his power to resist diminished ever further. As he reached the door, Alistair's heart thundered in his chest. Incapable of turning away, he attempted to peek through the opening. He could see nothing.

Before he had the chance to think, he found himself pushing his way inside. A flickering candle was the source of the light, and before it in the claustrophobic room stood a slender woman, dressed all in white. The face reflected in the bathroom mirror made his blood run cold. It was his wife, eyes closed, the very picture of serenity. The door behind him slammed shut.

"Maria?" Alistair spoke softly. Innumerable copies of Maria's silhouette seemed to twist and twirl on the walls around him. The figure did not respond.

Alistair's mouth became as dry as old bone, his bare body shivered in the icy cold. Breath turned to frost in the air as he exhaled. He reached forward with a trembling hand, his eyes never leaving the motionless face of his former love reflected back at him. She looked so much younger than she had in her final years. Her stillness reminded him of an open casket. His outstretched fingers were less than an inch from her. Then it happened.

All at once, a deafening low-pitched drone drowned out the moving chimes. The eyelids of the static figure peeled back, and the mouth opened wide. Viscous black tar poured from each orifice in congealed lumps, Alistair stumbled backwards and fell leaden upon the tiled ground. The candle flickered, shifting the whole room momentarily into an impenetrable darkness. The face was upon him then, staring right at his own. He cried out, but it was impossible to hear over the deep thrum of the noise that enveloped all others. He felt the vile and putrid substance fall upon his exposed skin.

The bathroom door swung open wide, and in the same instant, the candle ceased to burn. A wiry man stood, clutching a candle of his own.

"Are you alright down there?" Mr Cooke croaked, his wrinkles deepened by the flickering flame.

■■

When the sun arose its light was smothered by a thick and heavy fog. Alistair hadn't gotten a wink of sleep since the incident in the bathroom. He talked himself into believing that it was a night terror, some kind of delusion, nothing of substance. Through bleary eyes, he dropped a fresh egg into a hot pan. "You damn near gave me a heart attack last night." George chuckled in good humour. "Prone to sleepwalking?"

"Aye, it's not unheard of." Alistair lied.

"Well at least I know that now, if I run into you in the halls again tonight it'll be less of a shock. I mean, don't get me wrong, I like the whole 'historical' vibe you've got goin' on here, but I'll be damned if it don't make things a little unsettling when night comes around." George croaked.

"You get used to it, and besides, you'll struggle to find another place like this one anywhere in the world." Alistair replied, in a weary attempt to keep the conversation flowing.

"Well, that's for certain." George smiled, and then paused for a beat. "Don't suppose I could trouble you for some bacon with those eggs, could I?"

"It would be my pleasure." The owner of the grand guesthouse gave a quick nod. The hungry old man offered a soft pat on the shoulder in appreciation, then swiftly left the kitchen.

Alistair prodded at the eggs absentmindedly. The sound was like static. Fat spattered his yellowing apron as he lit another of the stove's gas hobs, and placed a fresh pan upon it. He added a splash of oil, and a loud hiss filled the room. He stepped over to the icebox to retrieve the cuts of meat his guest had requested. As the box opened, a single musical note seemed to ring out.

Alistair leaped back in horror. He collided with a towering shelf, sending decorative glassware tumbling to the ground. He approached the box again, against his better judgment. When he peered inside, masses of writhing flesh squirmed upon the ice. They were coloured with deep reds and putrid, infected looking yellows. Bile rose in his throat, and the stench of death overwhelmed his senses.

"Is everything alright in there?" George yelled, sounding concerned as he approached. Alistair slammed the lid of the icebox closed as the old man entered.

"Yes, everything's fine. I'm just a little accident prone today, it would seem." Alistair glanced over his shoulder, still crouched by the icebox. He could hear the wriggling monstrosities within. He prayed that George could not.

"Jesus, you really did a number on these, huh?" George mumbled, eying the shattered glass spread across the kitchen floor. "I'll help you clean this up."

"No, no, it's quite alright." Alistair stood. "My mess, I'll clean it up." He sighed as he retrieved an ancient looking dustpan and brush from under the sink.

"Well, at least let me give you a hand with the breakfast." George reached for the icebox.

"No, don't you o-" Alistair began, but it was too late.

"Honestly, it's no trouble. You need to relax a little my friend. I can whip up bacon with the best of 'em, I assure you." George held the frozen bacon aloft, and winked. The crow's feet around his eyes momentarily became deepest chasms.

■■

With that, the safety of the day seemed to dissipate. Alistair began to consider the notion that he might be losing his grip on reality. He needed rest, surely that would be the cure, but something would not let him sleep. Over the following days, he continued to hear the scuttling feet from within the walls, to see things that he was certain, could not be.

As sleepless night followed sleepless night, the world itself seemed to take on a warped, twisted quality. A sense of the surreal began to permeate the old guesthouse, still isolated by the dense fog. To Alistair, the walls were in perpetual motion. Fluid - like the rippling of gentle waves, lapping silently at icy shores. All sound had become distant, as though he were drowning beneath the surface of that same, frosty water. All that is, except for the music, which seemed to haunt him whenever he tried to snatch a moment of respite. The instant he closed his eyes, the music would return, and along with it came paranoia.

His guests noticed nothing out of the ordinary. They went about their business, occasionally disappearing for a few hours, becoming hazy, distorted figures as they disappeared into the mist. It was in these moments that Alistair felt at his most vulnerable, and he feared that what lurked within the walls might smell his weakness, might taste his fear in the air. After five days, he was convinced something was stalking him. And whatever it was, it had to be the cause of his misery.

■■

Alistair was alone. In a daze he wiped down the front desk with a dirty rag. It felt soft and pliable. What he knew was solid wood seemed to give beneath his hand. This was his sixth day without sleep. The grainy surface appeared to twist and tangle itself between his outstretched fingers. He clumsily snatched his hand away from dark, oaken tendrils. His eyes watched them retreat, but saw little.

The sound of a cawing crow enflamed his otherwise dull senses. He spun around and stared blearily at his beloved oil painting. The crow's unblinking eye stared back. Alistair struggled to focus, mouth hanging open vacantly. Every blink only seemed to further diminish his already muddy view. He staggered forward, and clutched the painting's frame. Soot-like dust clung to his palms. He squinted at the bird on the canvas, for a second the image became clear. The bird's head jerked towards him.

All at once, the malicious melody burst into existence again, this time at a deafening volume, and countless shadowy crows flew from the canvas in a torrent of black feathers. Alistair was thrown off his feet. He crashed painfully on his aged hip. The birds dived towards the ground and, instead of crashing into it, seemed to be absorbed by it. They combined, becoming an inky black mass that spread outwards, growing as though organic. From the pool of darkness, the music box arose. The headless dancer twirled, and from beneath her delicate feet, vines began to grow. From them sprouted golden leaves. They clung to every surface, taking root where they could.

Alistair leapt to his feet, and rushed towards the cupboard under the staircase where old tools were stored, long since retired from use. He tugged the door open violently and grabbed the closest thing to hand – a grubby sledgehammer. His soft hands gripped the handle with purpose as his eyes fell upon the music box, the trinket his wife had held so dear. Alistair lunged toward it, raising the hammer high above his head. He swung it down with all the force his weary bones could produce. The box shattered, and the room fell silent.

The vines had ceased to grow, the dancer no longer twirled, and the branch in the painting was now without a resident. The sound of laboured breathing was all that could be heard, until the tell-tale scuttling from behind the bricks, began anew.

"You bastard, not this time!" Alistair cried out, enraged. He swung the sledgehammer again, aiming for what moved behind the brickwork. Each thunderous blow left a fresh hole in the stone of the old guesthouse, and each one seemed to be a fraction too late to stop the unseen creature.

He chased the sound up the stairs, and to the second floor hallway. As he tore through the building the doors to the rooms around him receded, disappeared as if they were never there, until only one remained. The door to room seven. He could hear the thing moving somewhere in the space beyond it. The hallway as he had known it was gone, it had morphed into a sterile, white, box like room. He rattled the handle aggressively, but the door would not budge.

"I'VE GOT YOU NOW, YOU LITTLE FUCK!" he bellowed, sending stringy saliva spilling down his chin.

Wheezing, he began to swing his sledgehammer at the entrance to room seven. The repeated strikes made his palms numb, but he refused to stop. Finally, a split appeared in the wood. Then with another strike, the door began to splinter. Alistair cast the hammer aside and furiously hurled himself at the barricade that stood in his way. It gave in, and he tumbled through, landing face down on the moist, pulsating ground.

As Alistair raised himself from the floor, foul smelling, mucus-like fluid clung to every part of him. The four walls that surrounded him were made of a familiar sickly flesh, with bloody crimsons and fatty yellows. Light gradually disappeared as the disgusting tissue expanded over the opening through which he had fallen, plunging him into darkness.

For a few agonising seconds, all was quiet. Then, an ear-splitting shriek as countless candles sprang to life. What appeared in the glow of the flickering flames was a distorted and broken thing. It wept loudly at the room's centre, shrill cries of anguish and torment. Countless clear tubes sprouted from its back, and through them flowed a glutinous biological liquid. The monsters mouth was covered, wrapped in skin that formed a hose. The hose hung down loosely, and then ran up into the blackness above. Its eyes leaked obsidian fluid, and yet looked disturbingly human.

There was a sadness in them. In its equally human hands, it clutched the fragments of the broken music box. Alistair fell to his knees. Tears he could not understand broke free, echoing the unimaginable sorrow that overwhelmed him.

"I'm sorry." He whimpered to the grotesque being in front of him. It still sobbed uncontrollably. "Forgive me." He pleaded, with hands clasped tightly together.

It screamed out for a final time, with such force that it could have split the very sky itself. Suddenly, the candles ceased to be.

A bright light blinded Alistair. When his vision returned, the doorway had reappeared. George and Sylvia Cooke stood in front of him. The sledgehammer was back in his hands.

"Hey Ali, what're you do-" George began, but then his words morphed and became an unbearably deep and troubling drone.

"NO! STOP!" Alistair cried, burying his head, but it was lost to that all encompassing sound. The foundations themselves seemed to shake beneath his feet.

George's arm began to blister. Then the blisters grew and merged, forming a raw looking red lump. More blisters began rise, this time on his face. They too grew to grotesque proportions, until he barely looked human at all. The strange phenomenon then spread to his wife.

"YOU'RE A PART OF THIS, YOU'RE BOTH A PART OF THIS!" The aging Scotsman yelled against the unstoppable noise, tears still falling. He squeezed down hard on the hammer's handle, and leapt towards the mutated creatures.

Alistair ran through the dense fog, near sightless.

"I have to hide, I have to hide. I need to be where it can't find me. I can never go back there. Never again." He wheezed to himself as he forced one flabby leg in front of the other, in spite of his heart that threatened to burst. The guesthouse he once knew was far behind him, and all was silent aside from his own shuddering breaths. A large form emerged from the void ahead of him. A farmhouse.

He dashed up to the front door and slammed a gelatinous fist against it.

"Hello… is… is anyone in there?" He asked, breathless. No answer. He ran for the window but it was shattered, behind it there was no furniture, and no sign of life. Just an old house, left in ruins.

"I can't hide here, it has walls. Walls with spaces behind them, spaces for it to be, spaces where it can get me." He rambled, still panting. Then set off slowly around the house to continue his search.

It was then that his sights fell upon a well that lay to the house's rear.

"That. That is perfect! It has walls with no spaces, nowhere for it to be." Alistair smiled widely to himself in jubilation. He sprinted over to the well with something close to a spring in his step. It had a bucket with a rope, and a crank to lower it down. It was impeccable.

Elated, he wound the crank, lowering the bucket down into the deep well that would be his sanctuary. It settled in the shallow water at the bottom of the shaft. Carefully, Alistair lifted himself onto the stone circle, muttering to himself the whole time.

"I'll hide here until it stops looking. Then when it leaves, I'll be free. I can never go back to the house, never go back there again, it knows there, it knows every inch of the place."

He took a firm hold of the rope, and with aching arms, he slowly lowered himself down. He reached the well's base with a faint splash. The freezing water came up to his knees, but he barely registered the cold. He gulped in great lumps of air, and breathed a heavy sigh of relief.

"It can't get me down here. I'm safe." He chuckled to himself, beaming. "Down here I can sleep."

He lowered his soft body into the freezing water, and leaned his head against the damp stones behind him.

"Yeah. Down here, I can finally sleep." He mumbled, looking up at the hazy sky from his safe place below the ground. The silhouette of the rope swayed lazily to-and-fro. Then, with a soft click, it dropped. He watched it fall, felt the weight of the rope as it coiled up on top of him, becoming heavier as it absorbed the water.

He grabbed a hold of it and held it aloft above his face, eyeing it carefully. Then, he laughed. He laughed harder and longer than he had ever laughed before, revelling in the joy he felt, in the hilarity of the moment. The rope had fallen, and he could not care less.

Alistair settled back down, still chuckling manically to himself. He got comfortable, and finally closed his eyes. The moment was serene; it was silent perfection, the purest bliss. In a flash, his eyes flew open again. His pupils grew large in the low light, as a familiar melody began to play.

Printed in Great Britain
by Amazon.co.uk, Ltd.,
Marston Gate.